CRUMBS

CRUMBS

by Marek Mann and Maria Martell

Copyright © 2006
by
Marek Mann
332 Zepp Road
Maurertown, Virginia 22644
(540) 459-4215
mstrauss@shentel.net

Library of Congress Control Number: 2006908573
ISBN: 0-978-9958-0-5

Printed by
WINCHESTER PRINTERS, INC,
Winchester, Virginia

Printed on acid-free paper

This book is dedicated to all those who work toward a world without brutality and hatred.

In the beginning there was a void. Now there are infinite galaxies with their multitudes of universes throughout the void. Here, on this micro-micro speck of matter, creatures live. Among those creatures, we humans kill and maim one another and other creatures of God. We make uninhabitable the speck of matter which we call earth. But we humans have a good side to us as well: we forgive, create, aspire, love, and remember.

I, too, forgave, created, aspired, and loved. Now I am fortunate because I am able to remember. I remember many things from the past and I want to share them.

—Marek Mann, *Chronicles*

To my "little darling" ELIza
on Oct 8th 2006 with
thanks for her
assistance
Mark R

The authors would like to sincerely thank all those who have made this book possible through their words or deeds.

Pre-World War II Europe, ca. 1930

Present-day Europe, ca. 2000

CRUMBS

Prologue

Am I among stars or am I on earth? Just above my head is no ceiling, but rather an entire Milky Way, while my feet are firmly on the wooden floor, next to a dark elevated stage. In front of me, barely illuminated by the stellar light, are rows upon rows of unoccupied seats. Utter silence prevails except for my booming voice as I lecture.

"The fall of 1941 was a critical time. Nazi Germany dominated almost the entirety of Europe; from the Arctic Circle in the north to the African lands along the Mediterranean in the south; from Spain in the west all the way to the environs of Moscow and Leningrad in the east. It was a heady year for the citizens of the Third Reich. Their armies appeared to be invincible. But—"

"But we don't give a hoot." A thin, soft voice from the stage on my left interrupted my discourse.

"Who are you?" I inquired politely, turning my head in the direction of the voice.

"She doesn't know me," the voice addressed someone invisible on the dark stage. "Isn't it a laugh? Well, maybe she hasn't met me yet, but Marek sure must have told her about me. Phil, put on the lights—let her see us."

Suddenly the stage blazed with light, illuminated by the various projecting beams. While, high above in the sky, among the stars, neon lights appeared. Successively, in red, white and blue, huge block letters wrote themselves across the sky: N-A-T-I-O-N-A-L-M-A-L-L.

The thin voice from the stage forced itself on me again. "Here we are, professor. I am Anna, the Lady Orange, not a normal woman, you'll see. There's Phil helping Violet to steady herself—she is trying to stand on her half-legs. They are like me—far from normal. There's Yulia, that slut, again arguing with Yvonne about who has had more men. I guess they're normal. Do you recognize them professor?"

I hear my voice again, now ringing with irritation. "I can see who you are. I don't need to know more. You are puppets, raggedy dolls. With your names stitched to your raggedy clothing. I can read your names—you don't have to identify yourselves! Why must you interrupt me? I'm about to talk about people in a very special town in Eastern Europe during World War II. Keep quiet and go away."

"We are not what we seem." Yulia and Yvonne spoke in unison. "None of us is a bad cookie, but where is Figarroo?"

Just then a voice from behind the stage sang out "Figarroo, Figarroo, Figarroo" as if performing in Mozart's opera. It was the voice of a man, but not a tenor—the voice was low and gravelly.

Lady Orange coaxed Figarroo to come onto the stage. "Come and meet the Professor."

"I have no use for her, and besides, I must fly up to heaven. And then I promised Marek that I would meet him in front of the National Gallery of Art. I have something to give him." The deep voice began to sing out the same melody as before: "Figarroo, Figarroo, Figarroo."

"Oh, shut up," shouted Lady Orange. "I know what you're up to. You're trying to crowd us out of the story. You're..."

A motion at the far end of the rows of empty chairs caught my attention. At first I saw only the red lights above the entry doors, but then I noticed the silhouettes of two uniformed soldiers wearing helmets, approaching me from opposite corners. They did not walk down the aisles, but glided over the chairs, on a collision course aimed at me. They were close enough so that, even in this dim light, I could identify their World War II uniforms and helmets. The one on the left was a German soldier from the elite

Waffen SS squad and the one on the right wore the distinctive insignia of a Soviet border policeman.

"Who are you? Who are you?" They yelled at me in German and Russian. "Why do you disturb the peace here? Who are you?"

Dread possessed me and I began to sweat profusely. I began to mumble: "I am Maria Martell, I am Maria Martell, I am Mar…" Then I was paralyzed by an uncontrollable fear because under their helmets there were no faces, only bleached-white skulls. My screams did not leave my mouth. I tried desperately to move but the terror arrested me as the skulls bent over me.

Then a child's voice penetrated my dream: "Mommy, mommy." The nightmarish specters disappeared as I awoke, still uttering "I am Maria Martell, I am Maria Martell, I am a historian" but now, thankfully, I could hear myself.

Chapter I

❦

The Artist and the Historian

My two-year-old Billy looked stricken by my fright, and I spent a few extra minutes in bed to hold him and stroke his blond hair. Soon, though, it was time to get dressed, to start the day and to prepare my lecture. I really didn't want to look in a mirror. My brunette hair is streaked with gray. A few liver spots have sprouted on my arms and my neck but fortunately not on my chest and face. This is all vanity, and anyway, how could I look young again? I am nearing forty.

I know my eyes are sunken, and I feel the stark lines of pain that etch my face. On few occasions of joy, when a smile smoothes my features, a rare photograph might still capture an unlined face, with full lips and sparkling eyes. Marek liked to observe me when, with a jerk of my head, I swept the unruly hair away from my eyes. To him, this motion represented inherent vitality. When he watched me walk, he would say, "You are deliciously sensual." I didn't appreciate his comment then, but I remember it now and shiver with a brief surge of emotion—a brief resurgence of lust.

I select my clothing in a manner similar to many women from decades ago: skirts and dresses, with nylon stockings or pantyhose. I remember how Marek found my legs shapely and irresistible, and how he wanted me to wear tight-fitting, long silky dresses with a slit up the side. Not too long of a slit, just enough to excite him. Then, when we embraced, Marek would press his maimed hand against the small of my back and slip his good hand under the dress, slowly moving it upward, exploring all the undulations. The sensation of nylon on smooth skin thrilled him.

Focus on the lecture, I told myself. Did that horrible nightmare mean anything? Was I dealing with something that was better left forgotten? I couldn't concentrate. At that early hour my mind wandered, and I thought about why I was drawn to study the tragic subject of the Holocaust.

As early as I can remember, I knew that I was a daughter of grateful immigrants. The Stars and Stripes flew in front of our house on all the major national holidays and even on some other days.

"Daddy, what holiday are we celebrating today?" I remember asking my father one day as he walked back into the house after inserting the flag into its holder. I was probably five years old then.

"I am celebrating the day I came to America." His voice quivered with emotion.

"You know that we are Germans, your mother and I. We came here after a terrible war. We were lucky to be able to start a new life here. We are happy here and we treasure the opportunity to live in America."

Father paused and, as if remembering something, added, "My sisters, your aunts, came here from Germany also."

I was emboldened by father's willingness to talk and asked him, "Do I have any uncles, Daddy? In Germany?"

Father became thoughtful. He turned his head toward the window and after a long while faced me again. His eyes were moist.

"No, I had three brothers and two were killed. Your mother had two uncles and they are dead—they would have been your granduncles."

I was startled by this revelation, but persisted.

"What were you and they doing during that war?" But my father merely said that I would know when I got older. He arose from the table and walked away.

My parents were good people with memories they didn't like to share. I didn't know much about their families when I was young, and as I grew up, I figured out that my father was ashamed that he grew up in Germany in a family permeated with Nazi ideology. The Martells actively supported the Führer, Adolph Hitler. My father and his friends were dutiful members of the Hitler Youth. Two of his older brothers died in World War II while serving Hitler's empire, the Thousand-Year Reich. Of course, he and his parents mourned their deaths. He lived through the destruction of his town and his own house by American bombs. He has spent his adult years coming to terms with the evils that Nazi Germany imposed on society, and his revulsion has made him an ardent believer in the American way of life.

In contrast, my mother's family—the Menkes from Berlin—were opposed to fascism. My mother and the Menkes are as proud of their resistance to Hitler's Reich as my father is ashamed of the Martell's association with it. The Menkes had liberal views, and they paid dearly for them. My mother's uncle Hans was taken to the Dachau concentration camp because he was active in the Socialist Party. He was never heard from again. Nor was he the first of the Menkes to disappear in those dreadful times. Even before Hans was taken, my great-uncle Willi had been arrested. Willi was an acknowledged Communist and we assumed that the Nazis had executed him as well. As a teenager, I was sympathetic to my mother's family, to Hans and to Willi, the German victims of Hitler's reign. They were my heroes.

But then I found the "Willi File" and learned that there was much more to Willi's history. Even later, after I met Marek, as we were pursuing our quests, Willi's astounding career came to light and had a role in what happened in Lwów.

It was in Lwów, two years ago, when my young friend, Irka brought to me the tragic news. I still vividly remember her coming to the Novikov's apartment where Marek and I shared a room.

"Maria! Open the door Maria. It is me, Irka! Pani Novikova? Maria? Is anyone home? Please, let me in!"

Irka's frantic knocking and the urgency of her voice woke me up with a start. I quickly got out of bed and reached for my robe and slippers. Sara and Vladya Novikov, my hosts, had left already.

I glanced at the clock. It was eleven in the morning. I almost never slept that late, but that had been my parting night with Marek. Full of apprehension and tenderness, holding onto each other, we hardly slept. Then Szmuel came before dawn and Marek left with him for Kiev.

"Anybody home? Open up!" Irka's voice was one of desperation. Is somebody after her, I thought. It wouldn't be the first time that bandits roamed through the dark staircase.

"I am coming, Irka. Are you okay? What is it?" I said as I struggled with the complex locks on the door.

Finally, the last security device gave way. I unhooked the chain. Irka burst in, perspiring from exhaustion, and she embraced me. As she kissed me on the cheek, I felt her face moist with tears.

"Marek is dead! A car accident near Rovno. My boyfriend, an orderly in the hospital, called me. They identified one of the bodies as that of your American friend, Marek Mann."

I wished that Irka's appearance was only a nightmare. No. I faced a tragic reality. Our romance was short-lived; an ephemeral glow, more like that a shooting star. Yet we had known each other for a long time.

If I had lived in Germany during Nazi years, I would have been tainted by the slur *eine Rassenschande*, meaning "a racial shame." I, a pure-blooded German, an "Aryan," loved a Jewish man. Even worse, he was twice my age. Irka told me that a powerful explosion had ripped apart the car in which he was riding and killed him. Marek had survived the Holocaust when he was a youngster in Poland. Just before the end of the war, he survived when a detonator exploded and blew away parts of five fingers. But ironically, more than half a century after that war, Marek had been murdered because his father was a Jew!

Marek's remains were brought from Ukraine and buried in the Blue Ridge Mountains of Virginia, where he lived and painted. His simple stone was inscribed: HERE LIES MAREK MANN, 77, AN ARTIST WHO DID WHAT HE THOUGHT WAS BEST.

Blue Ridges

The Mall in Washington, D.C. brought Marek and me together. We met on the path between the National Gallery of Art and the Air and Space Museum in July 1987. After his burial, I was relentless in pursuing Marek's final ambition: to have his paintings exhibited here, at the National Gallery of Art. In doing so, I have walked this path many more times—pounded, trod, and shuffled on my dedicated mission to have his work exhibited in style. After all, his work was well-received by ordinary people, and now he was dead. Artists are given more consideration dead than when alive. Odd, but true. Over three hundred of his original oils and over ten thousand prints grace homes and offices throughout the world, primarily in the USA. Yet, while he was alive, the art world refused to have his work juried in a meaningful and impartial manner.

He had no formal training. He was not of this school or that school. I pleaded with the museum bureaucracy, petitioned them, yelled and cursed. I clawed the U.S. Park Service policemen when they arrested me for protesting on the street and for carrying angry signs along with Marek's prints. All in vain. Not until my doctoral dissertation, "The Jews from Lwów," based in part on Marek's history, became publicized, did Marek's wish come true. The art establishment capitulated under the pressure of public interest—its self-serving critics, curators and their emasculated cohorts gave in. The minimalists, the maxi-faddists, finger painters and the believers in the fabled "Emperor's New Clothes" must have despaired.

This week, a temporary exhibit of his painting will open to the public in the National Gallery of Art. Tomorrow evening there will be a reception at the Gallery to honor Marek. I will be there savoring our triumph. I will dress the way that Marek liked: a long silk dress of bright hues with a slit over the right leg, wearing nylons, heels, and a ribbon around my hair. If only he were there. If only I could feel his hand caressing me once more.

I am standing on the steps of the fabulous marble stairway of the West Wing looking down to the path from the Air and Space Museum on the opposite side of the Mall. The Mall is nearly empty. A few pedestrians can be seen scurrying at this late hour to their cars on Madison Drive. To the left gleams the dome of the Capitol; to the right looms the towering National Monument. Time passes quickly as I reminisce. Although there is still daylight, it certainly is late, perhaps nine o'clock. I am as if in a trance. Memories assail me as I look down at the spot where Marek showed his painting skill and exhibited his wonderful creations. He persevered here for twenty years, every Saturday and Sunday of each summer. I remember the first time that I met him. It was a Saturday nearly twenty years ago. Throngs of people were drawn to the Mall attractions. There were families, groups of students with teachers, young couples holding hands, platoons of tourists, and some solitary visitors like me.

I had come from Oregon, and to me, the Mall was like a candy store. Would it be the Air and Space Museum, or Natural History, or may be art museums? I got off the tour bus at the National Gallery and immediately saw a display of colorful and imaginative pictures across the street. Next to the display, several onlookers surrounded the artist, observing him paint. I crossed the street to see him at work. The artist was kneeling along the gravel path. The patches of grass around him were trampled down by tourist shoes and parched by drought. A stretched canvas lay on the hard ground in front of him and he was brushing oils onto its linen surface. Unusual, I thought, don't artists use easels? Next to him stood two elaborate aluminum stands with paintings and prints affixed on their frames. Near the stands was a table piled with matted and shrink-wrapped miniature prints. An empty lawn chair beside a large cooler under a shade of an oak tree completed the artist's encampment.

I was intrigued and stood next to the artist to observe. His brush did not have long tapered bristles like those I saw in art stores; the bristles were rather short, widely arrayed and were squared off at the end. He was using a squat brush, about half an inch in width, to spread oil pigments. I watched as he imbedded thick, orange oils into streaks of white oils. The orange hue lightened as the brush stroke lengthened. The result was a gradual transition, gently rendered. Narrow orange furrows resulted from one very long, slow sweep of the artist's hand. The separated bristles of the brush gave the orange-white streak an elegant texture. It was hard to determine what the artist was painting. Perhaps it was a plowed field or tongues of fire.

Even though the artist focused intensively on his work, he was explaining to the viewers that he was using two metallic pigments: cadmium orange and titanium oxide. He spoke with an accent. I could not tell where he was from, but he was easy to understand. At first I thought that the artist was a meticulous, plodding person because his explanations were so detailed and carefully phrased. He told us that he really should not have used titanium oxide as a substrate pigment because it was lighter than cadmium oxide, weight-wise. For white pigment, he should have used lead oxide, which was heavy, but it was not sold those days because of safety considerations. But, on the other hand, he said, titanium oxide was brilliantly white—and he liked that.

He stopped talking, looked for a long moment at the canvas and then, with surprising speed, wiped the brush on paper toweling. With a vigorous motion of his entire hand, he plunged the brush into the newly created orange-white field. Twisting the brush from a wide aspect to a narrow one, he plowed a perpendicular, wavy wedge across the beautifully textured field. Then, faster, without pausing, at a slightly different angle, he created another wavy wedge. Throughout, he anchored the canvas, pressing it downward with the palm of his left hand, thus preventing it from sliding on the ground. The canvas did not budge under the assault of the squat brush.

Because the canvas was held down forcefully, it took a while for me to notice that something was wrong with the artist's left hand. Parts of the artist's fingers were missing. No nails, just thick stubs above the knuckles remained. The sight of the amputated fingers startled me as the artist continued to deftly make energetic strokes, gracefully dragging the orange-white pigment of the field onto the dry linen of the canvas. He lifted the brush when the pigment was spent. The newly stroked paint shone like menacing flame. The contrast was such that the tongues of flame, with their sharp points, marred the placid beauty of the original, elegant streaks. Once more, with an even greater burst of energy, he wiped his brush, ready to strike again.

"Don't," I blurted, unbidden.

The artist turned his head from the canvas toward me. His glittering eyes locked on mine, and I felt a peculiar sense of being examined, exposed, and penetrated into my private being. Later, when we became intimate, Marek always claimed that I stooped and bent low to intentionally show him my bare breasts under my partially buttoned blouse. I did no such thing. Men: I thought of them as the seniors in my high school. Twenty years ago, I did not know the workings of a primal, worldly man who was in touch with his feelings, a man who had been abused in life but who burned with an inextinguishable flame for lust and love.

For many years to come, neither Marek nor I would know how prophetic that Mall encounter would be. Eventually, our lifelines crossed again when our quests merged. I, a historian, was researching the success and tragedy of a unique town in Ukraine, a town that was once Austrian, and then Polish. Marek sought an answer to a family mystery in the same town. The town is called Lwów in Polish, Lviv in Ukrainian and Lemberg in German.

I have written this story based on my memories of recent and distant events, the recollections and documents of my family members, and my archival research. Into my story, I have woven segments of Marek's unfinished chronicles—infrequently recorded observations of his later life—and his partial memoirs—memories of his Holocaust past. A true artist, he incorporated sketches and photographs of his paintings into his chronicles.

*　　*　　*

The full moon had just risen above the hills surrounding Lwów on that night when I first learned about Marek's chronicles and memoirs. At half-past seven I had put on lipstick and walked up to Kupol, the restaurant where Marek and I had agreed to meet. The host guided me past a well-stocked bar and seated me on a heavily upholstered bench. On the wall beside me hung an old, decoratively printed Polish menu, but the menu handed to me was in Ukrainian, Polish, and English. On the other walls, I could make out a 1938 diploma from Jan Kazimierz University, now called Ivan Franko. The diploma hung amongst a sword, a photo of a Polish general, and a painting of the Ossolineum, the Polish cultural institute here in Lwów.

Marek appeared as if emerging from this prewar era. "Cześć," he said in Polish. "Hi." Clearly, he had made arrangements with the bartender, because wine and brandy appeared and soon loosened our tongues.

"I don't see a wedding ring on your finger," Marek said.

I smiled. "You know, I'm still working on my dissertation. I don't have time to think about getting married. And besides," I paused, "maybe I haven't met the right man. What about you?"

"My wife and I live separately. We used to share so much more than we do now. The children and grandchildren...well, they are busy with their lives. Not much time for me or even for their mother. Their families are typical American middle-class. Music lessons, sports, summer camps, time-share place on the shore..." Marek's voice trailed off.

He looked down toward the wine goblet coddled in his hand. Then he raised the goblet and playfully clinked it with mine.

"You probably don't know that I have thought about you often," Marek said. "I might have been a little bit in love with you. I wanted you to come back to see me on the Mall. Without that other man, I mean." He laughed dryly.

For a moment I couldn't look into his eyes. When I did, I changed the topic. "I feel awkward being an American abroad. I feel as though people are suspicious of me, or want to take advantage of me—or both." I had intended to start a neutral conversation, but I felt vulnerable.

Marek took my hand. "You should be proud that you are American. Of course I wasn't automatically patriotic myself, but my experiences made me that way. I came to America right after World War II ended, on the SS *Ernie Pyle*, an American troop ship named after the war correspondent. Have you heard of him?" I nodded.

"Would you believe that I don't even know exactly how my parents traveled to the USA, and I am supposed to be a historian. I think also by ship. Well, they don't talk much about their earlier lives. But go on—I am interested."

"It was good ol' Harry who brought us here."

"You mean Truman?"

"Yes. We anchored at night in thick fog, directly under the Statue of Liberty. Several hundred Holocaust survivors—Jews and non-Jews alike—were crowding the deck, awaiting the morning to have the first glimpse of America. As the fog slowly began to dissipate, it was the symbol of liberty that first revealed herself to us, hovering above in all her imposing size and beauty. I believe that upon seeing the Statue, many of us cried unashamedly. I know that I had tears in my eyes." Marek was lost in the memory.

"An hour or so later, as the fog lifted, we saw the panoramic silhouette of New York City. Then and there I knew that this would be my land, a country for me to cherish and a place to prosper. My journey from Lwów to New York City—from Holocaust to freedom—was over. On the day that we finally docked at the pier on the Hudson River in Manhattan, I was sixteen years old." Marek's eyes looked straight into mine.

"But you know, Maria, let me tell you a little story. In Marienbad, in what's now the Czech Republic, I spent a few weeks under American occupation before I crossed the border to

Germany. It was the fall of 1945; I was fifteen. I met a beautiful German girl about my age who was working for the hotel where we were staying. Dark hair, dark eyes, and just a lovely face. Plus....oh, well. She always smiled at me, and in my shy adolescence I thought she looked at me invitingly. But there was a big problem. She was German. In my hatred of all things German, I refused to acknowledge her existence"

Marek stopped for a second, lowered his head, perhaps seeing that girl again. Barely audible he added, "And to this day, I regret it."

We were quiet for a little while. "Now I have another beautiful German woman sitting across from me," Marek said. "And I'm not going to make the same mistake. No, not as long as I remember Figarroo and his cookies."

"What do you mean by figrookies?" "Figrookies" stroked my funny bone and I laughed. Marek also laughed.

"Wait, be patient. You will know it all." We laughed again and clinked our glasses.

Later, I told Marek about my research of the diverse cultures of Lwów, and that I was also searching for information about my relatives, Willi and Gerhard. He told me that he also was delving into the history of Lwów. I did most of the talking. What I said about my personal life, I don't remember, but we both felt upbeat by the prospect of working together. Indeed, we did, and the mutual attraction from our first meeting was slowly resurrected.

Over an excellent coffee, I told Marek that my grand-uncle, Willi, was probably in Lwów during the Soviet occupation right after Poland collapsed under the German onslaught in the fall of 1939. I assumed that Willi, a former inmate of a concentration camp for Communists in pre-World War II Poland, was rewarded by the Soviet state, and most likely became a political official, perhaps a commissar. His letter to Grandma Menke from Lwów in 1940 hinted that Willi was a member of the Soviet Communist Party apparatus. These were still the days of partnership between Hitler and Stalin, and Grandma Menke lived in Berlin.

That evening, Marek and I parted with a promise to meet again soon. Marek assured me that he could readily postpone his departure from Lwów, indefinitely.

"When we meet again, hopefully tomorrow, you will know what really brought me to Lwów. My legacy, so to speak. Tonight, I did not want sadness to diminish the joy of being with you." Marek said. He affectionately kissed my hand as we parted.

"Sleep well, Marek," I bid him.

The next evening at Kupol Restaurant, Marek brought a plastic envelope with handwritten sheets of lined, yellow paper.

"Here, Maria. I brought you my memoirs and what I call 'chronicles.' You are a historian. You may be interested in my impressions of events and of some people I came to know. Mostly, you will learn a lot about me. You are also mentioned."

Marek, embarrassed, looked down at the yellow sheets as he handed them to me. I touched his hand and his blue eyes enveloped me. There were tears in his eyes, but with a business-like voice, he continued.

"Actually, I began writing the chronicle years ago on the Mall in Washington. You will know who Figarroo was or still is. You do remember my stands with the exhibiting panels. Don't you?"

Yes, Marek. How could I ever forget, I thought to myself. I turned the packet of sheets over in my hands, feeling its thickness. On the back I noticed the word BOGDAN written over and over, big and small, all in capital letters—something Marek had doodled exquisitely. The Os were layered across the Bs and filled with swirling animal-like shapes, as intricate as an illuminated manuscript. All the letters moved across the page in vibrant curves. Suddenly my eye caught one O which contained a single, unadorned swastika.

"Who is Bogdan?" I asked.

"He is the reason I am here. You will read about him. I am sorry that I must leave right now. I have to meet a man. I am sure that you will meet him too—sooner or later. Good-bye, Maria." Marek hoisted his backpack and was gone.

I went back to the room I rented in the apartment of an elderly couple, greeted them, and quickly excused myself, telling them I was tired. I wanted desperately to know who Bogdan was but realized right away that Marek's handwriting was too messy to skim. Methodically, I started with the first words:

I am Marek Mann, an artist.

*   *   *

In the beginning there was a void. Now there are infinite galaxies with their multitudes of universes throughout the void. Here, on this micro-micro speck of matter, creatures live. Among those creatures, we humans kill and maim one another and other creatures of God. We make uninhabitable the speck of matter which we call earth. But we humans have a good side to us as well: we forgive, create, aspire, love, and remember.

I too forgave, created, aspired, and loved. Now I am fortunate because I am able to remember. I remember many things from the past and I want to share them. How do I start? Actually, fate compelled me to write. Fate jolted me yesterday when I opened up a squashed box of animal cookies. My frequent visitor, Figarroo, brought me the box of cookies as a gift. He calls himself Figarroo but explains that it is an adopted name. In reality, he insists, he is the Messiah who descended from heaven to be a harbinger of good will on earth.

"The animal cookies came from heaven also," he told me. "God created heaven and earth, and then on the seventh day he created animals to prowl the earth freely, and some animals he created as cookies to be eaten up," said Figarroo.

I knew better than to correct him. After all, if he is the Messiah he should know the biblical events and their sequence. However, I definitely knew that the box of cookies did not come from heaven but was scrounged by Figarroo from a trash can.

"Here are the animals. Open the box and look at them," the homeless Messiah sternly told me. So I did.

Mostly crumbs fell out of the box, but also a whole tiger, an elephant, a pig and other animals. They arranged themselves on the marble pedestal of the colonnade, guarding the portal to the West Building of the National Gallery of Art in Washington, D.C. Whether it was the constant gaze of the Messiah that embraced me and the contents of the box, or the influence of my festive gin, I will never know. But, the animal shapes began to resemble human heads. I could even identify the mustachioed features of Dali, Harry Truman with the bow tie, and the composed wise face of my benefactress, Franciszka, with her reading glasses on top of her nose. There were also bits and pieces of other heads that were now mostly crumbs. Family heads popped up among the crumbs. There was my likeness! I was a cookie! We, the unknown and the famous, were cookies! It made sense: We are all fragile. We are all different, obviously not shaped by the same cookie cutter but all destined to be eaten up or to crumble.

"That's the way the cookies crumble," exclaimed Figarroo, interrupting my fantasy.

I opened my eyes to look at him just as he was picking up the tiger, then the elephant, and lastly, the pig. I noticed how delicate his hands were and how agile his fingers were when he rummaged among the crumbs. He stuck the three cookies into his mouth with one swish and munched them audibly. Then turning his head skyward, he bid me good-bye saying, " The rest is for you. Eat them. Eat the crumbs, too. I have to go and look for pure water to drink. I hope it will rain."

*　　*　　*

The enchantment brought about yesterday by the Messiah is gone but the feeling of being a brittle human being is not. Who could be more emotionally vulnerable and economically fragile than a self-trained, self-proclaimed artist? A painter, at that.

For more than an hour now, I have sat on the "cookie pedestal" overlooking the Mall. The crumbs are gone, eaten by pigeons. The realization that not even crumbs will remain from my life jerks me. Unfortunately, I have time to reminisce and to feel sorry for myself. Some days I have lots of time for blues. When I don't mope, I experience life intensively. With me it is either famine or feast. Either I have emotionally charged interactions with people and my pigments, or I suffer from inactivity, accompanied by the feeling of rejection, followed by depression. Rather than sitting idly alone when my artistic ambition and patrons desert me, I am resolving to substitute a pencil for a brush. Both of these implements feel fine in my hand.

Today I am starting to write, before the fate of a cookie catches up with me. I will write a chronicle—perhaps more in the nature of a diary. I hope that this new endeavor will absorb my mind, just as the act of painting possesses my faculties. I am also prodded to write by my sense of self-importance. I am obsessed by the notion that my work will eventually attain the fame of past masters such as Dali, Van Gogh, and Rembrandt, or, more likely that of M.C. Escher, a contemporary artist who has achieved genius status. His recognition is proof that the success of a no-nonsense artist is possible in our times. Thus, as an additional incentive to write, I am anticipating the day when art historians may find this chronicle to be interesting and instructive in learning about the life and work of Marek Mann.

Reverberating in my mind is a nagging premonition that I will not see the day when my work is finally acclaimed. Should that sadden me as it often does? What manner of death will come to me? Sometimes at night, I am tortured by my dreams. Yet another explosion tears my body apart. Am I a psychological mess? Maybe.

But, aren't many of us, each of us carrying a different mental burden? Aren't we all subject to different fears? As I said, the same cookie cutter did not shape us all. Certainly, the experiences that molded us made us even more diversified. How will my remaining years alter me? What does fate have in still store for me? Enough of this—I am supposed to begin a chronicle but, at first, a bit of my past.

For the biblically significant period of seven years, as Figaroo would certainly put it, I exhibited and promoted my work every weekend each summer on the grassy grounds of the National Mall in Washington, D.C. This chronicle is an attempt to record the events and tribulations of an aged artist endeavoring to bring his work in front of the public. As I write this, I promise to truthfully portray happenings as they occur and to dutifully dredge out of my soul all feelings and thoughts, be they self-serving or embarrassing.

I am beginning this chronicle after four decades of living in America, but my thoughts dwell mainly on the past seven years. Seven summers on the Mall in Washington, D.C. On Saturdays, Sundays, and sometimes on weekdays. Early in the morning, during the day, until late in the evening, I interacted with passersby: homeless and mentally disturbed denizens, demonstrators for various causes, as well as visitors from all over the world who came to this focal crossroads of our Capitol in order to see our treasures and to experience our culture.

*   *   *

Today, this Saturday in July 1987, at about 7:30 in the morning I parked my rusty old Chevrolet sedan right where I always park on Madison Drive: by the two public telephones, three car-lengths away from the pedestrian crosswalk. The three-hour parking restriction is not enforced strictly on weekends but it is better to not to be the first or second car parked nearest to the crosswalk. Park Police officers may just have enough time or energy to ticket one or two cars but not the third or fourth.

It is hard for me to believe that my new Dodge minivan wouldn't start in the morning, completely upsetting the scope of my exhibit today; that is, if I will be able to exhibit at all. It just ceased to pour and I am sitting in the car, writing instead of being out there in "my" place, setting up my stands. Well, I don't have my stands—the rusty sedan is not configured to carry them like my minivan. But I could set up the few paintings and prints I squeezed into the sedan; some I could lean against the trees; some against the folding table and chair. But I don't. It looks like it will continue to rain. I must wait and hope. So, I sit cramped in the driver's seat and write, surrounded by my canvases, prints, and painting paraphernalia with my new muse urging me onward. Who is the muse of writers? Perhaps it is Erato. I should learn her name.

Many strollers have seen me on the Mall here, on the corner of the Madison Drive sidewalk and the path from the Air and Space Museum. Thousands have walked past me in the last seven years. Has it really been so long? Almost a decade! Many stopped by to look at my work and to see me paint. Some bought my postcards, large prints, small matted prints and even original oils. Of course, I, bent down over a canvas, seldom see the faces of those who observe me paint. I remember well a few of those who were especially attracted by my work.

The face of Maria appeared in front of my eyes today. She had the attractive face of a girl in her late teens with hair tightly pulled back into a ponytail. But it was her breasts that she so coquettishly exposed to me while observing me paint that I vividly remember. Was it two or three weeks ago that I first saw her? My first impression of her was that she was trying to pick up some "business." Talking to her for a while, I realized that she was an intelligent, seemingly decent girl who apparently didn't mind exposing her beauty.

"I am Marek Mann, an artist, as you can see."

"My name is Maria Martell," she responded. We talked for a while and then she told me that she was of German descent. As she was saying it, her pretty, smiling, girlish face acquired the seriousness of a mature adult. She looked at me quizzically with apprehension and became silent, expecting a response to her revelation. "Yes," was my only reaction to her statement.

I continued to lead the conversation along the usual touristy topics. I had to admit to myself that forty years ago I hated Germans, all Germans. Since that time, my hatred has gradually waned. After all these years I now consider Germans like any other nationality—a few good, some very bad and most in between. So I treated Maria as if she was just another pretty girl visiting Washington. Seeing no change in my behavior toward her, Maria's eyes relaxed—her face became smooth and soft again. She told me that she is an avid student of history with a special interest in World War II. I talked to her for a while about Poland and Ukraine. I was then abruptly interrupted by a man who asked me for directions to a coffeehouse in downtown Washington. After disposing of this very talkative tourist, I looked around for Maria. She was gone.

*   *   *

These last two weekends I have been hoping that Maria would reappear. But no. I was attracted by her youthful good looks and her curiosity regarding Eastern Europe. Maybe she will come today or perhaps tomorrow. I know that this hope made me drive here today in spite of the threatening forecast. I have a strange feeling about Maria. Was she real? She appeared like Venus from the sea foam and then she submerged into the crowd of tourists. Will she reappear? Maria, Maria, where are you?

Well, back to the struggle of an unrecognized artist on a rainy day. It is already nearly ten o'clock in the morning and water is again pouring from the sky. Nobody is on the Mall except—here he is again as usual—Figarroo, the Messiah. But today he seems to be taller, lankier, and more black than usual. He dances to the silent music that only he can hear, with arms and head pointed skyward, his mouth opened, as if he were catching droplets of rain.

"Thou shalt drink water from the sky," I heard him say to no one in particular.

I could not tell if he was misquoting the Bible or simply drinking the "pure" rainwater. Most likely he was singing. I have seen him and heard him many times before. What an irony—he is wet and happy with his song. And I am dry but miserable with my thoughts, sitting and waiting for the clouds to leave. He has plenty of nothing and nothing is plenty for him, it seems. I lived a prosperous life in the business world, but I foresee an unpromising future as an artist. Yet I persist, hoping to be noticed, hoping to...

Hey! Figarroo noticed me and approached the car. His curly long hair and his nose dripped water. He motioned me to roll down the window. I did as he bid, thankful for the interruption in my self-flagellation.

"Figarroo, does the water taste good?" I asked him just to be saying something.

"I am the Messiah and you should know it. Here is the proof!"

Figarroo stuck his hand into one of the recesses of his drenched overcoat and brought out a miniature print of my painting, which I titled "The Messiah."

The Messiah

"You see, here is the heavenly evidence. This is the document!" He shouted at me, pointing to the soggy, crumbled paper, with his likeness still discernible. The picture showed Figarroo lying on a bench with pigeons around him and a Bible under his head.

Last year, he wanted to be painted by me and so I did it. Later, I signed and gave him a small print of the painting. He carried it with him and proudly showed it to all he met on the Mall.

"Give me that picture. I will exchange it for another one—a dry one," I offered.

"No. This is mine—it came from heaven."

Figarroo turned around and danced away, deluged by "pure" water coming from the sky.

The sun finally did come out yesterday and, today, Sunday, was a gorgeous day but Maria did not come back. I sold some and painted some but it wasn't worth the effort of driving all that distance. "Damn it," I swore under my nose. If the weather forecast would be as bad for the next weekend as it was for this one, I was determined not to come and exhibit, Maria or no Maria. Then, as if to convince myself that I should leave Maria out of my considerations, I blurted aloud, "By the cookies of Figarroo, I will come only if the weather will be good." That tragi-comic man, the pathetic Messiah, imbedded himself in my brain. I uttered my newly adopted oath, even louder, "By the cookies of Figarroo."

By my public invocation of Figarroo, I must have startled two middle aged women who were just then walking by. They stopped talking and looked at me. "By Figarroo," I swore even louder. That scared them and they rapidly resumed their walk.

Enough of the Mall for this weekend. For now, I have to pack my rusty Chevrolet and drive back to the Blue Ridge Mountains.

Chapter II

Some of the Cookies

Yet another weekend. It is Sunday afternoon with nothing much to report. Phil showed up. As usual, he squatted by me, and with the utmost concentration, looked at the unfinished painting of colorful fish frolicking in the water. The painting was leaning against the cooler. He seemed to be studying it. On past occasions, he has made at least one or two truly profound comments about my work, but not today. He was silent and he really stunk badly. I moved a few feet away from him but remained within hearing distance.

"Are you okay, Phil? What's new? I brought you some tomatoes."

I attempted conversation. Phil did not respond. He was not in a talkative mood. He pulled a small plastic box out of one of the many pockets of his large, heavy overcoat. He opened the box and poured coins into his palm—mostly pennies and nickels he had found on the ground. He collects them and doesn't seem to spend them. He spread them carefully on the top of my cooler. Then he tenderly picked them up one at a time, and examined each one very closely. The rustier and crummier they were, the more carefully he examined them. Perhaps Phil was remembering the circumstances related to finding them. I don't know and never will. Sometimes Phil talks—very, very little; mostly he tells me about his day, but never about his former life. Once he even brought me blackberries that he had picked along the railroad track next to the Capitol, at the spot where the tracks go underground before they emerge at Pennsylvania Station.

Phil is a handsome man, tall and lanky, between twenty and thirty years old, with long, matted blond hair and a scraggly blondish beard that covers his entire face. Years ago, when I first noticed him, he acted be-deviled; his body seemed forced into constant motion by his tortured mind. He would walk up and down the steps of the West Wing of the Gallery. Up and down. Down and up. Again and again and again. I wondered how he could sustain the strain without collapsing. It must have been due to his youth and strong constitution. As the years have passed, Phil has calmed somewhat. Still, the inexplicable torment motivates him, making him restless. He always has to get up and walk. He can never sit longer than a few minutes. Phil's presence brings on me a strong urge to urinate. The effect of his visits is like that of a dog to a hydrant.

"Phil, I need to relieve myself," I told him. "Watch my stand. Don't let anyone touch my wet canvas." These were my parting words and off I went. Phil didn't look at me. He concentrated on his coins. But I knew that he heard me. He has guarded my encampment many times.

I ran quickly across the road and dodged tourists as I climbed all sixty steps. Finally, I reached the massive bronze portals and entered the cool, air-conditioned art palace. Quickly, I ran to the men's room. As I relieved myself, my mind dwelt on trivia. I imagined that if there were a contest for the most entries through those fabulous portals to the Gallery during one's life span, I would be the winner. I have relieved myself here at least three times a day, every day, during every weekend in summer, for a score of years. How many times is that? A lot.

One may challenge my claim to championship in that department. What about the Gallery employees coming every day to work? Well, they have a service door on the street level. They don't use the imposing Mall entrance. I continued in my trivial pursuit while zipping up my trousers and watching two uniformed Gallery guards in conversation. One competition that I would certainly lose, I thought to myself, would be for record use of the bathroom. The first prize for that competition clearly belongs to one of the security guards. The guards are always using the men's room or occupying the only two public telephone booths in the anteroom.

Mission accomplished, I was ready to return to my encampment. First, though, I needed inspiration. I am compelled to communicate with those who are considered to be great masters. By habit, I walked to the nearest exhibition hall, to the right and again to the right. There they were: "Doña Teresa Sureda" by Goya, and the tutor from "Young Man With His Tutor" by de Largilliere. Teresa is beautiful and the tutor is wise. What were their lives like? The models don't live anymore; neither do their famous painters. I will cease to exist also, but what about my work? Will it ever reach those exalted halls?

Back to Phil. He waited until he saw me crossing the drive.

"Thank you Phil. You are a good man." I announced my return.

He walked away with eyes to the ground, without a word or wave of a hand, on his endless search for dropped coins.

Of course, Maria did not show up. It has been a long time.

*   *   *

This is Saturday, early in the afternoon. Young adults, mainly senior high school students from the Soviet Union were strolling about the Mall. A group of them approached me and I had an opportunity to show off my extremely rusty Russian. The students left after a few minutes of chitchat to look for other attractions. But Yulia, a girl from Poltava in Ukraine remained and kept me company for several hours. Alone with Yulia, I learned that she is one of the recruits to Reverend Moon's cult. About two hundred of them are in her group, some even to be married to "randomly" selected partners in a mass ritual wedding. However, she told me that most of them did not believe in the nonsense spewed by Moon; they simply pretended to be converted in order to get a free trip to the USA. Yulia was exceptionally erudite, with a keen knowledge of World War II history. A neatly dressed girl with a fair command of English, she is likely a very good student. She prodded me to tell her about my experiences during the German occupation.

I stopped painting and dipped into my memory. For some time, I dragged out some of the painful, but crucial, events from my life: the experiences of a Jewish boy between the ages of eleven and fourteen. Yulia listened intently and respectfully, and interjected carefully phrased questions.

I told her how we, the Jews in Lwów, were hunted by German special police units and Ukrainian militia in what was known as "actions" or akcias in Polish. I described how Jews were transported to nearby sand pits for execution and how Jews were brutally beaten to death on the streets of Lwów by police, militia and civilians. Yulia was especially interested in our life in the Ghetto. I told her about the filth, starvation and ever-present fear; how my mother and I were hidden in a hole in the ground, which my father dug for us in the Ghetto, where we stayed for many hours during the akcias. The Ghetto was hell, I told her. It was nothing but a cage where Jews were forcibly isolated from the rest of the population. I explained that I was smuggled out and that my life was saved by an elderly Polish woman who hid me for twenty-two months in a tiny room in her apartment.

"Were you ever taken to a concentration camp?" Yulia asked me.

"If I was, I would not be talking to you today," I answered. "Concentration camps were really extermination camps where Jews were starved, worked to death, and executed. Boys like me would have been killed immediately."

Describing those events to Yulia I realized how infrequently I talked about that tragic period. My father Karol was mute to the subject of the Holocaust. He would never mention the suffering that he endured in a concentration camp. Nor would he respond to questions when someone asked him; even to me he would reveal little. He destroyed the few documents that he managed to save except for several small family photographs from pre-World War II days. Father wanted to forget all the brutalities, but my sense is that I should have preserved my ugly remembrances. I shoved much of what happened in Lwów under a mental carpet where the details of those days are slowly dissipating. Perhaps returning to Lwów and seeing the various sites would help to restore my memory so that I could relate it to youngsters such as Yulia. Yes, I think that I should inform the youngsters of our country what it was like.

I must go back. The thought of traveling to Lwów and getting away from here grows on me and excites me.

*   *   *

Yulia returned early this Sunday morning. Today she came alone. She told me that she had made a "woman's health" excuse to the leaders of the Moon group and was left behind in the hotel to minister to her discomfort.

32

"A ruse to see you" she told me.

I was flattered. She was a different girl today. To start with, her hair was not neatly combed and braided but loose and flowing. She wore a miniskirt instead of long shorts, exposing shapely legs. More startlingly, her demeanor had changed radically. What yesterday was a studious, stiff, attentive countenance, today turned into a smiling face with dimples in her cheeks. What happened to the serious, respectful student from Poltava? Yulia did not fire questions at me as she did yesterday but began talking about herself, about her life in Ukraine. Even though her parents were relatively well-off, and even though she was accepted to a prestigious architectural institute for the fall semester, she saw nothing but gloom ahead. Not much hope for a good job, for comfort or even for excitement; yet she wanted all three. She said that she would gladly stay in the States but not as a Mooney.

"I want to live it up. Isn't it what they say and do in America?"

I said nothing and Yulia paused for a while, looking away from me. Perhaps she was remembering something or trying to phrase what she wanted to say.

"I don't want to marry one of those hairless men without balls. I heard from one of our girls that they have little between their legs," she ventured finally. She jolted me with these vulgar statements, but more so when she added, "Do you know a man who will buy me?" I thought that she chose her words poorly. But no, she meant what she said.

"I want to marry a man who would bring me to the States legally. I would leave him afterwards, but I would give him fun for his money and trouble. Marek, do you know such a man? If you do, tell him that Ukrainian girls can be a lot of good time. If we want to, we can fuck well."

Then Yulia opened her handbag and pulled out a manila envelope from which she took out two large photos of herself in very coquettish poses. Her smile was warm and inviting. She looked glamorous in a cocktail dress. She wore a necklace around a well-exposed neck and a bracelet on her naked arm, plus a lot of make-up. I was impressed. It must have cost her a bundle because professionals had shot those photos, and the salon could not have been cheap either.

"You will show them around to rich American men, Marek, okay?

The use of my first name upon such short acquaintance was highly irregular in view of the difference in our ages and especially from someone brought up in Eastern Europe. After I took the envelope from her, Yulia seemed satisfied and reverted back to yesterday's self.

"Tell me more about the Ghetto, Marek. In that hole in the ground where you hid with your mama, what did you do when you or she had to piss?"

*   *   *

Ever since Yulia left to rejoin her group, my mind has focused on the narrow hole in the ground where I sat on my mother's lap. My father would cover the hole with some rusty sheet metal and a sewer lid before he reported for work at the Ghetto gate. Now, as I sit here and write, a vision forms in front of my eyes—I imagine what it would be like if a policeman were to kick aside that sheet metal and discover a boy sitting on his mother's lap. Certainly, the policeman would probe below with his bayonet. He would wound us, inflict pain, prod us out. What would we do? I imagine that our hands would rise in a gesture of surrender, perhaps begging for mercy. Yes, now I can see a painting, portraying our last moments on earth, for certainly he would kill us there and then. I see a somber painting of dark hues except for the two raised right hands, which will be created out of patches of yellow, orange, and violet pigments. It will be a mosaic-like painting. I will start tomorrow and I will name it "Last Day in the Ghetto."

Next weekend will be Labor Day weekend, and another year on the Mall will be ending for me. Maria must be graduating from college by now. No use thinking of her.

I really should travel to Lwów now or next year in the spring, to learn what has happened to those who helped us. Perhaps I could arrange for a show of my work there. This would be a good time for such a trip since the Soviet Union just ceased to exist. Travel would be easier. It would be the first time in many years that I would see Lwów. Forty-five years is a long time. Perhaps I could meet Yulia on her home ground. It would be a good diversion from the Mall and my thoughts of Maria.

Last Day in the Ghetto

Chapter III

————◆————

Maria's Legacy

*I*t was strange how I came to meet Marek Mann.

My father's business required him to travel from our home in Oregon to Washington, D.C. We—my mother, my older sister Kathy, and I—attached ourselves to my father in order to tour the capital for a week. We stayed at a motel in Bethesda, Maryland in a primarily residential section of this vast metropolitan suburbia. From our motel, the three of us traveled to see many of the historically important sites. Once, when his business permitted, my father joined our excursion.

On the last Saturday of our stay, I ventured to town by myself and took the mini-touring bus which circulates through the downtown section. It was steamy hot.

"It is a typical Washington day. Every time I am here it is like a sauna," said the lady who sat next to me.

I got off at the West Building of the National Gallery of Art. I was terribly thirsty and right away I noticed a black woman carrying three frosty-cold bottles in each hand. She wore a very loose blouse made of many colorful patches and an equally vivid turban, unmistakably of African design.

"Water, soda, cold water, icy-cold soda. Only a dollar, one dollar." She stepped up to the bus, looking cautiously around as if she were being followed.

Through the bus windows, passengers were handing her money while they grabbed a thirst-quenching, cold drink. Before

I had a chance to dig out a dollar bill from my purse, the woman turned tail and ran across Madison Drive. A Park Police cruiser swerved from the street after her. The car didn't even slow down for the curb but drove across the sidewalk onto the green area in full pursuit. The black woman disappeared behind the stands of an exhibiting artist. The police cruiser quickly reversed and, in a cloud of dust, drove backwards to begin another forward tack. I don't know how the woman peddler evaded the police because my eyes became absorbed by a profusion of colors and shapes displayed on the artist's stands.

My eyes immediately focused on two paintings composed of vivid geometrical figures that gave the illusion of three-dimensional space. In both paintings, I observed the symbols of the Jewish religion: the menorah and the Star of David. The artist must be Jewish, I thought. Yes. A biographical brochure displayed nearby mentioned that the artist, Marek Mann, was born in Poland. He was a Holocaust survivor, no less.

The artist knelt on the grass in front of a canvas that lay flat on the ground. I stood next to him, being mesmerized by his energetic brush strokes. His forcefulness seemed too much for me, and I suddenly said "Don't!" But, pulled in by that same force, I bent down for a closer look when a button let go on my blouse, exposing my breasts. I became aware of this when the artist stopped painting and steered his eyes toward my bosom. I reddened when droplets of my sweat began to fall on his canvas. For a shy, well-brought up girl this was a calamity. I quickly stood up, trying to pull the blouse together. I was ready to turn away and run when the artist's eyes moved up to my face and arrested me.

Then the artist stood up and introduced himself to me. "What is your name?" he asked.

"Maria," I replied.

"I like your work," I managed to stammer while still clutching my blouse.

Marek talked to me but I don't remember what he said or what I said. It was a very guarded and polite conversation, I am sure. I think that I mentioned that my parents came to America from

Destroyed Temple

Germany. I wanted to ask him some personal questions like how he lost his fingers and what moods motivated him to portray both whimsy and tragedy. But after this embarrassing incident I didn't dare to ask. I wanted to know a lot about this intriguing and imaginative artist but I was trained not to be inquisitive, certainly not to be forward. In fact, I was trained by my German parents

Holocaust

to be a modest young lady. So, I just listened to Marek's discourse on the history of Eastern Europe.

Thankfully, this seemingly superficial but, to me, somehow titillating interview came to an end when other tourists approached us and attracted Marek's attention. I walked away with a wave of

my hand. Marek was looking at me even though he was explaining something to a young man who was questioning him. He beckoned me, saying, "Stay. Don't go yet."

I continued to walk away and did not turn back, but I was definitely pleased and thrilled to meet a working artist.

At the bus stop, the same woman was peddling cold drinks. She was undaunted by the recent police pursuit.

"A dollar. Only a dollar for my bottles," she sang out.

She was a virtuoso performer. With her head whirling in all directions, she was giving change, stashing the bills under her ample colorful blouse, and handing out bottles—all in matter of seconds. I was parched with thirst and quickly bought a bottle of water, unscrewed the top, took several sips, and the hot muggy day felt good; I had met a man who puzzled me and stirred me. I hopped up to the Gallery entrance, skipping some steps in my exuberance and entered the marble coolness of the Gallery interior.

Inside, I reproached myself for not buying some of Marek's postcards. At least then I would have known his address and could have been able to write to him. I made a mental note to stop by his stand on the way out and buy something. It didn't happen that way. After some time in the Gallery, I walked out through the Pennsylvania Avenue exit, a good distance from Marek's stand. I figured that if I came back it might seem brash. Girls like me must not appear to be fresh, I thought. Anyway, we were to fly back to Oregon the next day so all this would be history.

*   *   *

But history it wasn't. Colors, shapes, Marek, and the whole scene around the Gallery kept popping into my mind. Last night, I had another dream about Grandmother Menke. She beckons me in these dreams; she seems to tell me the way I must go. She sends me back to Washington, back to see Marek.

As fortune would have it, my father had to travel to Washington again. To the complete surprise of my family, I insisted on accompanying him. The reasons I gave to my parents were flimsy: I was beginning my senior year in high school, and I wanted to visit Georgetown and American University. Secretly, I wanted to see Marek again. I was attracted to this old but charismatic man, and to his life stories. Underlying this desire was my need to appear in his eyes, as well as in my own, as an assertive young woman. It bothered me that I sort of ran away from him that time on the Mall. I needed to learn how to converse, how to acquire social graces, especially vis-à-vis a mature man. I must admit that mature men appeared in my fantasies more frequently than boys. Besides, I was still on summer vacation and I was getting bored at home.

Father and I left on Wednesday and I had two full days to tour the area before I would venture to Marek's exhibit stand on Saturday. I visited Corcoran Gallery. (What trash!) In the Phillips Gallery, I saw an excellent, large Renoir that portrayed a lusty group of picnickers, and then I walked through Georgetown. With great curiosity, I inspected the Georgetown University campus. Its architecture denoted a long history and venerable tradition. I thought about how different it was from the University of Oregon, where I planned to attend. I found American University to be less imposing and more accessible. Perhaps I should apply there, I thought.

The next day on the way to the Holocaust Museum near the Washington Mall, the pavement steamed. I was telling myself that I should have known better than to come back to this built-up swamp at this time of the year. My long, brown hair was tied back in a ponytail, but beads of sweat still gathered where my hair met my skin, and fine, salty lines trickled down the sides of my face and the back of my neck. How unladylike, I couldn't help thinking. Some years ago, Grandmother Menke's elegant sister Liesl had told me that ladies didn't sweat, while moisture actually wet her own brow as she walked in two-tone heels down the promenade of the spa town Baden-Baden. The unsaid German phrase was that sweat on men was sexy, but my great-aunt let that thought go with a twinkle in her eye and a slight blush that might have just been from the heat.

Wiping my cheeks and neck with wilting tissues, I continued to walk toward the Holocaust Museum on a mission motivated by a mess of confusing questions. I thought back to one of my earliest memories: a night at the Menke's house, my grandparents' beachfront house in Maine. It was a farewell party, actually, before my parents packed up the Volkswagen 411 and moved us to Oregon. Maybe that was where my questions began. I was seven years old then.

That night, the record player was on and everything was whirling around as my father guided Grandmother Menke around the living room. His movements were studied and responsible, her fingers awkward in the cupped palm he offered. My grandfather's large arms were wrapped around his daughter—my mother—and the couple flew by in a burst as the next polka started up. It was the last song before the record would need to be changed again. And there was my older sister Kathy, with her gleaming eyes. She was running alongside the spinning dancers and bending over as if she wanted to unwrap them and see between them.

The music stopped and my grandmother smiled as my father bowed, only partly in jest. He never was quite comfortable with his mother-in-law. Even though her strong body had gotten her through seventy-five years, she was glad for the short rest. She wanted to sit down for a little while with a martini and a cigarette. She wasn't used to nights like this, though she enjoyed them.

My grandmother walked over to the dark brown baby grand piano which doubled as a sideboard, and poured a drink out of the pewter martini shaker that stood there. My father looked guilty as he stood over the record player and called out that he hadn't realized she was "dry." The furniture had been pushed over to one side of the room, and as she settled herself against the piano, I ran across the floor from my perch at the top of the staircase where I had been resting after twirling through so many polkas already that evening. My feet barely made a sound in the electric blue slippers that I thought were appropriate dress shoes for that night's dance, maybe because of their metallic silver trim. My face was red and dripping then, just as it was when I walked on the Mall to see Marek again.

Others were dancing as my father approached Grandmother Menke and they began to talk seriously in whispers. Several times "Willi" and "Halya Laski" entered their conversation. I also overhead them mentioning another name: Gerhard.

"Lets not talk about Gerhard," said my father in German.

"Why not?" interrupted Aunt Hedwig, my father's sister who joined the conversation. "At least our brother Gerhard and others in the Martell family died honorably, fighting for Germany. They were not like Willi—that brutal Communist."

Silence followed and Hedwig, feeling rebuffed, walked away. My father looked away toward the record player and my grandmother lit a cigarette. She was clearly agitated.

"Kurt, wait," she suddenly said, interrupting my father before he could put the needle on the record. Grandmother's eyes swept the room, pausing for a moment on my mother.

"I have something for you to take with you."

From the small bookcase behind the piano she pulled out a soft, worn cardboard file tied with a blue ribbon.

"Here are some old things and some new. I don't want them anymore," she said in a tone I recognized. It was the tone she used when asked about her past, about her family, about what was just referred to as "the war." My mother would pose the questions anxiously, anticipating the inevitable discomfort they caused. But she would still try, again and again. Without saying a word, my grandmother would cross her arms over her limp breasts and grip each side of her torso with stiffening fingers.

But that night she answered, in the simple gesture of handing a well-bound file to my mother. And that night my mother remained silent. She put the file aside and looked at my father expectantly. He started another record and the dancing resumed. All the adults were enjoying the waltzes and tangos except for Aunt Hedwig, who sat apart coddling an empty martini goblet in both hands. She was always cheerful around company, but there she sat alone, gazing at the floor, apparently deeply in thought, perhaps thinking of Uncle Gerhard and her other brother who had died for Germany.

Months later, after we arrived at our new home in Oregon and I entered a new elementary school, the file sat on our upright piano. I untied the ribbon, opened the file, and saw German script on the first page. I could make out the words "Willi Menke" and "Lemberg, Schätzchen." The last two were the name of a town and a term of endearment. I quickly browsed through and saw letters and newspaper clippings. My unsanctioned deed scared me and I ventured no further, but re-tied the file and left the room. Willi Menke, familiarly Willi, my great-uncle. What about him?

Now back in Washington, waiting to visit Marek's stand on Saturday, I went to the Holocaust Museum. I couldn't do otherwise—too many questions swirled in my brain. As a diligent student, I viewed everything conscientiously and found the experience revolting. The thought that the Nazi beasts might have cut off Marek's fingers in a camp gave me goose pimples. This time, when I see Marek I will ask him, I thought to myself. I must know, no matter how embittering that knowledge may be. To be sure, not all Germans perpetrated those atrocities, but those who did and directed others certainly were German. The families of both my parents were German living in Germany during the war. Could any of them have had something to do with those atrocities? I was troubled by that thought. What about great-uncle Willi? What was Willi's role during that terrible period?

Saturday finally came. In order not to appear overly eager to see Marek by being at the stand early in the morning, I tarried. The fabulous space technology and the intricate engineering feats on display at the Air and Space Museum overwhelmed me again, but could not completely captivate my mind. Marek's likeness permeated through every display. After wandering about the exhibits for about an hour, I walked out onto the Mall, directing my steps toward the National Gallery of Art.

It had rained very hard during the night. Water had inundated lower lawns and created large pools on the gravel path. Tourists were not discouraged by the drizzling rain. It was about eleven o'clock in the morning and already multitudes of them jostled past as I slowly made my way toward Madison Drive. Diverse races, different languages, young and old were rushing to see, to photograph and, later, to remember.

Groups heading in the opposite direction were making their way to the Air and Space Museum. Blocking the flow of walkers were hustlers selling umbrellas, T-shirts, or simply soliciting money for various causes: help the drug addicts, become a flower girl, be a part of human race. Do not eat meat, do not wear animal fur, do not use cosmetics, and other dos and don'ts. They targeted me who was alone and walking slowly, and I tried to shake them off politely. But where were Marek's stands? I reached the area where Marek displayed his work only to find a few shabby tables loaded with T-shirts, protected from the rain by long, plastic sheets. I beheld a homeless man with his head turned upward. He was swallowing raindrops while his body swayed to a silent music.

I lingered, walked up and down on the sidewalk of the Drive but saw no Marek. I felt unfulfilled and sad, as if I had lost something that I didn't even know was precious to me.

Dejected, I walked away aimlessly. It stopped drizzling but the steamy air drenched my body with perspiration and my mind with confusion. I was wet but didn't care—I was miserable among all those people. Out of this confusion, my brain wove together a pattern—a vision of myself with a purpose. It was an intricate pattern created by thoughts of myself, Marek, my family, the Holocaust, and events of the past. A life to be explored formed before my eyes. At that moment, I knew that I would study history: the history of Eastern Europe, the history of the Holocaust, the history of my family. I might have lost contact with Marek but not the memory of him. The intricate pattern marbleized into a ball of bright hues. The ball fell onto the ground and I kicked it forward with all of my strength. It rolled, but it did not fall apart. It was as solid as the resolution born within me. My step quickened as I remembered to meet my father for a late lunch before we flew back home.

* * *

I was sitting next to my father, flying across the country. I was deep in thought. My kind father tried to coax me into conversation by telling me about his professional dealings in Washington but he got little response from me. Sensing my reluctance to share my thoughts with him he gave up somewhere over West Virginia, probably attributing my silence to a romantic interlude during my previous visit. Why else would I insist on traveling with him again to the same place we had visited just three weeks earlier? To visit the area universities? Bah! It must have seemed to him that his seventeen-year-old girl had met a young man and deserved to have her privacy. How wrong he was! My thoughts were profound—they belabored the terrible history of the twentieth century. My walk to the Holocaust Museum on the steamy sidewalk did not begin when I met Marek. That walk began a long time ago. It began with Great-uncle Willi's file.

As a girl on the verge of starting the first grade, I was already an avid reader. But that day that I opened the file, it overwhelmed me. A page that I pulled from the middle displayed no words that I recognized; only later did I realize it was Russian. The German script on the first page looked like what I had seen in Christmas songbooks. Struck by the same awe with which we observed Christmas Eve and sang carols, I put the file back down. Within a few days it was gone, probably stashed away somewhere with other family papers. I never heard my parents speak of Willi's file, and amidst the distractions of settling into our new house, I forgot about it.

Some ten years later the file reappeared. I was in high school then, and in history class we were discussing World War II and the Holocaust. I came home from school one day, upset. Over dinner, I told my parents what had happened that morning.

While driving to school with my newly earned license, I had gotten into an argument with my classmate, Shana, who lived nearby and rode with me. Shana had said that the class discussions had aroused new feelings in her about her Jewish identity. She was struggling to comprehend the terror unleashed upon the Jews during the Holocaust. She could not understand how the perpetrators could have done what they did.

My response was naive, I now see, and insensitive. "But the Germans suffered too," I said. I told her how my father's two brothers had been killed fighting for Hitler's Germany. As she and I grew more and more agitated, I tried to make my way through my own confusion. My mother's aunts and uncles had resisted Hitler and died; my father's parents and sisters had raised their arms shouting "Sieg Heil!" for the Führer while their sons, brothers, and husbands were dying in battle. Now I had implied to my Jewish friend that the personal pain caused by my uncles' deaths was somehow equivalent to the suffering of the victims and survivors of the genocide. Did I really believe that?

It was around that time in high school when Willi's file unexpectedly reappeared on our upright piano. I do not know if it was my mother or my father who brought it back out. When I got home from school the house was empty; my parents were still at work, and my sister Kathy was away at college. I took the file to my bedroom. With one of the quick, shallow breaths that make me lightheaded under stress, I opened it.

The papers were stained and deceptively smooth. I envisioned my grandmother's arthritic hands pressing over them, just as she would rhythmically and absent-mindedly smooth out her place mat at the dinner table. Usually the motion signaled that her deep convictions, often suppressed out of shyness, were rising to the surface. Sometimes she would then shyly but pointedly state her case after she and my father had disagreed over a political issue. But while smoothing out these papers Grandmother Menke surely was alone and remembering her past.

I again saw a number of letters, still in what looked like their original envelopes, and also sheets of paper and some clippings

50

from what appeared to be a West German newspaper. One of the clippings was very large and contained two artistic renderings of the same man. One showed him with a kind smile, in fact a handsome smile, the smile of a successful man. In the other, he leered; his head was turned but his eyes directly challenged the viewer. The bold headline caught my attention: IS WILLI MENKE REALLY THE MAN HE SEEMS TO BE? It was a front-page story; the title of the sensational but still respected weekly, *Die Welt*, stood above the headline. The date was December 3, 1956. The story claimed that Willi Menke, the outgoing and seemingly friendly East German Politburo member, was also the head of the committee that crafted policies—oftentimes severe—regarding escapees from East Germany. The reporter had interviewed recent successful escapees who consistently mentioned Uncle Willi as the cruelest proponent of brutality. I was startled, intrigued, and plunged eagerly into the lengthy article.

There were also two clippings of photographs that pertained to the article. The one that caught my attention first was taken with the Brandenburg Gate in the background. On the picture, a tall, uniformed man was pointing to a large concrete plate on the ground with several military or police officials watching attentively as uniformed personnel affixed a gigantic slab in a vertical position to a standing assortment of metal beams and other slabs, forming a wall. The sarcastic caption read: WILLI MENKE, "CHARMING" CHAIRMAN OF POWERFUL INTERNAL SECURITY COMMITTEE SUPERVISES STRENGTHENING OF WALL IN BERLIN.

The second photograph showed the same tall man with a broad smile, this time wearing a civilian suit with a tie, standing in front of a group of children. The children were laughing and each extended a long-stemmed rose in his direction. The man focused his attention on a well-dressed woman, a group leader, whose hand he grasped. In the background was a solid black curtain with a sign: WE PIONEERS ARE THE FUTURE OF OUR SOCIALIST STATE. The caption under the photo differed somewhat with that statement. It read: THE FALSE WILLI MENKE AND HIS ILK ARE BOTH THE PRESENT AND THE FUTURE OF A SOCIALIST STATE.

After these initial revelations about Uncle Willi, I wanted to finish the article right away but I worried that one of my parents would see me. In any case, I needed time to make my way through the entire file and all of those German words, especially the handwritten letters, which looked hard to read. I saw what looked like the Cyrillic alphabet on some of the pages, but I could not make any sense of it. I turned back to the old German script and I started to read painstakingly when another short newspaper clipping in the same font as the Die Welt article caught my attention. It stated: WILHELM MENKE DISAP-PEARS FROM POLITBURO SCENE.

I heard the doors squeak. I put the file together and left the room. The file was not there when I returned.

Just then, as well as the time when I walked across the steamy Mall on that July day on my way from the Holocaust Museum, I knew that I was driven by a belief that it was up to me to complete Willi's story and certainly the mystery of his disappearance. My parents and grandparents' anxiety about the past had seeped into me. But surpassing that fear was curiosity, and anticipation of an adventure that would carry me out of my family's embrace.

Chapter IV

———◆———

Marek Remembers Lwów

It is the fall of 1991. I departed from Dulles International Airport for Europe on United Airlines, and in Frankfurt, Germany, I transferred to a Ukrainian airliner bound for Lwów. On descent, the Ukrainian jet burst through the clouds and I beheld the landscape below.

It is definitely not the picture of Germany or even that of Eastern Germany. Here, in western Ukraine, there is little regularity in the shapes of the fields. The colors are not delineated but appear to merge into each other, as if rational man had little influence in altering the landscape. Even groups of houses look as if they were randomly tossed together without a plan. In contrast, fields in Germany have distinguishable, angular shapes; they are generally large and each exhibits a different hue of green or yellow. Even the forested areas seem to have been planned—trees planted and grown in an orderly manner. In Germany, the network of narrow and wide roads along the edges of the fields indicates ease of transportation, an important attribute of industrialized civilization. Here, over western Ukraine, I see few roads and many of these show colors darker than the reflected color of a paved road. These obviously are dirt roads. The most striking difference between those two countries, however, is the scarcity of motor traffic on the roads below me.

As the plane descended, buildings and communities in large numbers came into view. We lowered even further and what a sight: a cemetery of Soviet aircraft. As far as my eye could see from the window of the jet, aircraft, fuselages, wings, and detached engines littered the fields like bones after a cannibalistic feast. Their greenish, rusty color almost blended with overgrown bushes and grasses. The seemingly intact aircraft were abandoned helter-skelter, different types, in different orientations. An idiotic thought occurred to me: this was not a vast junk dump, but the Ukrainian Air Force, well camouflaged against an enemy attack. Another equally facetious thought came upon me: these were clever decoys to lure enemy planes. But who could be the enemy? The Cold War is over, and this year Ukraine became an independent state. I did not have time to pursue this line of thinking because our plane lowered its wheels and in a moment, we were taxiing on the runway. "Welcome to Sknilów," I said quite loudly, using the Polish name for the airport, and the other passengers looked at me as if I were crazy.

Little do they know that I am indeed out of my mind, crazy for coming back here where we suffered so much. But the lapse of decades has mellowed the bitterness and an invitation to exhibit my work in Ukraine, to give a lecture at the Art Institute of Lwów, has helped to draw me back to the town. Actually, my advancing age has made it imperative for me to finally find out what has happened to Pani Franciszka, the one who saved my life by hiding me. What happened to her husband and to our Polish and Ukrainian neighbors? What was the fate of dear Pani Natalia and helpful Pani Cwik? When I think of them, I still use the Polish word Pani meaning "Mrs." Normally, Pani is a polite form of address, but when used with the first name, it expresses fond respect. I am hoping to learn about those of my generation: Misko, Bolek, Lesia, and certainly Bogdan. Once, we all lived and interacted on Lyczakowska Street, the street where our apartment house was located.

Marek's chances of meeting former neighbors, even ones from his own generation, were slim. Ninety-seven percent of Jewish residents of Lwów were murdered. Most of the Polish residents were resettled by Soviets at the end of World War II. With the Allied victory, the Soviet Union incorporated eastern Poland with Lwów, its largest town, into its vast land empire. As compensation, Poland was awarded Silesia and Pomerania, which were part of the German Reich. Thus Polish residents of Lwów were shipped en masse to those two provinces. Although some Ukrainian residents took refuge in Austria and Germany as the Red Army approached, most stayed to face Communism.

Lyczakowska Street is a thoroughfare radiating eastward from the defensive walls of the historic town of Lwów. The street was handsomely paved with square cobblestones in which trolley rails were laid for Line #1. From the origin of the street, and for several short blocks after, one sees old, massive—but not tall—apartment buildings. Some of these have large, twin-door gates with drives that tunnel through the house into the courtyard. Decades ago, the courtyards accommodated carriages and stables for horses. These tunneled passages from the street into the courtyards are dark. They are not lit now and most certainly never were. Further up, as the street climbs away from Old Town, newer houses appear among blocks of old ones. Prior to World War II, facing the street were small retail stores, tradesmen's workshops, restaurants, and even a nightclub. A farmer's market, a hospital building, churches, a synagogue, a school for the speaking and hearing impaired, public schools and a movie theater were all within a few blocks from 41A Lyczakowska, where Marek lived. This was an apartment house where Poles, Ukrainians, ethnic Germans (later called *Volksdeutsche*) lived together under the same roof, often cooperating on a daily basis. Though they harbored hatreds and prejudices, lied and were false to their neighbors, they also loved with dedication and passion. This was the Mann family home since before Marek's birth, through the Soviet and German occupations, until the end of summer 1942, at which time they were forced to leave it for the Ghetto.

If one would fly over the region of Lyczaków, the Mann house would be seen as an equilateral, rather stubby-angled, self-standing building among gardens and courtyards, surrounded by houses fronting Lyczakowska Street and its tributary side streets. Marek's house could be entered from the street only through the hallway of number 41, which itself was one in a row of ten adjoining buildings that lined the street. From the air, these houses would be seen as a block of pairs of buildings, each pair consisting of two L-shaped houses, joined by a common wall. At the shorter leg of the L, like Siamese twins, they were mirror images of each other. This entire block was built at the beginning of nineteenth century.

The house at 41A Lyczakowska was considered to be a new house. It was built by Marek's parents in 1928 behind the row of houses fronting the street. It was ideally located—a short walk to the middle of busy Old Town, and yet quiet, in a parcel of land with trees and flowers around it. The house had three stories. On each floor were two apartments: one four-room with a kitchen and one two-room with a kitchen, as well as two one-room basement apartments. Each kitchen had a balcony. Being at the ends of the angle legs, the balconies faced each other across a small garden and a small yard below.

During and after his initial visit to Lwów in the fall of 1991, Marek finally forced himself to write his memoirs. The visit was motivated by his melancholic outlook on his future prospects and his realization that the events of the brutal past had to be accounted for and recorded. I did not edit these memoirs, nor Marek's observations about his final visit to Lwów, which he wrote as chronicles. I merely arranged them in an order most conducive to the flow of the story.

*   *   *

Growing up, I played in the little garden and the little yard enclosed on two sides by my house. Towering almost directly over my head were six kitchen balconies, the place where neighbors and parents talked to each other, hung wash, beat carpets, or sat leisurely, sometimes peeling potatoes. Before World War II, my world was small, intriguing, and comfortable. My mother took me on outings to Old Town where many enticing smells permeated the air. The basement stores were full of delicatessens: Sour kraut, stuffed herring, pickled tomatoes, and cucumbers. I relished all of these. Often we would walk or take a trolley to Zamek. Zamek was a wonderfully wild park on the hills right under the remains of the castle that guarded the town centuries ago.

Mother's cousin Paula, who lived close to us, and her daughter Ella, a year older than I, would join us on those excursions. Mother and I would first stop at Paula's. She would just be getting out of bed. I didn't mind waiting for her because this gave me an opportunity to learn about female anatomy. Paula invariably would greet us in her underwear and she would finish dressing in our presence. The final touches required her to lift her skirt several times and pull her garter and majtki upwards—they must have been somewhat loose. This procedure gave me an excellent view of Paula's voluptuous calves, of her ample behind, as well as of the angle where her legs came together. Paula did not seem to mind when I stared at her, while my mother was so engrossed in talking about her own problems that she probably forgot about me. Although I did not experience an erection until a few years later, Paula's exposure of herself excited me tremendously. When, emboldened by what I saw, I asked Ella to lift her dress for me, Ella only scolded me and told me that I was a bad boy. If intense prepubescent curiosity is bad, so be it.

Yes, it was good to have family around. My paternal grandfather was a master of sheet metal work. Essentially, he had a roofing business, but in his shop, the workers also made and repaired pots and pans. His workshop occupied the entire basement floor of number 43, next door. In the summer, larger jobs such as tinning very large cooking pots would be done in the combined courtyard of numbers 43 and 45. There was always lots of activity in his workshop. On market days, peasant women would come and bring their leaking milk cans and other metal utensils for repair, or buy new ones. It was my grandmother who presided over that aspect of the business. I spend many hours in that shop, fashioning swords and shields out of scrap sheet metal. There were also other members of my family who lived on this block. On Jewish holidays we all would gather at my grandparents' apartment to celebrate. Their house was on one of the small streets around the corner. In fact, I could see their kitchen balcony from our garden.

I would have gone on to the third grade if the war had not devastated our lives. Yes, my circumstances were certainly pleasant prior to that apocalyptic event. Even the little anti-Semitic bullying to which I was subjected was more than compensated for by what, at that time, I thought to be the genuine friendship of older, non-Jewish boys who were my neighbors. There was Bolek who was Polish, and Misko and Bogdan, both Ukrainian. I remember how these bigger boys took me skating in winter and how I flew on ice between them, holding onto their hands as they propelled themselves with incredible speed. How our all lives altered with the advent of the war! Human relationships began to change drastically with the coming of the Soviet occupation, which began in the final days of September 1939.

Prior to that date, we lived a middle class, town-based life. My father, Karol, was at that time a journeyman in a sheet metal guild and he worked for my grandfather. We lived in a four-room apartment on the second floor. Although my parents did own the apartment house, they were perpetually deep in debt. I understood that it was because they built the house at the wrong time. I did not know the difference between the "wrong" and the "right" time, and it was of little consequence to me when I was eight or nine.

My parents never did have ready money and had to sublet one of the front rooms to a succession of out-of-town medical students. The Lyczaków section had a vast complex of public hospitals as well as a university and a medical school, and therefore a housing need for students and interns. My grandmother paid my father's salary, part of it indirectly. She did not trust my father with money, my mother even less so. She considered them to be frivolous, so instead she would give our maid the cash to make food purchases. That way she assured herself that I would have something to eat. At least that is what she thought.

To be sure, my parents were partygoers; they gave receptions and they went to parties while I was obliged to go to bed. They seemed to associate a lot with Paula and her husband Wilek, a physician. I think that the association was considerably intimate, at least that is the way that it appeared to me. My father and Paula went together to a watering place every summer, while I saw my mother and Wilek together frequently. Well, they are all gone. It hardly matters now.

I have since learned that Captain Wilhelm Engel was taken as a prisoner of war by the Soviets in September 1939 and was one among 10,000 Polish officers shot in the back of his head at Katyn in 1941. The fun-loving, gentle physician met his end. Paula and Ella were taken by Soviet police to one of the most inhospitable places in Siberia, but they managed to survive. At the time they were being taken, it was considered a tragedy, but as events proved later, it was a blessing. Germans or Ukrainians would have brutally murdered them.

In contrast to my parents, I always had ready cash. My very dear grandmother would give me ten groszy, the equivalent of ten pennies, every day that I stopped at the sheet metal shop. She gave me a coin and a kiss. I did not spend it frivolously. I saved it. It was Bogdan, whose friendship I cherished, who would often "borrow" the money from me, never to return it. He also encouraged me to remove small sheets of tinned sheet metal from the store and give it to him. He was my idol and I obeyed him.

I had a small room in our apartment next to the kitchen where our maid had her bed; that is, whenever we had a maid. I was told that years ago I had a nursemaid. Today, I vaguely remember our domestic help. But the image of the courtyard and the garden where I played is imbedded in my mind. I also retain vivid images of our neighbors in this self-standing three-story house at 41A Lyczakowska Street.

* * *

Even before I was nine years old, I knew that our immediate neighbor on the second floor, Pani Cwik, lived together with Pan Burek without being married. I heard that she stole Pan Burek from his wife and their two sons. Pani Cwik and Pan Burek were patriotic Poles and, like nearly all Poles, they were Catholic. I also knew that they never went to church services because of their sin. Pani Cwik was a dainty but extremely energetic woman of thirty-five or forty. She always walked fast, talked fast, and furiously beat the carpets with a trzepaczka, a carpet paddle, on her balcony. Clouds of dust would emerge under Pani Cwik's powerful strokes. When I saw Pani Cwik cleaning, I was glad that she was not my mother. My mother would not beat me with a trzepaczka as was the custom, but would lightly smack me on the face when aggravated, which happened often.

Despite Pani Cwik's violent cleaning method, her demeanor toward Pan Burek was always gentle and caring; she was totally devoted to him. She called Pan Burek "Tatuniu," little dear father. I was sure that Pan Burek was very precious to Pani Cwik—after all, I thought, he must have been worth a lot because she stole him away from his family. Pan Burek, an imposing, heavy-set, bald man in his sixties, he was neither her Tatuniu nor the father of her children (she had none). "Tatuniu, don't do this. Tatuniu, don't stress yourself. Tatuniu, let me help you," was a constant admonition to Pan Burek. This is when I learned the words "angina pectoris." Pan Burek had a heart problem—at least one.

He was a well-respected intellectual, always with a book or a newspaper in his hand. With all the ominous news surrounding us Jews at that time, Pan Burek assiduously tried to discover a hopeful word or a phrase in a local, four-page pro-Nazi rag. If he indeed found a shred of good news, he would happily accost my father to tell him that the situation was not terribly bad. He was an incurable optimist. At one time, Pan Burek was a high-ranking official in the Polish regional government (Wojewodztwo), so his views were correspondingly well-respected. Even so, the man was deluding himself and others. The German army was invincible at that time and hope for its defeat was unjustified.

Underneath us, in another four-room apartment, lived an unmarried couple with a dental practice. They were a Jewish man and a Polish woman. Pani Doctorowa Yanka was a dentist and her partner, Daniel Szapiro, was a dental technician. She received and treated patients in the front two rooms and he had his workshop in the third room. The last, smallest room was their bedroom.

Pani Yanka had a beautiful face but walked with the help of leg braces. I don't know what her disability was, but she limped very badly. She called her partner "Tusiek." He was a smallish man who talked quietly and walked softly. He was kind of a mousy person. He didn't look Jewish but which Jew really did? Tusiek had blue eyes and thin, blond hair like my mother and me—perhaps we were throwbacks to the Khazars or perhaps had genes of Cossack rapists. Pani Yanka and Tusiek were outwardly cordial and affectionate with each other;

60

they must have been deeply in love. Later, she tried to save his life by hiding him in the apartment, but they were informed upon and both were arrested. She, along with sixty other people, was executed by a firing squad. Tusiek was most likely murdered on Piaski, the sandy, precipitous, uninhabited ravines in Lwów near Lyczakowska Street, a place where Jews were slain en masse.

I remember that Pani Yanka and Tusiek smoked a lot, and that they never left the apartment. Oftentimes, after work, they sat with a friend or two on the kitchen balcony. They would still be wearing their white smocks. They all studied horse racing magazines. I suspect that one of the frequent visitors was taking their bets. Playing in the little garden, I had an excellent view of their balcony. It was only three feet above the garden level. It was easy for me to look underneath Pani Yanka's lab coat and dress, but after seeing the complex metal and leather contraption that embraced her leg, I ceased to look. I reserved that kind of exploration for the first girl who interested me: Lesia.

*   *   *

Lesia was Bogdan's sister and Bogdan was my friend. Lesia was about two years younger than me. She was blond, blue-eyed, thin, and lithe, I might add. She would merely chuckle when, occasionally as we played, I would stick my hand under her dress and feel her legs all the way to her majteczki, her panties. Once, she began to lower them for me, but I was too timid, and I told her not to bare herself. Actually, I liked her a lot, and she was the princess of my fantasies, like the princesses in fairytales. I thought that she should not expose her private parts.

My younger playmate, Kazik, felt differently. He was not a dream-er but a doer. Although he was a year younger than me, he was my mentor when it came to sex education. Gleefully, he told me that Lesia had taken her panties off for him and had showed him her pizda. I thought that he was bragging; I didn't want to believe that my princess would do it for anyone, not even for me. But Kazik convinced me by describing the coarse material of Lesia's majteczki. I had felt their coarseness myself. I realized that Lesia was not a fairy princess and that she had betrayed my affection. But her betrayal was nothing in comparison to how Bogdan behaved toward me later.

Lesia and Bogdan were the children of an improbably-matched Ukrainian couple who lived in a two-room apartment on the third floor. Pan Kapista was a tall, aloof, older man with little remaining hair plastered to one side. He was always properly dressed in a suit, with a buttoned shirt and a tie. I think that he was an accountant or some sort of a senior pencil-pusher. He wore a pince-nez and carried himself erectly, exuding an air of respectability, prosperity, and authority. For as many times as I visited their apartment prior to the German occupation, I seldom saw Pan Kapista and doubt that he ever noticed me. He never said anything to me, even when he was around.

Pani Natalia Kapista was the extreme opposite of Pan Kapista. First of all, she was pleasant to behold and to be around. She was of medium height with curly, dark hair. Her eyes, I think, were blue. She wore simple, neatly fitting dresses with colorful flower designs that accentuated her gentle curves. She was not beautiful in the sense of the movie stars I saw in American film magazines; she was plain but definitely pretty and a nice person. I was always pleased to hear her speaking to Lesia and Bogdan in Ukrainian and to me in Polish. Like all the Ukrainians I knew, they spoke both languages well. In comparison to other neighbors with whose children I played, Pani Natalia treated me better. She allowed me entry to their apartment early during the German occupation at a time when other neighbors had already forbidden me to visit them.

In contrast to the fair-colored Lesia, Bogdan was dark and stout. Although Bogdan was three or four years older than me, he took an interest in me. I often came up to his apartment and he invited me to watch him build tiny models of naval ships. Bogdan was a very creative boy. In constructing his truly Lilliputian navy, he used anything that could be scrounged: buttons, needles and metal scraps, small bottle tops, and tiny bits of plywood. He would let me help him arrange his tin soldiers in battle arrays or parade formations. We also traded postal stamps. He had already accumulated a large collection by the time that I began to emulate him and start my own collection. Bogdan's ingenious creativity was matched by his ingenious unscrupulousness. Bogdan traded stamps dishonestly, always to his advantage. He would also cleverly steal my stamps. He would lick the palm of his hand, and while examining my loose stamps, he would stick the more valuable to his palm. I saw it and knew what he was up to, but I did not complain.

Within the first month or two of the occupation, the Jews of Lwów were assessed some millions of zlotys to be paid in gold or silver. This was called reparation, a fine for "crimes" committed by the Jews! The repercussions would have been dire if the Jewish community had failed to produce that huge amount in a very short time, perhaps two or three days. Our apartment was designated as the collection center for the Lyczaków area. I distinctly remember how Jews flocked into our apartment depositing their jewelry, coins, silver items, and other valuables on our large dining room table. Some of our non-Jewish Polish neighbors also stopped by and left donations to show their solidarity. I can still picture gentle Natalia entering our apartment and depositing a piece or two of her jewelry on the table. She came and departed without a word, very quickly, perhaps not wanting to be seen. Because she was Ukrainian and because Pan Kapista was an ultranationalist, her action surprised me, but I was grateful.

At the end of the second day, the table bulged with donations. It was piled with tall stacks of gold and silver coins, American dollars, Russian tsarist rubles, Polish coins, and all sorts of precious objects. The highest stacks were of the three denominations of Polish silver coins: 10, 5, and 2 zlotys. I was marveling at this accumulated wealth when Bogdan slipped into the room.

"There is so much money here and it certainly will not be missed if we start a coin collection with some of those," he told me. "Go ahead. Grab some," he told me sternly. "I will take a few and you take some—it is alright. Go ahead, take them and give them to me," he demanded.

I obeyed him. I stepped up to the table and, pretending to examine some of the Polish coins, I took a handful of them. I gave Bogdan most but I did retain some pieces for my collection. I still have those three coins today. The memory pains me and reddens my cheeks as I write. Yes, Bogdan corrupted me.

A day came when the Kapista's apartment door was closed to me, gently but with finality. I surmised that it was because Pan Kapista probably admonished his family. Bogdan then became a constant visitor to our apartment, which by now was reduced to two rooms denuded of most furniture, but loaded with sheet metal tools that my father Karol had rescued from grandfather's shop. (At that time my grandparents had already been murdered.) Bogdan's visits were not friendly in nature. We did not do things together. Bogdan merely came to browse among the tools and then would simply take some with the statement, "You will not need them."

My father Karol must have known about the pilfering, but neither said nor did nothing to stop Bogdan. I thought that he feared Bogdan or Pan Kapista, but perhaps Karol had realized already that we would be forced into the Ghetto and would not be allowed to take anything with us. So, it did not matter to him. But it did matter to me. Bogdan's calls, even under selfish pretexts, still meant a lot to me; being favored by Bogdan's visits still meant prestige for me in the eyes of my non-Jewish friends, especially Kazik.

*   *   *

Kazik Kieda, his parents, a baby sister, and a fairly large dog lived in a one-room (with a kitchen) basement apartment in our house of odd couples. Kazik's parents were no exception. Pan Kieda was a Ukrainian and Pani was Polish. Pan was not religious, but Pani was; at least he did not insist on bringing up Kazik according to the Ukrainian Greek Catholic rite, which differs from the Polish Roman Catholic rite. Pani Kieda was raising both Kazik and his baby sister in the Polish language and as Roman Catholics. Since Pani worked by helping Pan in the shoemaking business, a young peasant woman who came daily to take care of Kazik and his sister became an important addition to their family. Kasia was essentially a baby sitter. Although nominally in charge, Kasia would let Kazik behave however he wanted. In the absence of parents, Kazik was actually the boss.

The Kieda's very congested quarters were decorated with numerous religious articles. I distinctly recall a picture and a figurine of St. Mary,

64

the mother of Christ. Not surprising, since Polish people adored St. Mary the most from amongst all the saints in the holy gallery. St. Mary received even more adulation than Jesus himself. Although Jesus did receive considerable adoration. A large picture of Jesus hung in a prominent place on the wall. It depicted him as a good-looking young man with long, blond hair, his bleeding heart protruding from his naked chest.

With Kazik screaming, we played various physical games—mostly rowdy chases and tumbling. Agreeable Kasia didn't mind. She enjoyed participating sometimes, too. It was a lot of fun, especially when their dog came into heat. The bitch would stand up on her hind legs and rest her front paws on Kazik. Then she would let herself go; her middle section would sway rhythmically, and she would try to satisfy her urge. That act apparently triggered Kasia's sex call. Kasia would lean against the upper section of a tall credenza and would emulate the bitch. Kazik, like a pedagogue with an all-knowing, superior smirk would look at me and point to Kasia. She, leaning on her hands, would thrust her pelvis forward so that she could rub her crotch on the corner of the credenza, and she would let herself go. All that time, Kasia would be stealing glances at the three of us, perhaps to assure her that Kazik and I were observing her or to get additional inspiration from the bitch. Yes, I watched with excitement as Kasia's ample buttocks pulsated and shook like gelatin. The bitch ended the ritual silently, but Kasia moaned several times at the end: "Oh daj, tak, tak. Oh…"

I didn't know what this was all about, but these doings stirred me—definitely not unpleasantly. Kazik, of course, did explain to me with appropriate gestures that females needed males and that our penises have a special place between female legs. Kazik was my mentor on erotica. It was actually he who first dared me to make advances toward Lesia.

Pan Kieda was a shoemaker who endeared himself to German occupiers. He and Pani opened a large workshop where they made boots for individual policemen and Wehrmacht (German military) personnel. The German occupation suited them and the Kiedas became quite well-off. Almost as soon as the Germans occupied Lwów, Kazik was prohibited from playing with me, and I was barred from entering their apartment.

For a while, we met in our little courtyard. Later, even that ended, and since there were no Jewish children left in the immediate neighborhood, I was left to my own devices entirely. This was with the exception of Bogdan, who continued to come by, but only to take whatever he wanted from our rooms. He did not bother to ask. If he didn't see what he wanted, in a commanding tone he would tell me to ask Karol to obtain it for him. And Karol continued to comply with Bogdan's wishes.

The Kiedas moved out of 41A Lyczakowska Street into a larger apartment, one that was left vacated by a murdered Jewish family. As the liberating Soviet front approached in 1944, the Kiedas and many others who collaborated with the Germans and thus feared retribution from the Soviets left Lwów for Austria or Silesia.

The description of our neighbors would suffer an important omission if I would not picture the Schoenhoeffer family on the first floor, opposite Yanka and Tusiek. They were true human chameleons. They were able to change their coloration with the regime in power and profit by it. Prior to World War II, Pan Schoenhoeffer was a senior sergeant in the esteemed Polish gendarmerie, the military and political police whose many duties included arresting and jailing Communists, German provocateurs, Ukrainian nationalists, and other real or supposed enemies of the Polish state.

Many in Poland feared the sight of their colorful insignia and embroidered uniforms. Under Soviet rule, members of the gendarmerie were caught and were either executed or sent to Soviet labor camps, Gulags. Indeed, Pan Schoenhoeffer was not to be seen during that time. Pani Schoenhoeffer and their two sons, Bolek and Tadzik, were not abused by the Soviets, as far as I could tell. But Bolek, who was Bogdan's age and who was friendly to me before the war, stopped noticing me even then. As soon as the German armies entered Lwów in 1941, Pan Schoenhoeffer re-appeared, fairly opulent and well-dressed with a flower in his boutonniere. What he did under Soviets we did not know, but he certainly did not look as if he was persecuted. Rumor was that he sold himself to NKVD, the Soviet secret police, and became an informer.

With the prospects offered by the "1,000-Year Reich," it was profitable for him to bring forth his German ancestry, and so he became an

66

ethnic German, a Volksdeutsche. As such, he was entitled to all the privileges that his superior race "deserved." Thus, the Schoenhoeffers had especially generous ration cards and Pan Schoenhoeffer became a minor official of the occupation bureaucracy. I saw him hobnobbing with the Death Commandos and Ukrainian police during an akcia when my grandparents were herded into an awaiting lorry and thus to their death. At that time, I was hidden in the attic of our house and witnessed the sordid scene.

Whether it was Pan Schoenhoeffer or another neighbor who pointed out our apartment to Commandos during another akcia, I never will know. I wouldn't be writing those memoirs if it weren't for the fact that one of the Death Commandos who broke into our room later convinced his colleagues not to take us to a truck full of captured Jews, for reasons I can only guess.

As the Soviets were nearing Lwów in 1944, to everybody's surprise, the Schoenhoeffer family did not run away with the escaping German army. They stayed. As it turned out, Pan Schoenhoeffer and his older son Tadzik, found good employment with the Soviets, perhaps again with NKVD. Once again, they didn't seem to be discomforted by regime change.

It is quite evident that in my house on Lyczakowska, people were not made by the same cookie cutter—some were bad, a few were good, and many simply applied themselves to their immediate lives without regard for anybody else.

The actions of many remain a mystery to me: Pan Schoenhoeffer, an ethnic German who collaborated with every authority in power; Pani Cwik, a Polish neighbor who was loyal to us but who would have liked to have seen a restored Poland without so many Jews in it; the Death Commando, a member of the notorious Schutz-Polizei, who came to our room to take my mother and me for execution but relented in the last moment. I believe he did so because he spotted a photograph of my father as an officer in the Polish army dressed in parade uniform with a saber by his side. Although this one Schupo and his ilk brutally murdered other Jews, I believe that he himself had served in the Polish Army and simply extended "professional courtesy" to the family of a former colleague.

Even the actions of my father Karol—a muscular Jew, a Polish reserve officer, an insolvent landlord, as well as a hard-working sheet metal worker—remain somewhat of a puzzle. At times he was a sports reporter; at times he sold printing inks; at times he whipped me badly, and at other times he patiently showed me how to draw faces with caricature noses.

By far, the most inexplicable person was Pani Natalia, a Ukrainian, and the mother of Bogdan. She helped us Jews by donating her personal jewelry to the reparation fund, even though her husband was an ardent Germanophile and a Jew-hater. Perhaps because of her hateful husband, she risked her life by visiting and comforting Karol and me while in hiding. Her actions remain a perplexing mystery.

Now all of these people are not even scattered crumbs. Why did the cookie cutter cut out such odd shapes?

*　　*　　*

The Ukrainian jet landed. The first encounter with the officialdom in Lwów came as soon as we alit unto the tarmac. The initial passport and visa control began even before we boarded the beat-up bus for the terminal. The terminal building was a one-story, formally ornate palace with large windows, now partially boarded with plywood. The eroded, marred, and dirty plaster was a mute witness to half a century of neglect. Inside, the very large room that served for both departing and arriving passengers was in no better condition, except for the ceiling. The tall ceiling suffered the least. It was arched and on it was painted the "heroic" view of the Soviet proletariat; the nationalistic Ukrainians didn't have sufficient time to erase these vestiges of Communism. Much more aggravatingly, they didn't have the time, funds, or motivation to expand and clean the sanitary facilities. The odor—or I should say a number of obnoxious smells—emanated primarily from two one-seat toilets. In addition, the floors of the terminal reeked because of the urine trampled out of the bathrooms by the foot wear of travelers.

Here we stood in the initial line. We were required to buy medical insurance, of course with hard currency. Then we stood in the second line—the second passport and visa control. Then a third line for currency and baggage check. I was loaded down with packing tubes and a large valise that contained my prints. The custom official went easy on me when I gave her a print and a formal invitation to my exhibit in the Lwów Museum. I like to think that she was genuinely appreciative of art and artists. That was the end of the process; I finally escaped from the authorities and into the outstretched arms of Szmuel.

"My brother, my brother, we are welcoming you," were his first words to me in Polish, which he spoke fairly well, as he took my valise from me and led me into fresh air in front of the building.

At first I thought that the "we" was a royal "we," but I had a surprise. Two hefty men in pseudo-military fatigues awaited us on the steps of the entrance. They took the valise from Szmuel and the tubes from me and marched us toward a decrepit minivan parked in a no-parking zone. That presented no problem because the policeman who leaned against the van was not there to give us a ticket but to protect the vehicle. One of my escorts slipped a banknote into the hand of the cop who returned the gesture with a sloppy salute. The other escort sat in the driver's seat and started the engine. It coughed a bit but, to my amazement, succeeded in propelling the van forward with the four of us inside. At first it seemed to me that all the attention that I had received was overdone, but later I realized that the two burly men were much needed bodyguards who seldom left me alone. They were in Szmuel's employ, and I was Szmuel's paying guest.

Down toward Old Town we rode. The fairly empty, wide streets were full of potholes; on both sides were large blocks of the Soviets' contribution to Lwów—massive apartment houses that looked exactly the same, one after the other: gray, scratched, unpainted. Ten stories of small, regularly spaced windows to which various electronic implements were attached. Some had window boxes with plants. Those potted plants appeared to be the only intrusions of nature on these overpowering building complexes. Although it was spring, the large, empty spaces around those apartment houses had no gardens, trees or bushes, just stretches of pavement and stumped over dirt with occasional recreational play structures for children.

The van shook and squeaked as we neared Old Town. Trying to recall the various district names, I asked Szmuel where we were. His responses did not enlighten me. The street names were different. Now they all belonged to Ukrainian notables. However, I knew that as long as we were traveling down the hill over cobblestone streets we must be going toward the center of Old Town. Indeed we were. The minivan stopped in front of the Grand Hotel, which I remembered as the posh hotel of Lwów, right opposite the statue of Adam Mickiewicz, the renowned Polish poet. I was surprised to see the monument intact since the chauvinistic Ukrainian administration was trying to obliterate any traces of Jewish and Polish existence in the town. All four of us got out of the minivan and my escorts took my baggage to the lobby, which left me face-to-face with Szmuel.

"Money. You will need our money," he said. Yes, I would need money.

"Here is the man," he said pointing to a giant of a man, modishly dressed in a Western-style suit over which was draped a sumptuous, oversized fur coat.

He was standing close to the curb opposite the elegant entrance to the Grand Hotel. Ten paces or so away from him loitered two body-guards with exposed pistol holders and a Ukrainian policeman.

"He will give you the best rate for your dollars if I talk to him," Szmuel informed me. "The more you exchange, the better." I wasn't sure for whom it would be better, but Szmuel continued, "You will need a lot of grivne."

So I gave Szmuel five one-hundred dollar bills in exchange for which the giant man pulled a sheath of bills out of the sleeve of his voluminous fur coat and gave them to Szmuel. Szmuel divided up the local currency between us, telling me that my transportation, protection, incidentals, and donation to the poor old Jews of Lwów would require that amount. He added that from then on, I would have no fear or needs; he and his "philanthropic" organization would take care of everything. So, now I was established in Lwów, ready to do what I came to do. My angel Szmuel would guide me and protect me, while at the same time the poor local Jews would have food and medicine. I hoped on all those accounts.

After sleeping off the jet lag for a few hours in my room at the Grand Hotel, I attempted to take a shower. Drops of lukewarm water came out of the showerhead and that was all. But rays of a setting sun entered the room and cheered me up. The telephone rang; Szmuel was downstairs.

"We are here to drive you to the house where you were hidden—the Bielys' house, right? We must go before it gets dark. The residents will not open the street gate to strangers at night."

Although it was just getting dark when the minivan stopped at the gate, none of the residents took the trouble to come down and talk to us.

"They probably shit in their pants seeing the four of us," was Szmuel's explanation.

That was a real catch-22. It was unsafe for a foreigner to be seen alone on the street but if he was over-protected, he was feared and not to be approached.

The next day, as we had arranged, Yulia from Poltava came to Lwów. She was escorted by a young man whom she introduced as her Russian husband. She obviously couldn't wait even a few months for her glamorous photo to produce a prospect for her bed in America. She was likely already married when she visited Washington. Or, even more likely, Andrey was merely her man-friend. Whatever his relation to Yulia, he was a good man and I liked him. He was not a Ukrainian but a Russian living in Ukraine. For Andrey, the highly chauvinistic Ukrainian Lwów was difficult to digest. As we walked the streets together, he would tear down the inflammable, jingoistic posters that plastered the town.

As I remembered her from the Mall, Yulia had two personalities, both were bright and likable. Today Yulia exuded an air of respectability. I, along with the attractively dressed Yulia and her handsome "husband," knocked on the gate of Franciszka's apartment house. We had left Szmuel's and his "we" waiting in the van a block away. Oksan let us in. As fortune would have it, Oksan was married to the Bielys' niece. He took us to the apartment on the first floor and to the seven-by-ten room where Karol and I were hidden. He knew about the Jewish boy and his dad, Pan Mann, whom Franciszka had saved. We both were glad to meet and scheduled to get together the next day, just the two "oldsters," as he said to me. He would show me photos and documents from the past.

"And, I will make us canapés," he added, which meant that there would be vodka. Fine with me.

*   *   *

My survival is primarily due to Franciszka and Piotr Biely. This devoutly Catholic, Polish couple hid me in their small apartment from November 1942 until the liberation by the Red Army in July 1944. At that time, they were both in the twilight of life. Franciszka was in her early seventies; Piotr in his late seventies. The risks entailed in helping Jews were incalculably great. Yet, thanks to the Bielys, I and my father (who joined me later) were saved. Very few trustworthy friends knew about our hiding place and they kept the secret. Only Bogdan inadvertently stumbled upon us, but he did not report this to the police and therefore, we lived. The Bielys truly deserve the honor of being designated "Righteous Gentiles." In fact, Pan Oksan, their only extant relative, received a medal on their behalf, commemorating their humanity and heroism.

Pan Oksan pulled an old photo album out of the lower drawer of the credenza. The drawer was filled with old documents and photographs, and more recent photos and papers that dated from the Soviet era. There was Pan Oksan in the Red Army uniform playing chess with another soldier; Pan Oksan, the outstanding lathe operator in Lwów's trolley car repair shop; soldier Oksan with other members of the Army choir. He was a highly praised, highly esteemed worker and soldier. The old photo album stood out among those loose mementos; it was leather-bound and I remember its musty smell. I opened it gently, with reverence, because it contained memorabilia dear to Pani Franciszka. In fact, the album contained Pani Franciszka's treasured keepsakes from long ago, glimpses of her youth.

There was Franciszka's baptismal certificate—born 1875 in a small village in Galicia, Austria; a marriage document from the Parish of St. Anthony—married to Piotr Biely in 1895 in Lemberg (Lwów),

Peace to Righteous Gentiles

both Roman Catholics of Polish nationality. There were also annual leases for a street-fronting store and living space on Piekarska Street and other official documents such as various permits to engage in business and even fines related to the operation of a grocery store located on Piekarska. I also noticed a few train tickets and a pressed white flower.

All this was of interest but I wanted to linger on the photographs, two in particular. The first was a group shot of about forty tourists standing in front of an old sleeping-train wagon, clearly identified by a sign, "Wien – Triest – Roma." Franciszka stood out in this group of mostly elderly women. Tall and statuesque. Long, light-colored hair in twin braids. A pretty woman of twenty-five. A typical broad Slavic face with a wide, upturned nose and widely set, pale blue eyes. Underneath the photograph the inscription stated, "Railroad Station in Rome – August 1900." That was the Jubilee year and the tourists from Galicia were coming to visit Rome with hopes for an audience with Pope Leo XIII.

In the other photograph, Franciszka appeared even more imposing. She was slightly bent, putting her arms on the shoulders of two teenagers on crutches who were with the group. To me, she portrayed an air of authority, physical strength, and compassion in this picture. She was also very independent. As a young married woman she had to leave her husband literally minding the store, and come across an international border with a group of tourists, pretty much strangers to her.

Franciszka indeed had a brain and a mind of her own. She dominated Piotr Biely and pushed this shorter, handsome, and vain man along the marital path from being an impoverished peasant to become an apartment-house owner. It was Franciszka's idea to open a small grocery store in the vicinity of Lwów's medical university buildings. It was her energy and business acumen that made the store famous among students for its tasty and relatively inexpensive sandwiches. Not being able to have children, Franciszka dedicated her life to the little store and as a result, she and her husband prospered.

The old album also contained an IOU note issued to my grandfather in the amount of 3,000 zlotys for the construction of a sheet metal roof. The Bielys did build an apartment house with the proceeds from the popular sandwiches, but not enough to pay for the roof. The note was never paid in money. Franciszka more than repaid it by later saving my father's life and mine.

After perusal, I gave the album back to Pan Oksan and he placed it again among his papers and photographs. Then, without a word, he embraced me and led me to a table in the kitchen. He offered me a buttered piece of bread and set a bottle of clear vodka on the table. With those gestures we became friends.

Oksan told me that he is not Franciszka's nephew but a nephew by marriage, on Piotr's side.

"Piotr was Polish but I am a Ukrainian from a village near Lwów." He pointed to several pieces of memorabilia on the kitchen cabinet, including a small bust of Lenin.

"I was better off under Soviets; my pension bought much more under Communism," Oksan opened up to me.

"Now we have independence, but there is just enough money to pay rent for this one-bedroom apartment and little leftover for food."

However, Oksan is thankful to be alive. He began recalling the Ukrainian uprising during the years immediately following the Soviet liberation from Germany in 1944. These were bloody years for the Carpathian Piedmont. The Ukrainian insurgents came to his village, hid amongst the people, and were nearly caught.

"We helped them to escape into the higher mountains," continued Oksan. "I remember distinctly one of them—Misko. His family lived not far from here, on Lyczakowska Street. Misko told us that he would rather be back home but that he had no choice. The Soviets would certainly have killed him in the mountains or, if he had returned home, somebody was bound to denounce him."

"What a great coincidence!" I yelled out excitedly.

"I knew Misko Fedan, the son of our janitor. Misko was a great friend of Bogdan, a boy who was nice to me during the prewar days. What happened to Misko?" I asked with curiosity. "Did you know that both of those boys ice-skated with me in the tow? Do you know what happened to Misko?" I asked again, nostalgia overtaking me.

Oksan didn't answer immediately.

"How about chut-chut?" he asked lifting a bottle of vodka.

Yes, I definitely needed a slurp. I was still startled that Misko had come into our conversation. Misko, Misko. Big, strong, simple-minded, good-natured Misko. Prior to World War II, I saw him competently sweeping the courtyard of our house and wearing a pleasant smile on his face. Then, when the proletariat ruled under the Soviets, Misko was advanced to sweeping horse manure from the street. He tackled his promotion dressed in a white apron and still retained that same pleasant smile.

"Misko came home to Lyczakowska Street. He must have deserted the insurgents very shortly after I met him in our village," said Oksan. "Somebody in Lwów who knew him well denounced him to the Soviets. They took him and executed him, probably in Kiev. We have people among us who would sell their own mothers; the Germans trained them well. Another chut-chut?"

"Yes, yes."

The Germans did train Ukrainians to denounce, torment, rob, and beat and murder Jews. But Metropolitan Andrej Szeptycki, the head of the Greek Catholic Church to which most western Ukrainians belonged, was a humane and wise cleric who was helpful to Jews during the German occupation. He foresaw the danger of brutalizing the rather unsophisticated Ukrainian population by giving them a taste of murder. In a letter to Himmler, the head of the German police, he asked the SS chief not to employ Ukrainian police in violent acts against the Jews. He feared that the murder of Jews would not stop Ukrainians from murdering others in the future. He was right. Numerous brutalities and violent crime still persist in Galicia, by Ukrainians and against Ukrainians. Money and alcohol hold sway.

Do fill our tumblers again, Oksan, my Ukrainian friend. Another chut-chut and those ugly memories of the ugly past will dissipate, at least for a little while.

Oksan shut his eyes. Was he remembering the past or sleeping?

*　　*　　*

I couldn't let the past go. The young and pretty Pani Franciszka of the sepia photographs metamorphosed into the septuagenarian and still handsome, grayish blond Pani Franciszka who welcomed me into her apartment on a dark and wet evening in November 1942.

That morning was dreary and it drizzled with rain. I said goodbye to my mother in the Ghetto. I fully realized that I might never see her again. My mother cried, but twelve-and-a-half-year-old boys, although terribly sad, do not cry. In fact, I felt exhilaration at the prospect of hope for myself, and certainly for a better life—better than this hellish existence was for us in the Ghetto. The constant overpowering fear, urinating in my pants when danger was near, the hunger, the fantastic filth and sickening odors, the bickering and fighting inhabitants of our small room—they would all be behind me.

I was smuggled out through the Ghetto gate with my father's work brigade. Luck was with us; the guards did not notice. Perhaps it was simply the dismal rain so early in the morning that made the guards less vigilant. Toward the end of the day, I separated from the brigade, discarded my white arm band with a blue Star of David, and began walking in the direction of Lyczakowska Street to the apartment house of Pani Franciszka.

As I neared the gate of her house, she opened the gate and then led me up a few steps to the door of her apartment. Nobody saw us and I hoped that nobody recognized me walking in the streets, just a few houses from where I had lived. She motioned me to the door of a little room and pointed to a cot on which there was a plate with food. The room was barely lit by a strobe of light coming from a crack in a door from an adjacent room. I only saw an outline of Franciszka's tall, erect figure looming over me. I met my angel in silence and in darkness. The next morning, I saw her clearly. She was a large woman, dressed all in black: black skirt, black stockings, black shoes, black sweater, and a black knit shawl over her shoulders. Only two graying blond braids enlivened the monotony of blackness. Her face was unsmiling and she looked at me with serious eyes. Her continence was stern. She was a brave, intelligent, humane woman, but she showed me no affection during that emotionally difficult encounter nor, for that matter, during my entire stay with her.

I met her husband Piotr the next day. A bedridden man with perfectly waxed, long, tapered Kaiser Franz-Joseph mustachios, he looked well-groomed with hair parted down the middle, plastered to his scalp. He said nothing to me then. I don't think he said anything to me during those many months until the liberation.

The infrequent times that I left my little room and did enter the Bielys' room, I saw Pan Piotr sitting in bed, propped up by pillows, with a well-worn prayer book in his hands. His eyes were closed and his lips moved steadily. Whenever he slept, he lay with his mustachios pinned behind his ears and fastened to the back of his head by an attached string. He was as conscious of his appearance as he was of his sickness—he suffered from a galloping anemia.

Both Bielys were very religious. I am sure that their faith in their God and in His protective powers made them less fearful of my being discovered and of all of us being executed. Pan Piotr and Pani Franciszka were a uniquely righteous couple. However, their demonstrable love was reserved for each other and for their God only. Yet they faced great risks to save my life, and eventually my father's life too. May they rest in peace together.

* * *

"Dear Oksan, you don't mind if I pour another shot for myself, do you? I'll fill another for you to drink when you wake up. I know you will join me in toasting our friendship. It is getting late. But then again, we don't have much to do, do we? All that is left for us is to reminisce."

I looked around Oksan's tiny basement apartment, located just below the first floor where the Bielys used to live—exactly under the small room where I was hidden.

"Of course, Oksan, you are my age. You did not live in Lwów at that time, but roamed the hills and woods of your village, while I, in contrast, was confined to a seven-by-ten-foot space."

* * *

There was a window at the end of the room where I was hidden. My room. It overlooked a grassy plot which was partly surrounded by apartment houses. The window afforded a narrow view of Lyczakowska Street. Across from the window was a door to a tiny vestibule. One long wall of the room was common with the staircase, while the other wall had a door to the Bielys' room. The third small room in the apartment was sublet to a young Polish man. Nobody was supposed to know about my existence. Certainly not the young man across the vestibule, nor any of the Bielys' relatives or neighbors. Fortunately, the Bielys had very few relatives, none of whom lived in Lwów. Franciszka's cousins lived in a nearby village. They were brutally murdered by organized Ukrainian militia gangs about a year after I entered into the Bielys' life.

In another village, somewhere west of Lwów, Piotr had a niece.

"She later became your wife. Right, Oksan?"

Franciszka's generally forbidding demeanor prevented close association with neighbors. The Bielys were considered unfriendly people. This was good because people seldom visited them and this reduced the risk of discovering me, as long as I behaved within my walls like an ethereal spirit and did not make a sound or show myself through the matte glass of the doors or through the window. I hoped and prayed that I would not be observed by anyone. This required me to live below the visual horizon. I spent countless hours on the floor or on the cot. I would slide noiselessly on a bit of a rug toward the staircase wall and listen with my ear glued to the masonry. I was always fearful that the next heavy footsteps would belong to police in search of Jews. At other times, I knelt in front of the cot and fervently prayed. Franciszka gave me a spare prayer book and a rosary. Believe me, Oksan, I used those articles. I recited the litanies and the repetitive prayers with the beads, pounding my heart with my fist in appropriate instances. I literally begged Jesus, St. Mary, St. Anthony, and St. Francis to protect me and grant me life. I would repeat and repeat and repeat my plea. Did it help me to survive? I know that it helped to diminish my fears somewhat. That, in itself, was a great benefit.

The window was the essence of my fantasies. To be there, beyond the window, playing with other boys on the weedy, green lot was my dream. I longed to touch the leaves and blades of grass, but I wasn't even able to see them well. I did not dare to come to the window during daylight for fear of being spotted. Franciszka couldn't even put curtains or drapes on the window because neighbors would become suspicious. Why, they would wonder, would she have spent a lot of money for even cheap curtain material after years of having the window undraped? That would have been very puzzling to the neighbors, indeed. The Bielys' life had to flow within the same channel as it did

The Window

before my coming. In essence, I felt as if I were in a cell, chained to the wall.

But when the neighborhood boys came to play soccer, I couldn't resist standing to the side of the window and listening to their joyful voices. There was Bogdan's voice, and there was Misko's voice, and there was Bolek's voice and the voices of others. Ukrainian, Polish, and German languages intermingled. Occasionally, German soldiers or police participated in those games. Several times Bogdan must have chased the ball very close to the window. His happy voice resounded in my ears. Did he see me standing just behind the window frame? Once, I had a feeling that he spent more than enough time retrieving the ball. Did he suspect something? Yes, he did, but he did nothing until about a year later when he boldly walked into our apartment and met me and my father hiding in our small room.

The encounter with Bogdan was horribly frightful. My father pleaded with him not to tell anybody about us, and I think that my father gave him money to keep silent. Bogdan left, but after that day we feared what Bogdan might do. We hoped that the friendly Pani Natalia would persuade Bogdan to forget what he saw and to keep his mouth shut.

*   *   *

Oksan stirred, awoke, and his eyes became fully alert.

"Did you know Bogdan?" he asked me. "You know that Bogdan and Misko lived in the same apartment house real close by. They were great friends."

"Yes, of course, I knew. I knew them very well. We all lived in my parents' apartment-house. They were my friends as well."

"They were both murdered by Soviets. Misko died, as I told you already, while Bogdan died fighting as a member of the SS Galicia Division."

Oksan looked at me knowingly. Locals either loved or hated the Ukrainian men who joined this SS division in 1943. Some believed the members were fighting for their freedom; others saw them as brutal collaborators. The division was short-lived, as most of it was decimated in battle near the town of Rovno in 1944.

Oksan refilled our glasses. We siphoned them. I mellowed considerably while Oksan assumed a patriotic mood.

"You know that Misko and Bogdan are now both local heroes—martyrs, actually—for the Ukrainian cause. Many people around here cite them to their children and grandchildren as models of Ukrainian patriotism. They fought and died for our country."

"So that's what happened to Bogdan," I exclaimed loudly. "You really think he was killed?" I considered Bogdan an unscrupulous chiseler, but I left that thought unsaid.

"Yes, most likely. Not many of them reappeared after the war."

Did that petty thief die for a cause? Why did Bogdan join the SS Galicia? He was too selfish and opportunistic to attempt a heroic role. Did he want to kill and rob? Perhaps. But he could have done it easily without endangering his life in war against the Soviets. He was not an idealist. So what was he, really? After all those years, I am still awkwardly touched by the memory of him and surprised at his decision to fight for fascism.

"What about Pani Kapista, Bogdan's mother? Did you know her, Oksan?"

No, of course not. It was a foolish question. Oksan did not live in Lwów at that time and he would have been only a young boy. He heard later that many people, and probably the Kapistas as well, ran away before the Red Army entered Lwów. Well, they all are dead, except perhaps Lesia, Bogdan's young sister. Yes, too bad for Bogdan—he was so bright and so very ingenious.

Chapter V

On the Mall Again

*I*t is a Saturday morning and I am back at my location on the Mall. *I am beginning a new exhibiting season, my eleventh year. The weather is fine but no visitors as yet. My travel to Lwów and the events that I experienced there have left a strong impression on me. My memories of Pan Oksan and Szmuel are still very vivid. With the passage of weeks, I have warmed up to the memory of the rascally Szmuel and appreciate more the candor and hospitality of Oksan.*

The exhibit of my prints at the Museum of Ukrainian Ethnography in the very center of Lwów was fairly well-attended. I funded a catered reception and paid for all the incidentals, including honoraria for the staff and the speaker who introduced me to attendees. The lecture at the Lwów Art Institute was more satisfying to me. I always enjoy talking to young people. The students truly appreciated my work; that buoyed me. Most importantly, I started to write my memoirs during my stay in Lwów. Perhaps I will incorporate my memoirs with these chronicles and write a book someday. Since the trip, I have felt far more cheerful and optimistic about the future, except that I worry about my father.

Yesterday, my father Karol was taken to the emergency room for the third time in the last several weeks. I am hopeful that his condition is not terminal. I called and learned that he is out of immediate danger. Perhaps it is nothing very serious. I will visit him Monday.

*   *   *

Now it is six o'clock on Sunday evening, and I am ordained by routine to begin dismantling my exhibit. But my thirst for alcohol counter-

mands that I sit down and begin to sip my cocktail—orange juice and gin—which patiently awaits in the cooler.

A half-hour and umpteen slurps later, I am ready. Nobody stopped to interrupt my R & R. I am in a mellow mood and now ready to evacuate my "beachhead."

When I think of my stand on the Mall, I tend to think in martial terms. Winning the permit to exhibit on the Mall was like winning a war—a struggle worthy of fine generalship. The Department of the Interior capitulated, and I have the right to occupy a strategic spot of grass next to a large tree.

I slowly unhook the large oil paintings in their heavy protective frames. "The Messiah" is a picture of a weary-looking, brownish man of undetermined age or race portrayed in a typical homeless posture, reclining on a bench with the Gallery as a background. In reality, the man who posed for me is Figarrroo. His head rests on a Bible. He is dressed in a "'uniform" of plaid material. To me, he epitomizes the wandering Jew of the past but also the homeless of today, without a place to call their own. I carry "The Messiah" to the minivan, place him between two sheets of large cardboard and walk back. Then follow "Nifty Fifties" and "Summer Barn." Next I carry a bag with prints in their tubes and other prints in boxes. I trudge back and forth, back and forth.

It is only 150 feet from my encampment to the van but I am already tired. Two folding tables later, it is time to sit down and have my special treat: straight gin. I save a small plastic bottle of gin for last. Being a sentimentalist, I use the same bottle all the time. It is multicolored now because of the many pigments that my fingers have imprinted over the course of the years. The cool gin tastes good. After several sips, I sense it penetrate my muscles and brain. I feel good; I had a profitable day. I take a bundle of bills and checks from my pocket and roughly total them. Not bad. Not bad at all. The worry about my father dissipates and, instead, I fantasize about being a really famous artist, admired by all.

But reality impinges on me. I have to convince myself that now I should get up and collapse the canopy. I don't get up, however. It is difficult for one person to lower the four supporting legs simultaneously.

I did it by myself in the past but I dread doing it now. I continue to sit and watch the sun disappear behind the trees in the west and I scan the hurrying passersby for someone to help me. While assessing the very few walkers, I notice a small person on crutches standing next to the two public phones on the sidewalk of Madison Drive. Another sip. Another glance at the phones. The small cripple apparently used the phone and moved a few steps to the curb of the sidewalk.

I spot and approach a young man and he willingly helps me with the canopy. In its collapsed form, the canopy is barely manageable to be lifted, but I carry it—all 150 feet—and shove it on the floor of the van. To my amazement, the little cripple is still standing on the same spot on the curb, looking at the street, periodically turning his or her head from left to right and back again like a radar. Apparently, the small person is expecting a ride.

I continue to stow my stuff away. I haul the two aluminum stands, one stashed within the other. They are awkward to carry and are fairly heavy. I heave them on the roof of the van and tie them to the racks. I sit down and take one more sip. My eyes turn inadvertently in the direction of the telephones. The person on crutches is still there on the same spot, looking to the right and left. The gentleness of the head motion suggests that the cripple is a woman. She is expecting something or someone. What? Who?

I take the last sip from the plastic "heirloom." I get up and fold my chair. With the chair in one hand and the cooler in the other, I look at what was my encampment. Did I leave anything? No, only mutilated grass with a few bits of trash. I am too tired to bend down and pick them up. I will leave them for the maintenance people to spear whenever they get around to it. It is already dark and I am feeling hungry; so, to the van. I look toward the telephones. The little cripple is not standing at the curb anymore.

Where is she? There she is in the distance, stomping her way toward Sixth Street. All I can make out on the poorly lit street is a short, wide, human bundle, slowly receding from view. I hesitate for some moments, then I walk quickly after her. Laboriously, crutch by crutch, she "walks." Right crutch forward. Left crutch forward. Now she is under the light of one of the lamps and I see that both of her legs are amputated. I am near enough to see the stump of a left leg swing as she lifts the left crutch. Actually, I only see a partly empty sock swaying with the motion. The stump of the right leg is firmly strapped to what I perceived to be the right crutch but actually it is a peg leg. She wields a walking cane in her right hand. I am close enough behind her now to see a mass of short, straight, black hair. I resolve to approach her.

"Hey, can I help you?"

The three supporting implements cease to move; she stops. Just as I am within an arm's length, the squat human shape pirouettes on the left crutch and, twisting her plump torso toward me, she looks up at me. Yes, she is female—a girl. She has a beautiful oriental face with bangs neatly cut over her round, black eyes. We face each other in silence. She is a beautiful child.

"Can I help you?" I ask again. She merely smiles. The smile turns into gentle laughter, exposing the most perfect set of gleaming, white teeth.

"No, thank you. I go taxi." Our eyes continue their contact; black overwhelming blue.

I lower my eyes and gaze at the pebbles on the sidewalk. I want to communicate that I am sort of a cripple also, and that she shouldn't be afraid. I make a gesture with my maimed hand toward the minivan.

"I will take you wherever you want to go."

"I go taxi," is her response, and to change the topic she adds, "You know Korea?"

"No. I never was there."

She ceases to laugh, but a smile lingers on her lips. The atrociously hurt cripple exudes cheerfulness. Well, not quite. I detect sadness in those expressive, black eyes. Yes, there must a great deal of pain within her. It takes one to know one, as the expression goes, and I should know.

I lift my eyes to hers. The black and the blue meet again. I desperately want to embrace her compassionately, to lift her up into my arms and flood that lovely face with kisses. Perhaps she sees the intention in my eyes. Her eyes leave mine and she gently twists herself on her crutch and turns away from me.

"I go taxi," she repeats with finality.

Before the three supports resume their laborious task, I stick my small brochure into her opened hand, hoping that she will get in touch with me.

Then I stand and watch her move away slowly. How I want to catch up with her again and tell her that it is I who needs her in my loneliness! It is I who needs companionship, consolation, and encouragement. But no. I turn about and walk to the van. I lean against the van for some minutes. My thoughts are with the crippled girl. A wave of sorrow and compassion sweeps over me—and also guilt. At this time in the late evening, the vast National Mall with its museums and monuments is deserted and is certainly not safe. I should have told her that. How far will she be able to get in her condition? Her hands will be hurting. I battle within myself. The modern man in me insists that it is not my business. The sufferer within me wins. I must find her and make sure that she is safe. If she will not get into the van, I will walk with her or behind her until a taxi shows up. I jump into the driver's seat, rev up the engine and speed after her. To the left on Sixth Street. To the right. Then farther up on the Drive. She is nowhere to be seen. The little cripple is gone. Will I ever hear from her or see her again? Was that child real or simply a chimera fantasized by my over-ginned brain?

*   *   *

No, my brain seemed to have been functioning. Today, two weeks after meeting her, a taxi pulled up to the curb. Violet Yun climbed out and made her away to my encampment. I was startled and overjoyed. I bend down and embraced the beautiful bundle of humanity and kissed her straight, black hair. She seemed not to mind and even clung to me for few moments, returning the embrace with the hand that held her cane.

"Thank you, thank you," were her words. "I go to Korea—want buy picture."

No, my lovely child.

"You may have one as a present. Which one do you want?"

She lumbered to the table where small matted prints were displayed and pointed to "Nifty Fifties," a vibrant and joyful composition of music and dancing that depicted a juke box and other items from that optimistic, happy era.

"I take to Korea, thank you. I like fun," said my terribly maimed Violet.

I assisted her back to the waiting taxi. As she situated herself inside and looked smilingly at me, I felt to be in seventh heaven. I had done something good. I knew that she was my friend.

*   *   *

Yesterday, Saturday, Maria showed up. Five or six years have passed since our initial meeting. She looked good in her well-fitting light-weight pantsuit. If her appearance has changed at all it is for the better. She looked even more attractive than on the day when I first saw her. Joy swelled in my chest at the sight of her, but as soon as my hands instinctively extended to embrace her, I dropped them to my side. I noticed that she was not alone. A youngish man with glasses stepped up to us and gently took Maria by the hand, which turned my joy sour. We exchanged some civil words during which she introduced her escort as a colleague-researcher from the Holocaust Museum here in Washington.

The veteran professional in me overcame my agitation and, like a recording, I repeated my usual spiel about my work. After my dissertation, the man asked me numerous questions about my Holocaust past, especially about my father's suffering in Obóz Janowski in Lwów. I had no heart to describe my father's brutal treatment by the Nazis, especially since my father has again been taken to the hospital, perhaps for the last time. Maria's escort was sensitive enough to recognize my aversion to this subject and ceased his questions. Instead, I veered toward pleasant recollections, telling them how my father used to take me to soccer games in Lwów, and how it was not terribly bad for us Jews under the Polish government. They listened politely, nodding. This pretty much concluded Maria's visit.

During all that time, our eyes did not meet, and I detected no warmth in her words or gestures. Nothing was said about meeting again. Maria came and Maria left, for what I obviously must accept to be forever. It will be easier now for me to eradicate her from my yearning.

Nifty Fifties

*   *   *

"You bastard! I hate you, you fuckin' son-of-a-bitch!" She is abusing me again. I am using cadmium orange and the bright, vivid pigment infuriates her. She spouts a few more expletives, and

with a hand gesture, as if pushing an evil orange emanation away, she turns around and leaves. In a few minutes she is back again. Even more pungent epithets come out of her. Now she approaches me quite near and, to my surprise, I do not smell the odor of sweaty clothing or that of an unwashed body such as is common to a homeless person. In fact, she smells slightly of lavender perfume. This is surprising since she is wearing a heavy coat, men's boots, and a thick-knitted beret, and she is carrying a large, bulging paper bag: a true picture of a homeless woman. Her words are coarse and loud. A few onlookers who are observing me paint are probably offended by her profanities and slink away, leaving just me and her.

How can I be insulted by someone who is so severely mentally disturbed. I am not angry with her. I feel sympathy with this small creature who is so terribly irritated by the orange color and, therefore, by me. I look at her closely, and here is another surprise. Locks of shiny, combed reddish orange hair escape from under the beret. Her freckled face is comely.

More expletives spew out of her mouth. Why does she hate me so much? What is her problem? She notices that I am staring at her. Instead of increasing the crescendo of abusive language, she stands silently, her face turned away from mine, looking toward the Capitol. Somewhat bent, perhaps under the weight of the big bag, she looks forlorn.

Hey! A mature couple is at my stand, examining my prints with interest. I approach them and give them my usual spiel: "I am not a representational artist, as you can readily see. I dramatize reality, hopefully making it more interesting to the viewers. As you see, I tackle many subjects: landscapes, the Holocaust, even football. Some of my pictures are whimsical, some are humorous, and some are serious."

They buy two small matted prints and, after a few words, they depart.

I turn back to see what the orange homeless woman is up to now. She is nowhere to be seen. She merged with the stream of visitors and is gone. I am glad, and yet...

*   *   *

Another Sunday passes with little to report. Perhaps I am simply tired and don't want even to think. I am not in a writing mood this weekend. But, I should record that the U.S. Park Police came to check my permit, and, as usual, found something to be wrong. This time, I had three tables with me instead of the allowed two. Quickly, I folded one table and they left satisfied. I am glad that they did not come a minute or so earlier to see a couple of British tourists buy and carry away tubes with my prints. I am prohibited from selling on the Mall, but there is no promotion without selling, so I do it on the sly.

I have to add that yesterday Lady Orange showed up toward the end of the day. She stood way out there for a brief moment, looking at me. Then she left.

*   *   *

Another Sunday has come and gone. There is nothing extraordinary to report, except that Lady Orange came again yesterday. She approached a bit closer and stood there a little longer, looking at me. She left as soon as I waved at her.

How I wish that Maria would appear!

*   *   *

Yet another Sunday. This was a much more eventful weekend. On Saturday, I met a young, physically fit couple who bicycled to the Mall. They live in downtown Washington and were attracted to my stands. Both the man and the woman liked my work very much. They did not buy anything, but expressed an interest in purchasing one or two of my original oils. My sense is that they meant what they said, but my past experiences make me a disbeliever. It is a long, bumpy road to an actual sales transaction. They promised to come back next weekend. I hope they will.

Lady Orange showed up again as I was packing in the evening. This time, she stood just across the gravel walk from me. As I was labori-

ously stowing my stuff into the van, she came even closer. I waved at her. This time she did not leave. She merely turned her head away. She looked at me again. I looked at her and waved. She turned her head away from me a second time. Again she looked. I waved. She looked away. We repeated this charade at least twice more. After the n'th wave of my hand, the Lady Orange slowly, hesitantly walked toward me and I, on impulse, walked toward her with an extended hand. To my utter astonishment, she grasped my palm. We shook hands exactly like two normal, civilized human beings living in the twentieth century, except that neither she nor I are normal, average people. Also, the quickly darkening, desolate Mall is not a normal setting for a social encounter. Greetings such as "How do you do?" or "Nice to meet you" don't even enter my mind.

Since we had already met several times and were already bonded by the color orange, I asked directly, "Do you want something to eat? Are you hungry?"

She nodded, still saying nothing.

"Come, I will clear off the passenger seat for you."

She nodded again. After some fidgeting, she sat down next to me with her large paper bag in her lap. Well, it looks like I tamed a wild human, I thought to myself. But I chose more practical words.

"I always eat on Pennsylvania Avenue. It is not far from here," I said. "It is right opposite the Gallaudet College for the Deaf and Mute." She nodded again.

I found a legal parking slot. We sat down at an outdoor table and I ordered red wine for both of us. We sipped our wine in silence. Well, I thought to myself, we are in the right place. We fit into the 'sounds of silence.'

It was odd: At the neighboring tables, heated conversations were taking place in silence. I judged the intensity of the conversations by the furiously flying hands and fingers of Gallaudet students and instructors, as well as the tempo of their moving lips.

By now, I savored her silent company. I did not need to talk. I did not need to impress her with my smarts or by being an interesting companion. Instead, I relaxed completely. This was a novel experience for me: wine, an hour or so of earned leisure, and a woman to look at. I altered the observations I made about Lady Orange when I first met her. The distorted features of a cursing woman altered too. She appeared a comely woman, though still harsh. I ordered chicken cacciatore for both of us without consulting her. She looked at me appreciatively with a smile and, at that moment, I knew that a human bond was forging between us. Her features were now totally relaxed and she actually spoke two words: "Thank you."

*　　*　　*

Another Sunday. I am writing in the late morning. Hardly any visitors. Those who do pass seem to be intent on getting to the museums and they do not stop. Yesterday, a tall, elegantly dressed black woman asked me for help. She wanted me to call some man and tell him that he had missed an "appointment." If a woman were to have answered the phone, I was instructed to tell the woman that I, not my supplicant, was waiting for the man at the designated spot in the Art Gallery. She introduced herself to me as Yvonne Black.

Black she was, and not only in name. I did as she asked, not knowing whether I would be calling a drug pusher who hadn't shown up for a sale or a married man-friend who had stood her up. The conversation between me and the man was to the point: he said that he would come. I related it to Yvonne, she thanked me, and that was that. Well, I must say that I was attracted to the Nubian princess, but I already had two women to think about; I did not need the intrusion of a third one. Maria was always on my mind, but now, strangely, I hoped that Lady Orange would appear at the usual time. Indeed, I looked forward to our mostly silent dinners.

Last Saturday, I learned Lady Orange's first name: Anna. She also told me that she used to teach and that she has a sister. I did not pry for additional information because I feared that I might scare her off and, like the wild bird that she is, that she would fly away. In fact, after a previous dinner she did disappear. To where she flew I do not know.

96

*　　*　　*

Anna did come yesterday, and again we ate together at what I began to refer to as "the mute restaurant." I learned that she, too, appreciates our dinners. She took my less-hurt hand into hers and gently caressed it. Then she placed my really maimed hand into both of hers and held it there. With the words, "Thank you, thank you very much," she arose, left the table, and walked away into the street.

*　　*　　*

It has been many weekends since I have written anything. Another summer is nearing its end. The reason for my inattentiveness is the very unfortunate conclusion of my relationship with Anna. She doesn't come in the evenings at the end of my workdays on the Mall anymore. Yes, I do miss her. In fact, I miss her very much. My conscience is pricking me and my loneliness impinges upon me. Now I realize how comforting it was to have Anna sitting next to me with wine glasses in our hands. It all ended, and now I have plummeted to the depth of despondency. Perhaps, if I unburdened myself…Could anyone empathize with an older man whose desire for the affection and companionship of a younger woman remains unfulfilled? With Anna, it was my fault. Now I suffer for it.

This is what happened: Since my last entry in the diary, I took Anna on several Saturdays to "our" restaurant where we ate, drank, held hands, and then parted. It was good until about six weeks ago. That evening began as a repetition of our previous meetings. Lady Orange came. I finished packing. We got into the minivan and started off in the direction of Pennsylvania Avenue without exchanging any words. It started out like our normal, relaxing routine, but that was not to be.

In the van, Anna took off her ubiquitous, heavy coat. For the first time, I saw her in a dress. What a dress! The satin fabric was a profusion of brilliant flowers arranged in an attractive design. To my surprise, the color orange was most vivid.

"You see, Marek, I am just a regular woman." She addressed me for the first time by my given name. I think that she never addressed me by any name before.

Unbelievably, she continued to talk, asking me to go to a restaurant on Connecticut Avenue in the vicinity of her place. This was another great surprise because that was a desirable, high-rent district.

"Please drive through Fourteenth Street and we will buy a bottle of vodka," she directed me.

That was not the Lady Orange I knew. I was a shocked because Anna always drank wine but never to excess. Now she wanted booze?

I stopped on the way at a liquor store and bought a bottle of Smirnoff. Anna unscrewed the top and we had a taste and another taste. Yet another.

"Marek, let's not go the restaurant now. Let's go to my place."

Anna took another slurp and passed the bottle to me. I did not pull on it. I just wetted my lips; I had had enough alcohol and I had still had some driving to do. We made it to a block on Connecticut with a large, well-maintained apartment house and parked. Then I took a gulp out of the bottle, but not Anna. She got out and motioned me to follow her. We did not enter through the main entrance but through a side door on the lower level leading to a basement. We walked through a narrow corridor with some janitorial closets and passed through a space filled with trash cans and more cleaning equipment. At the end, we arrived at a door. Anna took a key out of her bag and opened the door. She switched on the light and then I saw how she lived: in a window-less room with a bed, a dresser, an open closet, and a sink with a water spigot. I remember this little cubbyhole well in spite of being medium-drunk. Perhaps that is because I had hid during the German occupation in a similarly austere, little room.

What happened then is well-registered in my memory, although I want desperately to forget it. I lay down on the cot; it was not a bed. Anna set down next to me. We had some more Smirnoff. She took my hand and kissed it, and then she took off those ugly, masculine boots of hers. My head sank into her pillow and I closed my eyes. Hazy images of the past agitated my brain. I sensed soft pressure on my hips and gen-

itals. Anna, who had pulled her skirt way up, was straddling me with her legs opened wide. Sitting on top of me, she was rubbing herself.

"Marek, fuck me. Please, Marek, fuck me. Marek, I am a regular woman."

Yes, very dear Anna, then in your room, and now as I write, I see you as a normal woman. Without the heavy coat, without the boots, without your heavy bag, dear Anna, you are a lovely woman.

"I want you, Marek. Take your pants off." The words ring in my ears today. I am hurting as I write these words and tears are streaming from my eyes.

I did not unbelt or unzip my trousers even though my desire for her was growing, and so was my tool. My tool was rigid, but my resolve not to risk my health was equally rigid. My brain was receiving cautionary signals: She was homeless. She probably slept with a lot of men. She may have been HIV-positive or infected with other venereal diseases. Anna's sturdy, well-shaped legs were promising moist heaven at their confluence. I wanted to be one with her badly. I needed her embrace. I needed those delights which I have not experienced for many years. However, I did nothing. My brain was getting sick and my bladder was pressing.

Anna stopped her movement, obviously unfulfilled, and her facial features hardened.

"You bastard, you fuckin' bastard!" she screamed at me. "You no-good, fuckin' son-of-a-bitch!" she screamed even louder. She dismounted, donned her heavy coat over her lovely dress, and pointed to the door.

"Get out, you fucked bastard!" were the last words I heard.

I ran to the car. Before I could open the door, I did two things simultaneously: I urinated and I vomited. I sat in the van for a long time and sobbed, just as I am doing now. Anna never showed up again. I lost her.

Through my friendliness she became a "regular" woman. Due to my cowardice, she reverted back to being Lady Orange. Perhaps it wasn't due to my cowardice but to my failure to recognize her as an equivalent human being. I judged her—I profiled her. To be sure, I was nice to her, but she could have been a pet dog. Now, I despair. Had I thought of her differently, I would have prepared myself adequately for our tryst and we could have relished and ravished each other without jeopardizing our health. I would not have been so lonely, but more importantly, perhaps our intimacy would have brought back Anna's memories of being a "regular" woman. That is what she wanted: to be a normal woman. Perhaps, she will still show up. I hope so.

Chapter VI

On the Trail of Uncle Willi

To be sure, normality was not one of my attributes. At least not in the sense they use *normalno* in most of Eastern Europe. There, or even here, I could not be described as steady or unchanging. In two words: unexciting and not troubled. Life in metropolitan Washington, D.C. was heady, and dealing with the personal and communal tragedies of Holocaust survivors was often deeply depressing. The mixture of the two was not normal for a woman approaching thirty. The thrill and the satisfaction of learning history compensated for infrequent contacts with my family. Of course, there were friends in my life. My graduate school adviser became my mentor and set my sights on western Ukraine, specifically on the historic town of Lwów. The direction of my research and the prestige of my adviser helped me to obtain a research fellowship at the Holocaust Museum in Washington, D.C.

My archival research at the Holocaust Museum was slow and painstaking, but it had its moments. In any case, I was earning a doctorate degree, and I got to learn a lot about the area from where Marek came. Was it normal to select his hometown as the study of my dissertation?

It had been a long time since my first walk to the museum on that hot summer day. Has it been eight years already? I wondered how Marek was. During my fellowship, my colleague John and I once stopped at his stand. Our conversation was stilted and short. Marek's mood swiftly changed from warm to officious. He sensed the romance between John and me. What he did not know was that the romance was superficial. At any rate, we had to go back to the museum for a seminar. So we left Marek, who looked distraught.

Shortly afterwards came one of those infrequent moments when I urgently desired the serenity and order of home. I needed normalcy. And thus I cleared my desk and went.

Upon arriving home in Oregon from my apartment in Arlington, Virginia, I was welcomed warmly by my parents and Aunt Hedwig, who was visiting us at the time. After embraces and a surprise kiss from my father, I was led to the kitchen, a place with many memories. To me, the kitchen was the symbol of home.

"I cooked your favorite noodles with butternut squash," said my mother. "Those and *Sauerbraten* are still your favorites, right?"

"Yes, I haven't had them for quite a while," I said. It was not easy to prepare a dinner in my studio apartment, and, in any case, I would not marinate a chunk of roast all for myself, or even for a couple of friends.

My father, pleased to see me after nearly a year, smiled and carried my bags to my room.

At dinner, the talk turned to family topics. Aunt Hedwig monopolized the conversation, but I did not mind. I found these recollections interesting. Munching on the tender *Sauerbraten*, Hedwig told us how difficult it was to obtain a good cut of beef during the war.

"You know, Kurt," she turned to my father, "you were too young to know about those things."

My father, sitting next to me, squeezed my hand gently, signaling me to be patient with Hedwig. "Let her talk," he whispered in my ear.

My mother, however, was annoyed by the focus of conversation on meat shortages.

"Don't you think that the bombing of Freiburg was by far more terrible?" she asked. "Kurt told me of the devastation from Allied bombers. Thousands must have been killed."

"Ja, ja," chimed in Aunt Hedwig, prepared to tackle the new subject with the same vigor that she gave to the topic of *Sauerbraten*.

"Kurt," she said, "remember the girl we used to visit on our bikes? She showed you how to milk a cow. You liked her, I know. She was killed in the bombing."

My father blushed and my mother got up from the table and busied herself by the stove. Hedwig, sensing tension, prepared to leave the table also, but I asked her to stay.

I turned toward her, "What do you know about Uncle Willi?" I found myself suddenly asking.

She appeared startled by the question and did not answer but looked quizzically at my father.

"How much does Maria know about Willi?" she asked.

"I know little," I said myself. "Dad, don't you have a file on him? I saw a box on the table years ago, and I actually opened it."

I remembered those letters and the German newspaper clippings, and the photos of a man who must have been Willi. He was handsome. I recalled the German script in the letters. I couldn't decipher the handwriting then, and wanted to come back to it later. But that time never came; I got distracted by college.

"Do you still have the file, Dad? Will you let me see it sometime?"

"Yes, yes, I'll try to find it," he said. "You're not leaving until next Sunday. We'll have plenty of time."

Time, time, I thought to myself. There never was enough of it. There certainly was too little now. When I lived at home, both of my parents worked. I frequently had to rely on my own company and that of the books I read. Then came college away from home, then graduate school. I lived closer to home but still my visits home were rare.

Friday came quickly. Long meals with my family and visits with my friends made the days disappear. My father did not mention the file.

Saturday was a cool, sunny day. Both of my parents were working in the garden. I felt at home. With my parents outside, I felt unusually relaxed. I went to my room to get my book and walked into the living room, which had always been my favorite place to read. I saw the file.

I opened it and spread the letters and clippings on the table. Right away, I noticed that the *Die Welt* articles were missing. I looked more carefully for the drawing of Willi's two faces and the memorable photographs, but they were gone.

Amazing, I thought. My parents (who else could it be?) were trying to shield me from Uncle Willi. Was he such a "baddie"? What else had my parents removed? I did not what to embarrass them by asking. Even though I was disappointed, I turned my attention to what remained of the file. With my father's permission, I took the pilfered file back with me to Washington, D.C.

Chapter VII

—◆—

Merlot, Chocolates, and a Rat

I finally got a chance to turn my attention to the puzzle of my great-uncle. At my desk in the Holocaust Museum in Washington, D.C., I pulled out the "Willi File" and, for the third time since I had learned about its existence, I untied the ribbon around it and opened it. I was certain that on this Sunday morning nobody would disturb me in my office cubicle. Researchers and other staff generally did not come on weekends, and the public was not admitted to research areas. So, it would be me, Grandma Menke, and Willi, all alone; together in spirit. Well, we were intruded upon by the ghosts of my father's brothers: Uncle Gerhard, member of the fighting arm of the SS, the Waffen SS; Uncle Heinz, a captain of Mountain Jaegers; and Uncle Bruno, the U-boat navigator. In the bundle of documents, there were several letters from them to my grandparents, the Martells. All three of my uncles were dutiful correspondents as well as dutiful sons and soldiers, two died for Germany. Gerhard wrote from Lwów while it was still under German occupation, so I set his letters aside for future use in my research.

With the newspaper clippings gone, there was not much material left about Willi, though four letters to Grandma Menke caught my attention. The most recent letter was mailed in New York City by Mr. Tomek Laski in August 1977. Mr. Laski introduced himself as a new immigrant to the USA, born in Poland. Laski's English was stilted and the handwriting was poor. In essence, he said that he knew Mr. Wilhelm Menke in Lwów during the Russian occupation in 1940–41. Initially, Mr. Menke did him some favors, and Laski considered Menke to be a decent man even though Menke worked for the Soviet police. Laski, however, was devastated to learn that Menke was, in reality, a double-dealing, false man.

Under the pretext of friendship, Menke made advances toward Laski's wife, Halya. And later, in the words of Mr. Laski, "That bastard abducted my beloved wife and took her to the Soviet Union with him." Laski ended the letter by pleading with Mrs. Menke to let him know what had happened to W. Menke and thus to Halya. If Menke were still alive, he asked Grandma Menke to "let me know his address because I adored my wife and, if she is alive, I will forgive her and will bring her to America."

The address of Mr. Tomek Laski was cut out. Possibly, Grandma Menke answered his letter.

As I was perusing the file, August 1977 came to my mind as the time of our family farewell party, just before we left for Oregon. No wonder Grandma Menke was agitated that night. She must have just received the letter from Tomek Laski, a letter which portrayed Willi as a debaucher and a Soviet policeman. It makes sense to me now.

The second letter was written on the back of a small mailing envelope with a Soviet stamp marked with an original cancellation date: Lwów (in Cyrillic), XI–VII–1939. The local German overprint showed that my grandmother received the letter in Berlin in early 1940. So, the Molotov-Ribbentrop Non-Aggression Pact between Germany and the Soviet Union promoted mail exchange, albeit slow, between the two countries. A short, half-page note inquired about "Dear Sister's" health and about the welfare of the rest of the family in Berlin. Willi sincerely hoped that the war had little impact on his family and, in any case, he said, "It will be over soon."

Today it would be of great interest to know what Uncle Willi really thought at that time. Clearly, he tried to couch his words in such a way that the censors would not block them out.

For himself, Uncle Willi said that he was in good health and spirit. Now that he had managed to survive the Polish "hospitality" in the Bereza-Kartuska "welcome center," he was gainfully employed by a very "philanthropic" state organization which had a working relationship with his *Vaterland* (homeland). "Dear Sister" should not worry about her Willi. "I am not a wild-eyed youngster anymore but a hard-boiled, mature man. In fact, I just celebrated my twenty-ninth birthday in the company of my new friends."

Obviously, Uncle Willi wrote tongue-in-cheek, hoping—and apparently succeeding—to avoid the censor's wrath and to direct suspicion away from Grandma Menke and himself. Of significance to me was the fact that between 1939 and 1940 he found himself in Lwów.

The third letter was from Herr Joachim Benek, an East German. The letter was postmarked: Berlin, Deutsche Demokratische Republik, 1966. It was in the old German Schrift, indicating that the writer was a scholar from the old German school, between fifty and seventy years of age, a contemporary of Uncle Willi. Herr Benek introduced himself as a colleague and comrade of Herr Menke and, at one time, a subordinate to Herr Menke. He considered himself to be Herr Menke's friend. As a friend, Herr Benek presumed on Wilhelm's sister, Frau Menke, and wrote this letter. The gist of the letter was that Frau Menke probably would not receive any communications from Wilhelm for some time, but that Frau Menke must not worry. Wilhelm was safe. Clipped to Benek's letter was a response from Grandma Menke who thanked him for the communication and inquired for additional news about her brother, Willi. Grandma's letter was returned. The envelope was stamped "addressee unknown," address incorrect.

Another letter to Grandma Menke in 1967 was more intriguing and equally puzzling. It was written by a young woman. It lacked polite phrases and the handwriting was modern German. Frau Hildegard Braun wrote that she was an intimate friend of Wilhelm Menke and, in fact, they had lived together for some twenty years with the intention to marry. They were happy years because they worked for the East German state, and Wilhelm was esteemed and highly placed in the government of the Republic. Frau Braun explained that, about a year earlier, Wilhelm did not return from work and all her initial inquiries were stone-walled. Later, Hildegard was made to understand that Wilhelm probably ran away to a capitalist country in pursuit of a romance. She was advised by no less a person than the secretary of the Communist Party not to pursue this matter; apparently, large funds allocated to the Foreign Office where Comrade Menke worked were missing. An official inquiry into the disappearance of Comrade Menke would surely point a finger at him. Frau Braun did not know what to believe, but if Wilhelm was alive somewhere, she wanted to contact him, hoping for reconciliation. "I beg you; please let me know where your brother is. I will treat his present location with utmost secrecy." The envelope had Hildegard's address: Berlin Mitte, DDR.

"What in heaven's name are you doing here, Maria?" A familiar voice interrupted my concentration. "It is Sunday morning and you should be in bed."

Oh hell, I thought. I liked Jon's company, but I wanted to be alone, alone with the ghosts of the past. Being a sensitive man, Jon realized that I need privacy; that is, in part, why I cared for him.

"One question, Maria, and I am gone to the bowels of the museum: When are you leaving for Lwów? Are you going to stop on the way?"

"Not now to Lwów. Berlin, definitely to Berlin," I decided on the spur of the moment. I had a week to get ready.

*   *   *

"I was nineteen years old, you know, when I met Willi. He was a very handsome, charming man. I guess it was love at first sight, at least for me," said Hildegard.

We were sitting at an outdoor table at the Sophieneck Café in Berlin Mitte. Around us were residential homes interspersed with small businesses. The May afternoon was just perfect for an outdoor get-together.

"You know, I was a very pretty young woman in 1950. Here, I'll show you my photographs." Hildegard reached into her handbag and pulled out a bunch of well-thumbed photographs.

The first one she gave me was of a young woman in a swimsuit and cap, dripping wet, reaching out to a tall man who handed her a bouquet of flowers.

"This is me. Look at the emblem on my swimsuit: FDJ—Free German Youth. I had just won the 100-meter breast stroke for East Germany. That's Willi there. At that time, he was in the Ministry of Culture. But, you know," her voice grew softer, "he was also in the special police unit attached to state security, the STASI. Here, look at this other picture."

The elderly woman across from me wore layers of make-up. She had obviously tried to preserve her youth. I wanted to be kind to her.

"You're still beautiful," I said.

She acknowledged the flattery with a nod and then looked directly at me. "I know you want to talk about Willi. There's not much I can tell you. I remember writing to your grandmother in America a long time ago. I never got an answer. Is your grandmother still alive?"

"No, she died in 1990. She lived just long enough to see news reports of the Wall coming down in her native Berlin. I found your letter to her and I wanted to meet you. I'm a historian. Someday I hope to do research in Ukraine. Perhaps I will learn something about Willi in Lwów. As he must have told you, he lived there during the war."

A shadow flitted across Hildegard's face, but she said nothing. The waiter came and addressed her, smiling familiarly.

"What would you like, Frau Braun? Your usual Merlot?"

"Yes, and for the young lady too, bitte," Hildegard said. She jerkily turned toward me and looked confused for a moment, her age showing. "What was your name?"

"Maria Martell. My mother's maiden name was Menke."

The waiter returned and filled our glasses. Hildegard took a sip and regained her composure. "Did you say Lwów? In Ukraine?

Willi called it by its German name, Lemberg. He spent a lot of time there." Her voice trailed off. She pulled out a cigarette. "Do you mind if I smoke? You know, Willi didn't smoke. In so many ways, he was well-disciplined. That's what they liked in the Party. He got pretty far up."

Her glass was soon empty. Mine was still almost full. The waiter appeared as if on cue and immediately refreshed our goblets. This time, he left the bottle on the table. Soon we would need another.

"Lemberg. I guess the women there must be beautiful."

I could not tell if this was a question or a statement. Gently, I prodded her for more information. "In addition to getting your letter, my grandmother got a letter from the husband of a Ukrainian woman. Do you know about her?"

"Yes." Hildegard's eyes focused on some indeterminate point on the red brick wall of the psychiatric hospital across the street. "Her name—I can't remember, something with an H."

"Halya."

"Willi was fighting for the Bolsheviks and wrote letters to her during the war. She never received them, and they came back. He kept them hidden in a locked drawer of his desk. When he left, the STASI came and took them, but eventually they were returned to me." Hildegard's eyes suddenly focused hard on me again. "So yes, I know about her."

Hildegard's abruptness made me hesitate to push further. I changed the subject.

"Do you know Herr Benek? I have an appointment with him. He was Uncle Willi's associate, wasn't he?"

Hildegard took the last sip from her glass and firmly set it down. "That man. General Benek. During the war he was as staunchly German as they come, and then suddenly he was one of the most ardent leaders among the Communists. Why are you bothering to see him?"

"My grandmother got a letter from him, too, even before yours came. He said Willi was fine. Maybe Willi told him to send it."

"Yes, sure, he was fine. He probably did tell General Benek to write, then stole government money and ran to the West. I'm surprised he didn't find your grandmother himself."

Her voice had become gritty with bitterness. "I never knew what he really did in his job," she said.

"He often stayed very late at the office, and sometimes he traveled for days. I would ask him to tell me what he could, but that amounted to just about nothing. We barely saw each other. I worked too. I had a good job in the Ministry of Culture. That's how we met, of course. I had friends and started to spend more and more time with them, going out in the evenings. Why come home to an empty apartment, right? But the evening he disappeared, we were supposed to go to the opera together. I waited and waited, and he never showed up. Not that night or the next or the next. I grew frantic with worry. But I'll tell you another time...." Her voice trailed off.

"Some more wine?" I held up the bottle and poured the rest into her glass. She sipped and looked across the street again. I knew the conversation had ended.

At five o'clock the next morning, I was already up and excited. My appointment with Herr Benek—General Benek, as Hildegard still called him—was not until ten, but I didn't wait for breakfast at the pension in Kreuzberg. I took a quick shower and walked out into the fine morning. The bakery next door was already open, and I bought some almond cookies.

I had time to wander the streets northward into Mitte, where I would meet Herr Benek. Shop doors were opening, husbands and wives were calling reminders to each other before they left for work: pick up the children from school, buy bread. I heard languages I didn't recognize. The stench from last night's wine-soaked carousing permeated some alleys. I wound my way to Hackescher Markt, a two-storied marketplace crowned by an elevated train station. As I passed one stand of used books, I suddenly heard a language I did recognize. A young man wearing a faded suit was speaking Russian to an elderly woman, probably his mother, who was wearing a housedress and scarf. They caught my look of surprise and stopped talking. To start a conversation, I asked what they recommended among the books in the eclectic collection on the table.

"Are you American?" the man asked, ignoring my question.

"Yes," I said, and jumped at the opportunity to find out more about them. "Where are you from?"

"Kiev."

"Someday I intend to visit Lvov in Ukraine," I said, carefully adhering to the Russian name of the city. "What brought you from Ukraine to Berlin?"

I learned that the young man and his mother had come to Germany after making contact with the daughter of a German journalist who had hidden the woman, then a small girl, and her father during the German occupation of Kiev during World War II. I had never heard such an incredible story. The journalist lived in an apartment building reserved for Germans, and hid the father and daughter under her neighbors' noses. The image of young Marek hiding in Lwów came to mind. I wondered where he was now.

The young man glanced at his watch, and the gesture reminded me that I needed to go to Herr Benek. I apologized for cutting short our conversation and, checking a slip of paper on which I had scribbled an address, asked him for the shortest route to Schokoladenhaus Fassbender & Rausch on Gendarmenmarkt. The look that he and his mother exchanged told me that it was a place they had heard of, but would never go to; it was out of their reach, a place for German elite and tourists.

"The chocolates they make are the best in Europe, we hear. But they're very expensive," he said.

"I need to meet someone there," I said, feeling a need to explain. He drew his finger along a map and smiled. "Do svidania," he said. "Do svidania," I answered, waving good-bye.

I crossed the Spree River and started down Unter den Linden. The May sun reflected off of the garish metal sheets covering the East German Palace of the Republic. To my right towered the Baroque cathedral. I thought about General Benek, who, like Uncle Willi, had cast aside traditional religious beliefs on the altar of Marxism-Leninism. Both Benek and Willi had held the fate of many people in their hands. I wondered what Benek believed now, and let my mind open up to the possibility that Willi might still be alive, maybe a changed man, maybe not. In my stomach I felt a knot of excitement and apprehension.

As I approached Gendarmenmarkt, I understood why the immigrant booksellers would not frequent this part of town. Cartier, Gucci… the names glistened from elegant buildings, well kept and some newly renovated. I felt a little tired. I was still jet-lagged and the walk was long. The tables of the outdoor cafés looked very inviting.

*   *   *

Under the awnings of Schokoladenhaus Fassbender & Rausch, the tables were filled with either white-haired, well-dressed patrons enjoying coffee, or tourists—mostly Americans—wearing jeans. I walked inside and spotted a man getting up from a table with some difficulty; one of his legs seemed to be slightly lame. He was looking at me; I had told him what I would wear—a conservative gray skirt and white blouse.

"General Benek?" I asked, careful to show respect.

"Ja. Bitte setzen Sie sich hin," he said, gesturing toward the chair opposite him. "Maria Martell? I used to know a Martell, Bruno Martell. We were on the Eastern front together. A relative of yours?"

"No, Herr General, I don't recognize that name."

"Bitte, please don't call me General. That's from times past." He waved his hand as if to rid himself of the title. "I was just a foot soldier in the German army when your great-uncle Willi was an officer on the opposite side. Shall we order some hot chocolate for you?"

"Yes, thank you. This shop is new, isn't it?"

"Brand new. Life has completely changed since *die Wende*," he said, referring to the collapse of the East German regime in 1989. "We never had such good chocolate," he added, smiling wryly.

The waiter came, and Herr Benek ordered our hot chocolates and an extra box of the German specialty, *Baumkuchen*, for me to take along after our meeting.

The memory of Uncle Willi sent him back to the war. "I'm from a worker's family. My father repaired streetcars. We were socialists until Hitler came to power. Back then, we didn't tell anyone what we believed. I was drafted and I didn't want to fight for Hitler but I did want to fight for Germany, my Germany. Did you notice my leg?"

I nodded.

"I was wounded at Belgorod, on the Russian front in the summer of 1943. That was it for us. Only idiots believed we could win the war after that. After the war, I returned to the ruins of Berlin, embittered, limping, and unsure of my future. But I had one hope. My father was dead, but he would have had the same hope: the creation of a German socialist state. And I have to say that while the Americans in Berlin were flaunting their cigarettes, their gum, and their bananas, it wasn't hard for us poor bastards to feel some solidarity with the Soviets. "

Herr Benek paused and I reached for my handbag. "This is so interesting, I really want to take notes, do you mind?" I started to pull out my yellow pad but, to my surprise, Herr Benek shook his head emphatically.

"No, no, definitely not. It's not necessary. I'll just tell you everything. It's nice to speak to a young lady who is interested in all of this, you know." He smiled again. I put away my writing pad, and he continued.

"I met Willi when we were both in the security service, in the STASI. You have heard of the STASI, haven't you?"

I nodded. "Yes, of course."

"He was already a major and I was just beginning my career. We became friends, but I moved more quickly through the ranks and, by the time he was a colonel, I was already a general. Still, we continued our association. We all worked, but I worked harder. I sacrificed everything. Willi had Hildegard and others. I, on the other hand, was alone."

114

"I saw the letter that you wrote to my grandmother, his sister," I said. "She must have been relieved to hear that he was okay. That was kind of you."

"Kind? No, I wasn't kind to him. We were friends, as I said, but we had our important differences. I wanted Germans to create their own version of socialism. When I saw how Moscow made us purge our ranks after the 1953 uprising, I realized we were stuck. I admired Tito for making Yugoslavia independent, and I knew that for Germany it was too late, but I still held it against Willi that he felt so much loyalty toward Moscow."

"Why do you think he felt that way?" I asked.

"Well, he served the Soviets for so long. He left Germany when he was still young, and never seemed to have much attachment to our homeland. And, I don't know, he probably had some lovers over there in the East. He had winning ways about him."

I smiled. I couldn't tell whether Herr Benek knew about Halya or not.

"The Politburo became suspicious," he continued. "They caught wind of some highly sensitive information reaching the Kremlin. It was the kind of information that could only have come from the highest levels, from one of us. Willi was the most obvious suspect. I didn't want to believe it, but it turned out to be true."

There was silence now. I stared at Herr Benek. "Wait," I protested. "How did you know it was true?"

"The evidence was overpowering—"

"Couldn't he have been framed?" I interrupted, pulling back into my chair, trying to regain composure.

"No. I was always watching his back. Three of us, including the secretary general, formed an investigative committee. And when I, too, finally became convinced that Willi was a traitor, I did everything in my power to keep him from being shot. For several days, his life was really on the line, but I finally managed to persuade the others to send him into exile among his bosses. The Soviets, of course, agreed, since part of our deal was to keep the entire affair quiet."

"Is…is he alive?" I could barely get the words out.

"I don't know. All I can tell you is that the last time I saw him was the day he was forcefully removed from his office and flown to Moscow on a special plane. I told him that a security detachment was on its way to arrest him."

"What was his reaction? You had been friends, right?"

"Yes. It was irregular, even a little risky, for me to go see him that afternoon, but I felt a need to tell him they were coming and to assure him that they would not shoot him. He did not seem surprised. He knew he was in some kind of trouble. He could tell I was hurt and angry, even though my presence there was a sign of friendship. I wanted to call him a traitor—a rat—to his face, and to tell him he had caused irreparable damage to our nation. But I didn't. And he knew that I had participated in causing his downfall. 'Do me a favor, Benek,' I remember him saying. 'Write my sister in the United States and tell her I'm alive. She's going to read in the newspapers that I disappeared. I don't want her to worry. We have lost everyone else in our family. Please, Benek, please.'"

The elderly man stopped and looked concerned. "You're so pale. Do you need some water?" I shook my head. He took my hand and squeezed it.

"It was a long time ago. Today I try to remember the things I can be proud of, and there aren't many. It's hard to live with this. My socialist utopia never materialized. Your great-uncle Willi wasn't any different. The Soviet Union collapsed also. We and our dreams both crumbled at the end."

These revelations knocked the wind out of me. We finished our hot chocolate in silence. I was thinking about Grandmother Menke and the night I first saw the file. All she knew was that Willi had disappeared abruptly, and still she was upset. I could not imagine my family's reaction should they learn the full truth.

"I'd like more chocolate, but you look like you need to lie down." Herr Benek said. "Let me call a taxi for you."

"I'm fine, thank you. I'll take the U-Bahn; it's easy. I should go. You have been so kind to meet me." At the word "kind," Herr

Benek seemed to flinch slightly. I sensed that his conscience bothered him.

"Really, by meeting me you are again showing your friendship," I tried to reassure him. "Thank you. May I call you if I have questions?"

"Yes, of course," Herr Benek said, pulling himself up on his good leg. He grasped my hand warmly with both of his. "Auf Wiedersehen, Frau Martell," he said.

"Auf Wiedersehen, und vielen Dank, Herr Benek."

I took the U-Bahn in the direction of Kreuzberg. My mind felt fuzzy. As I walked up the stairs at the U-Bahn station near my pension, my bag slipped out of my hand and another passenger stepped on it as he rushed by. The *Baumkuchen* was secured by the box, and seemed intact, but the almond cookies were smashed.

* * *

I stood on the doorstep of a two-story apartment building in Mitte and rang the bell to Hildegard's apartment.

"Wer ist da?" her voice came over the loudspeaker.

"Maria, Maria Martell," I said.

"Come upstairs. The door is open."

I was surprised that the door was unlocked, and walked into a dimly lit stairwell. Hildegard's head appeared on the second floor. She looked down at me and smiled. "The landlord always tries to save on electricity," she said.

There were only two apartments on her floor. It was a narrow, small building, but the stairwell was clean and freshly painted.

She led me into her living room. On her coffee table rested a plate of fruit. An old typewriter sat on a small desk against the wall. Sheets of paper lay scattered across the surface, the only disorderly spot I could see. My eyes wandered to the medals encased on cushions in a cabinet with glass doors.

"You remember that I was a swimmer," Hildegard said. "I'm writing a book about sports in East Germany. We had such tremendous teams. It needs to be documented. All this business about our using steroids, that's nonsense, Western *Quatsch*."

I burst out into laughter. "*Quatsch!* I haven't heard that in so long. Grandmother Menke would say it all the time, and we grandchildren used to tease her and mimic her. I'd like to read your book. You and I are both writers. I would like to write about Lemberg, too, sometime." I noticed Hildegard's shoulders loosening as she smiled at me again. I felt my own apprehension melting away.

I had seen a bottle of wine on the kitchen counter, and went to get it. "Please, tell me what you know about Willi's disappearance."

"Dear Maria, I don't want to think about it, but I will tell you. When he didn't come home on the night that we were supposed to go to the opera, I just thought to myself, that's Willi. He was probably called away on official business. But by the next night, I was concerned. He would have told me if he had had to leave town. On the third day, I called his office. His usual secretary was gone. A female voice on the line said that Colonel Menke did not work there. I called all the officials that I knew and got exactly the same answer. If anyone recognized my voice, they pretended not to—." She stopped suddenly.

"Did you see Benek?"

Before I could reply, she went on. "I tried so many times to reach him, but he was never there—never there to take my calls, anyway. Damn him. Did you say he's well? Too bad."

Hildegard seemed unaware of my presence. She started to talk about people I had never heard of. Bastards, she called them. All bastards. Willi, too. She poured herself another glass of wine. There was no way to interrupt her until the phone rang and startled her out of her soliloquy. Someone was calling to confirm an appointment for the next day.

The old woman put down the receiver and turned to me saying "That was Antonina. She came here from Romania a couple of years ago, thinking she'd be cleaning houses and sending money home to her parents. She was tricked and sold into the sex trade. You've heard of that, I'm sure. Her bosses threatened her.

She was working out of the building next to my friend Bertha's place. One day she appeared at Bertha's door, terrified, crying. Bertha called me to ask if I would take care of Antonina until we could be sure she was safe. She's been living on her own now for a year, and cleans for me once a week."

Hildegard drank from her third glass of wine and sighed.

"The secretary general's office phoned me and told me to come after work. The guards would be expecting me, I was informed. I was astounded when they led me to the secretary general himself. Comrade Honecker got up from behind his desk and extended his hand to greet me. I shook his hand reluctantly and he began to tell me how much he admired my skill in swimming, and that he had seen me compete. Then he got to the point. 'I have bad news, Frau Braun. Colonel Wilhelm Menke, whom I liked and respected, embezzled large funds and escaped to the West. We have reason to believe that he did this for a woman. But we do not want to besmirch his name, or your association with him, by spreading this knowledge. Frau Braun, please refrain from contacting this or any office.' And so I was ushered out."

A few tears had eroded the layers of powder and rouge on her cheeks, creating small rivulets of mascara-stained salty water. Suddenly she seemed a shriveled old lady.

"I always knew there were other women," she said slowly. "You came here for the letters, didn't you?" Slightly stooped now, she walked to her desk and pulled a large envelope out of a drawer. I took it and thanked her.

"I will make copies for myself. I will bring these back."

"No, no. No need," were her parting words. She waved me toward the door. Our meeting had ended as suddenly as it did when we first met at the Sophieneck Café.

*　　*　　*

As I sat down in the U-Bahn, I clutched the envelope and felt the knot in my stomach again. The letters felt somehow sacred to me; I wanted to treasure them as much as any precious handwritten letters of a lost relative. But they were written by a man who had betrayed his country, his comrades, and his women. I could not wait any longer. I tore open the envelope and begin to read. The letters were written in Russian.

3 April 1944

My Heart of Hearts,

It is a long time since I have heard from you. I was uneasy that something untoward happened to you. I was happy to hear that you are well, but your words in the letter were guarded and not as loving as I am used to. Am I imagining, or is there someone else in your life? I am hoping that your next letter will relieve my doubts. In fact, I apologize now for being jealous. From the date of your letter, I am concluding that its lateness is the fault of our mail service. Well, maybe not completely, for we are on the move all the time. We go west and further west, and so catching up with us is not easy. We have the Nazi armies on the run although they are still capable of stoutly defending themselves. Being German, I can't help but to admire their resilience and fighting spirit. My feelings do not extend to their allies, the Ukrainians.

By the time I finished the first paragraph, the train had arrived at my station. "My Heart of Hearts." What a wonderful expression of devotion, I thought. I ran back to my room at the pension and continued.

Right now, I am in western Ukraine. Marshall Konev, with Comrade Khrushchev as commissar at his side, prods us forward. They smell final victory and are hoping to outpace our other Armies, especially that of Malinowski. I am fine and have plenty to do, translating for the staff of our division and interrogating prisoners. You might have read in the newspapers about the Order that distinguished my Ninety-eight Guard Infantry Regiment near Lwów for its heroism in battling the Ukrainian SS Galicia Division. We surrounded them and wiped out the fascistic beast. Those Ukrainian traitors brutally murdered Communists, Jews, and Poles, and now it was their turn to be filled with lead.

Frankly, we gave no pardon to those bastards. We took no prisoners, but I saved one who fell to his knees crying, begging for his life, and claiming to be a Jew. This was not the way to appeal to my partner, Captain Grigoriev who hated Jews only a bit less than he hated Ukrainian fascists. He was ready to shoot but I pushed his Pepesza aside while landing a powerful kick on the Jew's jaw, to soften him for interrogation. He talked without further inducement. I determined that he would sell his own mother if given something in return—a perfect candidate as an agent in our security apparatus.

I am yearning to be with you, Halya. Do you remember how we loved while escaping from the Nazis and from your husband? I hope that we will someday relive such a thrill. With all...

The ink was smeared and I could not read anything else. The letter's creases told me that it had not been folded in the triangular shape that conformed with Russian field post requirements. As I opened the second letter I learned that Willi had handed it to an acquaintance so that it would be delivered in person, uncensored. It read:

My Heart of Hearts,

It has been a few more weeks since I handed a letter for you to Comrade Himonov but I have received nothing from you in return. Was I right in my suspicion? I wish you would just let me know that you are well and that you have tied yourself to someone else; perhaps to one who is exempted from that front, one who has found a profitable, safe niche far away from battle. Those are the bastards who screw the sweethearts and wives of our fighting men. I am bitter, yes, but do write me the truth. It will hurt, but I will understand. I know that you were lonely. What else can I say? Perhaps now I will respond to the flirting of some of the comely Polish panie. *One infidelity deserves another.*

As for the news: we are across the Polish border, but you probably know that already. That Ukrainian Jew whose life I saved is useful to us. SMERSH suits him well. He has no scruples and will go far.

SMERSH, short for "Death to Spies," was the Soviet counter-intelligence department formed in 1943. I felt a shiver run down my spine. I continued reading:

But the war may swallow us all—him, me, and many others. The road to Berlin is strewn with corpses.

I ache for you but you are not mine anymore. Somebody else wraps himself around you and cups his hands over your small, hard breasts. Well, no use torturing myself anymore. I'll make this letter short and final.

Why had Willi given up on Halya? I wondered if he was right about her infidelity. War wreaked havoc on relationships, I knew. Maybe Halya had taken a lover, but maybe she had died. Or maybe Willi wanted an excuse to leave her. I read on.

I am reopening the letter to write you of the latest news. Comrade "U" from the German political committee in Moscow visited me today and offered me a Politburo membership as well as a high governmental position in the future German Democratic Republic. It is a big compli-

ment to me. Even more important was a call from Comrade General Khrushchev urging me to accept the offer. So it looks like shortly I will travel to Moscow and eventually to Berlin.

That's how Willi returned to Germany, I thought. Comrade "U"—that must have been Ulbricht, the first leader of the GDR, or DDR in German. Then Willi changed voices again, no longer the functionary but now the lover:

All I can think of now is how the war brought us together, and how it is tearing us apart. How we once were true and ardent lovers...I'll drink to those memories tonight.

Still your Willi

I pulled another slip of paper out of Hildegard's envelope. I could not tell where it had come from, whether it was attached to one of the letters or perhaps a fragment that was never mailed:

...But of course, as a Major in SMERSH I myself have a number of unpleasant deeds under my belt but certainly not on my conscience. Remember what I told you about the four years in Bereza Kartuska camp? Yes, the nationalist Poles tortured all of us who were dedicated Communists, and abused us in many creative ways. When one is so treated, one gets brutalized, one loses regard for human life; at least I did. The concentration camp run by the German SS brutes in Oranienburg had not much more to offer than Bereza Kartuska. Understandably, as a German it is poignant to me that the Polish government could be just as inhuman as the German government. Now on the front, as I learn about the atrocities committed by Ukrainians, I am convinced that most people are murdering scum. You do understand, don't you?

Yes, Great-uncle Willi, you're mostly right. And at that time you didn't even know about Hutus and Tutsis, about Darfur or Cambodia. You didn't even have an inkling about your own idol, Stalin. Or did you know? You certainly did his bidding.

So. Wilhelm Menke, major of SMERSH, ranking member of the Socialist Unity Party of East Germany, in fact, a member of the Politburo, the smiling, handsome, persuasive advocate of the Communist way of life had at least two additional faces. Officially, Colonel Wilhelm Menke of the Feliks Dzierzynski Wachtregiment, an elite military unit dedicated to internal security, was one of the four deputies to the head of the Ministry for State Security, better known for its security service, STASI. In secret, Comrade Menke chaired successive committees dealing with the repression of anti-government activities, the Wall and the related escapee problems. He seemed to have fit well into this vast hydra-like network of denouncers, spies, interrogators, border guards and jailers, and yet...

I needed to get out of my room and I found myself again at the Sophieneck, sipping a glass of Merlot and imagining Willi there with Hildegard. I pictured him being whisked in his black ZIS limousine from meeting to meeting. I saw him in the crisp uniform of an officer, and other times wearing a well-tailored business suit with an open-necked Oxford shirt.

He had worked nearby, in the Berlin–Lichtenberg area. In that central location, the STASI occupied a large complex of well-guarded, forbidding buildings. I visualized Uncle Willi spending his time in gray, austere offices and file libraries amongst six million dossiers, most collected on suspected GDR citizens, but many on those who were loyal. He walked on the tile floors with heavy boots that reverberated in the hallways; he was constantly saluted by the underlings. Uncle Willi, I mused, what were you imagining when your cohorts were surveying and attempting to control several hundred thousands of tagged human beings, sifting and analyzing periodic reports on them by anywhere from 100,000 to 200,000 informers? Was there ever laughter in those edifices where suspicion and ruination of human lives was the raison d'être?

How could this highly regarded, East German Communist *apparatchik* have been unmasked as a super-spy for a fraternal government, the Soviet Union? There surely was a carefully updated and monitored dossier on even this master of STASI intrigue. No mystery. Those big shots were also spied upon. Some false colleague or a truly fanatic, chauvinistic German Communist, or even a jealous husband, might have denounced Willi. Could it have been General Benek, in spite of his professed friendship?

If Uncle Willi was that super-spy, it was because of him that the Soviets learned a lot about the unpublicized thinking of their prodigy: the German Democratic Republic. Perhaps because of Uncle Willi's pipeline to the Kremlin, the Soviets were motivated to occasionally "spank" their obedient but knotty Warsaw Pact junior partner.

It is certain that directly or indirectly, Uncle Willi was responsible for the deaths or incarcerations of East Germans who attempted to flee to the West. Bad-Man Willi, to be sure. But was Uncle Willi truly a plant in the GDR government, a traitor to his kind, a super spy, a super rat? A twinge of doubt crept into my subconscious. Could there have been another reason for his sudden disappearance, like a flash that leaves behind only smoke? But which way did the smoke blow? If I were to believe the hurt and jealous Hildegard and the disenchanted secretary general, Willi was having a good time chasing women in the West, perhaps in America.

Herr Benek's silver hair, clear blue eyes, and steel handshake gave veracity to his parting words, "Willi was working for the Soviet Union. He was a rat and deserved to be cashiered."

I sensed hatred in the word "rat."

"No, he was not murdered. He was just pensioned off and sent somewhere to the Soviet Union," Herr Benek forcefully told me.

I tend to believe him. Even more, I believe Willi's words to Halya: "You will always be in my heart and perhaps we will embrace again." I desperately want to believe that there is a crumb of goodness in Willi's makeup.

———◆———

Chapter VIII

My Brother Bogdan

*T*he Labor Day weekend approaches. It is late morning on this Saturday in 2000, and I am simply reading the entries in my chronicles. My father was hospitalized again. I was given to understand that his heart is finally failing. I will not stay in the metropolitan area overnight for tomorrow's exhibit but will drive home to be with him in the intensive care facility. Actually, this is one of my last weekends at my encampment. I was given to understand by the authorities that next year they will not issue a permit to me, even though I have exhibited on the Mall for twenty years. They accuse me of shielding hustlers who prey on tourists. They are referring to the illegal water, ice cream, and soft drink vendors who occasionally hide their coolers filled with goods behind my stands. Despite warnings from the police, they have continued to use my encampment for their staging area and I am being blamed for it. No matter. I am weary of dealing with government bureaucracies and I do not intend to fight them again. The officialdom has finally won. I am very depressed. I have already imbibed my cocktail, which I normally save for the end of the day.

The alcoholic spirits were not lifting my spirits. As I contemplated resorting to my "final solution" of straight gin, Phil interrupted me. As if by heavenly design, Phil materialized from behind "my" tree and squatted in front of me as was his habit. Since I did not have a new canvas upon which he could rest his eyes, Phil gazed toward the Air and Space Museum in the distance. Phil, who needs to be in constant motion, began to nervously rake the skimpy, burned clumps of grass around him with the fingers of both of his hands. My depression lessened as I looked at this tortured, discarded human being.

"Phil, are you still searching for lost coins or are you simply caressing the grass? It sure needs some loving care." I did not expect an answer, but the prospect of one-sided conversation appeared to be more cheerful than reading my chronicles.

"Phil, where are you coming from just now?" Phil remained silent. "Phil, did you see Figarroo today? Once more and no response. So I quickly got up from my chair and began walking away toward the West Building stairs, still holding onto the yellow pages of my chronicles. Seeing Phil had the usual effect on me.

"By Figarrro, this will not do," I said aloud to myself. "Where I am going, it will be easier if I have my hands free," I shouted toward Phil and began to walk back to stow the yellow sheaf of paper in the cooler.

Surprise of surprises! Phil raised himself to his full height, pointed to me with his right index finger, and barely audibly asked me, "Are you going to Ceylon again?"

Hearing him actually speak was a rare event; but why Ceylon? I nearly dropped my yellow sheets.

"Will you be examining the bottom of the Palk Strait between Ceylon and India? It is deep water there. We did some soundings there in—"

"Palk Strait?" I interrupted. Now I was truly astonished.

"When did you read about the Palk Strait?" I asked, knowing that Phil frequented an air-conditioned library somewhere to cool off.

"It was an oceanographic research ship, a schooner. They are by far more useful than steam ships or any motor ships," he said with an air of authority as if he had served aboard all three types.

Strangely, it all made sense to me. As he spoke, he straightened out. His face acquired stronger lines and for the first time I actually saw his pale-blue eyes. His shining eyes were temporarily unobstructed by masses of blond, tangled hair and by his deep-seated ski cap. I saw Phil perhaps as he once was: a tall, muscular, suntanned young man swaying on the deck of a sailing ship. Actually, smiling; he was smiling as he beheld the hills of Ceylon across the greenish blue waters of Palk Strait.

The moment was gone. Phil squatted again and I, assured that he would mind my stand, turned around, crossed the street, and walked up the steps of the Gallery, as I had done numberless times before.

*   *   *

I am back on the Mall again, my very last day here, and back to reading my chronicles as well. As I read some entries, I see that many describe my boozing. I am afraid that I am giving the wrong impression. Certainly, I do drink, but mostly here on my battleground, the Mall, and mostly at the end of the day. Still, I do consume a lot of liquor. I feel apprehensive, weary, and lonely despite the people around me and despite a fair measure of commercial success. These three dark sisters—apprehension, weariness, and loneliness—have hovered over me for some time. I feared the approaching summer storms, I despaired having my permit revoked, and I resented altercations with the Park Police. Mostly, though, I feared the effects of my failing memory; I still do, perhaps even more so. Yes, mostly I fear the maladies and isolation that come with old age. These are poignantly visible in Karol's slow decline. This man, who was strong and virile at one time, is nearing his end. So will I. So must I. How soon? I experienced an explosion once. It was so quick that it was painless. Could I be so fortunate as to end my life that way? Could an explosion strike twice?

*   *   *

I notice that my chronicle entries are becoming fewer as the months and years have advanced. Many interesting things have happened to me but I am losing the motivation to record them. Would anyone be interested in reading about a struggling, aged artist? Likely, they would only take notice if my work were to become famous. This is the one hope that I do not dare to abandon, lest I die spiritually. I have given up all other hopes. To be loved by Maria, or a young woman like her, seems to be nothing but a dream, a wonderful dream. But that is all that it is. To make my work recognized nationally became my raison d'être. The many who admire my work make me believe that I do have that chance. But when? How? What more can I do? What must I do with the few remaining active years of my life?

There is not much left for me to do except to examine my past. How did I arrive at this stage of life where there are no discernible roads ahead of me? Outside of this occasionally thrilling but mostly exhausting life of an exhibiting artist, I lead a fairly normal existence. I am married, I have children, and I had fairly prestigious business prospects once. Why can't I now enjoy the simple pleasures of life? Why have I endeavored to conquer such a capricious, possessive, yet unfaithful mistress as art for so many years?

The Holocaust taught me that life can be unexpectedly and brutally terminated, so "live and do and let live" became my motto. My exposure to human perfidy, hatreds and savagery was partly compensated by witnessing some humans at their best, risking everything for others. The result is that I see the human race as it is. In fact, there is no human race. We are all individuals: a gigantic firmament of unique likes, dislikes, passions, lethargies, melancholies, depravities, smarts, and stupidities. Among those galaxies of human traits we navigate the best we know how. We try to locate those individuals with whom we can share friendship and life alike, often temporarily, but once in a great while for the duration of our trek.

My journey really began during those many, many months when I was hidden by the Bielys in the small room. Constant fear expanded my ability to fantasize to a towering height, to a wide breath, and to a profound depth. Fantasy was my antidote to insanity during that frightful period. Hour after hour, day after day, for weeks and months, I escaped the realm of reason. I flew the lofty sky in a fighter plane, shooting down German aircraft; I gorged German submarines in murky oceans with Captain Nemo. My imagination also took me into the embrace of Barbara, a girl one year older than me. She lived on the same floor next to the Bielys. I never saw Barbara but only heard her voice across the staircase, muted by the walls between us. My vivid imagination propelled me and navigated me later in life as I aimed toward my star: art, painting.

Imagination outlined the direction but my vast store of energy fueled me onward. Imagination and energy are my curse—they gave birth to my abnormal ambition, and thus did not allow me to settle down into a predictable and comfortable routine. However, neither energy nor talent is capable of breaking the barrier of inculcated bias and cupidity that resides in those who rule the art world. Now I feel exhausted and empty, unable to dream. I can still fantasize, though sadly, this often happens under the influence of alcohol.

Dejection did not come to me suddenly. As the summers have passed, I have become more depressed and lonely. Now I do not even attempt to reach out to people. I am morose, jaundiced, locked in my shell. Maria is gone and someplace in this world she is building a life for herself. Even Lady Orange no longer shows up. I yearn for them. To be sure, the elegant, ebony-tinted Yvonne Black visited me here on the Mall several times. She brought sandwiches and drinks. I learned that she lives in Maryland near Annapolis and that she was an airline stewardess, one of the first black ones. She is married to a white man, a minister, and she has two teenage children. Yvonne invited me to visit her telling me that the liaison she had been having with the man, the one who she had me call on the telephone, did not work out. I responded noncommittally. I didn't want to start anything that I might not have been able to finish. To be sure, I learned the Lady Orange lesson well. But today, I am not that sure. I desperately need companionship and I know that she likes me. It would be good to visit her next week. Yes, by golly, I will see her. Let the capricious, unknowable fate take over.

*   *   *

Indeed, fate did interfere. My father Karol, expired. His healthy organs struggled to keep him alive but his condition worsened. He was in and out a coma. At times he was conscious, but mostly not. The medical prognosis was death. It was simply a question of when and how. I consulted the internist and we agreed that my father should be allowed eternal respite.

They scheduled to drug him out of the last bit of life before that very night descended. I stayed beside him in his semi-private, austere, windowless room. The other bed was unoccupied, and the bluish green glow of the monitor display, punctuated by a pulsating red light, gave me an eerie feeling.

I sat on his bed and watched Karol's gaunt face and his sunken, closed eyes. I heard his labored, raspy breathing. Hours passed as my thoughts dwelled on the unimaginable terror, pain, and humiliation that he suffered during the German occupation. A large patch of darkened skin on his damaged nose testified to the whipping Karol was given in the Janowska concentration camp. Other scars, I could not see; those were psychological. Yet he had retained a lust for life, and if he retained hatred, it was not for Germans or Ukrainians as nationalities, even though some of them treated him brutally and partially destroyed him.

As I sat watching the old man, I also began to wonder what joys he did experience in his life. On the balance, was his life worth living? Suddenly, my father stirred, opened his eyes, and recognized me. He tried to move his head but succeeded only in moving his lips.

"Marus," he whispered, using an endearing form of my name. "Marus, I must tell you. Marus, understand: Bogdan is your brother. I loved Natalia. She saved our lives. Bogdan was..."

His words became inaudible and trailed into silence. His lips stopped moving and his face froze. Two tears appeared below his closed eyes and slowly trickled down his cheeks. His tears looked almost like two droplets of blood as their glisten reflected the red hue of the near-by instrument panel.

My mind exploded with old memories that, like shrapnel from a bursting shell, tore into my brain. Sadness gripped me and I began to feel a chill in the room. Then a nurse entered. She took me by the arm and led me out of the room. She told me that it was time to give him the injection.

I remember Karol's two reddish tears glittering in the bluish green light, and I remember Bogdan from decades ago. I also remember stories that Karol told me about a Ukrainian boy named Hryniu (a diminutive of Gregory) who lived in a village nearby and who Karol said he would bring to live with us if I didn't behave better. At that time, I was sure that he said it in jest in order to impress upon me the need to be a good boy, or else I would not be the only child whom he would love. I remember that whenever my mother heard Karol tell of

Hryniu she would become upset and irritable. Now I know that she suspected something, or that she actually knew the truth. I will never know, but I do know what I must do. I must learn what happened to Bogdan, the Hryniu of my childhood, and how Natalia saved our lives. What was her fate? I have a new lease on life and I will take it.

* * *

I am sitting at the window of an Air Ukraine jet streaking eastward toward Lwów. We left Frankfurt about half-an-hour ago. I assume that we are still flying over Germany. I see nothing but gently rolling clouds that bask in the rays of a mid-morning sun and hide the features of the landscape below as well as towns, buildings, cars, and lots and lots of people. They are Germans doing their daily chores, in pursuit of material things, and who feel a modicum of happiness. These are people with hopes, with problems, some perhaps in pain. Some are laughing and some are crying. They are the descendants of the World War II generation.

I am of the World War II generation, and so was my father Karol. He no longer pursues a daily routine; he no longer hopes for the comforting rays of a mid-morning sun to warm up his old bones. Karol is dead now. I think of my father back when he was alive, as well as of Natalia and Bogdan: the not-so-holy trinity is intimately related to me. We are all bound together because of human passion. I knew Natalia and Bogdan very well, but not in the context of my family. I must learn in Ukraine about their final lot. Was Bogdan actually killed in action against the Red Army? Did my brother and former friend die in battle, or was he executed, like most SS men, upon capture by Soviets? Did Bogdan really join the SS, that band of murderers? Why? These thoughts gnaw at me. I will have to see Oksan again. Perhaps he will lead me to someone who will know. I plan on contacting Szmuel immediately. He and his minions can ferret out any historical documents, especially now; it is a decade since the Soviet Union collapsed and Ukrainians are not mindful of bringing out some skeletons from Soviet closets. I am bringing several thousands of dollars with me—that should be enough to pay for Szmuel's services.

Thinking of Karol, Natalia, and Bogdan, the picture I see shifts abruptly from the placidly blown clouds to the drama of the little room in Lwów during the winter of 1943 and 1944, to my ten-by-seven-foot "cell" where I was hidden from the prying eyes of Jew-haters in the small apartment of Franciszka and Piotr Biely. Late one evening that winter, Franciszka entered my room. Agog with excitement, she told me that my father was in the kitchen and that he had escaped from a work detail on the way to Obóz Janowski.

"He is eating something in the kitchen" she told me. She immediately warned me that Karol was not the same man that I knew a year and a half earlier. She cautioned me to be prepared for a shock.

I was indeed shocked. The man who limped into my room was a scrawny wretch, a ragged, bloodied, filthy, bent-over version of his formal self. His right hand pressed a bloody handkerchief against his face while the left hand tried to embrace me. I instinctively drew back. Was it blood or the stench of his unwashed body and the rags he wore? Nevertheless, I noted two yellow triangles sewn to the front and back of his outer coat. He also had two other patches; one was his camp identity number, the other was the designation of the place where he was ordered to work.

Karol collapsed onto my cot, adjusted the bloody handkerchief against his nose, closed his eyes, and fell into a deep slumber. From then on, Karol and I hid in the little "cell" together. Pani Natalia began to visit us, bringing food and a smile to my father's slowly healing face.

I have no idea how Natalia saved our lives. Was it during those visits? I probed my memory in vain throughout my transatlantic flight and continue to do so as I cross the European continent. I must find out, but how? Because of my age, my memory may be failing me now. I will have to write down my experiences as a child up to the liberation in 1944 by the Soviet army. It is not too late to do so. I hope that re-visiting the apartment where we were hidden and other sites in town will focus my mind on the past and will allow me to remember events that I stored in my brain, never to retrieve.

My father's face never healed completely as a result of the savage beating at the hands of the SS guards. A week or so after he escaped from the camp to Franciszka, the blood ceased to flow out of his nose; open cuts were becoming scars while the brown areas on his arms and face began to turn bluish. At about that time, Karol came down with typhus. At first, Franciszka and I didn't know how to explain his high temperature. Karol was hallucinating, calling out to his comrades in the work detail: "It is not my fault. I had to run. I had to run. I wanted them to shoot me but not you. They would have starved me in the pit. Don't you understand? I had to try to get shot—it would be less painful."

Of course, I do not remember his exact words, but the gist was that Karol was being taken back to the camp and would have been tortured until the last for supposed disobedience. Instead, he broke out of the group on its way back to camp and ran. Guards shot at him and missed. He escaped and came to the only place where he could hide. In his delirium, his conscience had the sway. He knew, even as his mind was afflicted by high fever, that all the others in his work detail would be executed when they arrived back at the camp. That was the rule: if one escaped the rest of the group would die.

After my father joined me, Pani Natalia came to visit. She brought news which she had heard via Pani Cwik, who had a friend who listened to the forbidden British newscasts: the allies were finally winning and the German towns were getting their taste of war. That was good news, but there was plenty of bad as well: Germany was developing new, powerful weapons, and here in Galicia, Ukrainians were butchering Poles in rural villages.

Pani Natalia would sit on the cot next to my father and touch him occasionally. I sensed something special between them. She never stayed longer than a few minutes but those minutes were precious to me, incarcerated as I was.

Karol's fever and hallucination were followed by his inability to urinate. Natalia pronounced it to be typhoid fever. Karol had to be made to relieve his bladder, she told Franciszka, or he would die.

The two women looked at one another and an unspoken message passed between them because Franciszka quickly left the room. Natalia told me to turn my head away and to look at the wall, but, of course, I did peek. Natalia took off the blanket from Karol and pulled down his long johns. She took his penis into her hand and began to squeeze it rhythmically as if milking a cow. I had seen enough, and turned my head away. I don't know whether my father did or did not urinate. Perhaps this treatment saved his life or perhaps it was saved by a young doctor who came the next day with a large syringe and emptied Karol's bladder. Somehow, probably through Pani Cwik's connections, Natalia contacted a Polish or Ukrainian doctor who was willing to risk his life to help a Jew.

Well, we eventually survived thanks to Franciszka and Natalia, Pani Cwik, and the young doctor who knew about us but who never revealed that knowledge. And the opportunistic, thieving Bogdan, too: although he spotted us once at Franciszka's, he did not denounce us to the police. Could it be that Bogdan had scruples? What did my father mean when, with his last breath, he told me that Natalia saved us? I will try to find out. The first step must be another visit to Oksan and then to call on Szmuel.

*   *   *

In Lwów, Szmuel Orloff again became my guide, my protector, and my "brother." He called me "brother" from the very beginning of our acquaintance, even in our telephone conversations prior to my first visit. In this part of the world, one accepts nicknames or endearing names with grace. I presume that "brother," at least in Szmuel's mind, was justified by the fact that we were both Jews because I definitely was not related to him nor did we look alike. Szmuel was a big and heavy man. His hugs, which he bestowed freely unto me, were like those of a bear as he almost lifted me off the ground. His hugs were accompanied by bear kisses; here it is okay for men to hold hands and kiss on the cheeks.

He was more of a Ukrainian-Russian bear than a Jewish bear. With a Yiddish surname of Szmuel and a Russian aristocratic name of

Orloff he was a nomenclature anomaly, a hybrid. Ethnically, his parents considered themselves to be Polish by nationality and Jewish only by birth. They were ardent, militant Communists who had nothing to do with Yiddish culture; as a statement of their loyalty to atheism, they did not have Szmuel circumcised as is ordered by scripture. Instead, they indoctrinated him in the shining wisdom of Lenin and the heroic leadership of Stalin. Before World War II, both his mother and his father were agents of the Komintern. They fought for the victory of Communism throughout the world, beginning with Poland. Obviously they did not succeed, but they died trying, and left a young Szmuel to fend for himself within the anti-Semitic environment of what was the Soviet Union. I think this was about the time that Szmuel decided to change his name to the Russian-sounding "Orloff." The name is derived from "eagle," that noble and ferocious bird that was the symbol adopted by many European countries, including Russia. What about "Szmuel"? A typical Yiddish name. I suspect that he recently selected Szmuel for the benefit of Jewish visitors like me.

Like the eagle, Szmuel was both noble and ferocious. He harassed me for money in order to fund his noble cause: the old and sick Jews of Lwów. Szmuel was unabashed in continually asking and taking money from me. During my stay in Lwów, he "brothered" me and hugged me without respite. To be sure, he was a well-informed guide, and I was well protected. He and the twin bodyguards showed me what remained of my hell, the Ghetto. They took me to the sand pits and the cemeteries were my people were executed. With my escorts I saw the double walls with barbed wire at Obóz Janowski, where Karol suffered. We also went to Old Town, where two groups of Jews survived by hiding in the sewers. We visited other notable sites such the Kleparow Station, where hundreds of thousands of Jews from throughout Europe were transferred for shipment to the gas chambers of Belzec. At Kleparow, I was profoundly affected by the remaining brick, the concrete, and the rusty metal that once witnessed brutalities, and likely were once smeared with the blood, guts, brains, and excrement of Holocaust victims. In a different way, I was deeply moved when I met some of the live remnants of German and Soviet atrocities. Szmuel introduced me to the few remaining old and sick human wretches whom he was helping. It happened when Szmuel "brothered" me to sponsor a catered feast for those unfortunates. How they ate and drank the best canapés and the finest liquor! It made me feel like Moses providing manna for the hungry Israelites in the desert. After that event, I didn't mind Szmuel's "brothering." I even alleviated the suspicion that a lot of my money, if not all, would remain in Szmuel's large palms.

Szmuel did, however, have other attributes that continued to repel me. He would laugh loudly and frequently, often without an apparent reason. I guess the causes for his laughter were often comical reminiscences. He seldom shared these, and thus listeners could not participate in the merriment. He was extremely secretive about everything, including his political adherence, if he had any. If one listened to his references to Stalin, one would surmise that the dictator of the Soviet Union was his idol and that Szmuel was an unreconstructed member of the Communist Party. I could not have imagined a man like Szmuel, who knew well the crimes committed by Stalin, as a commie. He was especially secretive when I asked him where and from whom he was obtaining the food and medicine for "his poor Jews," or when I inquired about the activities of Moris and Boris when they are not with us. For that matter, I know little about his entourage or about his own personal life except that he is married to the daughter of a Soviet general who has an Asian ancestry.

Even though Szmuel's character remains unattractive to me, I use him. He accomplishes things. This was especially evident when we visited the town archives. His two men waited in the parked van next to the gate while Szmuel and I climbed to the office of the director of the archives. We were very well received. I sensed that Szmuel was highly regarded here, or else highly feared. Of course, the twenty dollar bill that the director accepted as a donation toward the archives' upkeep also had some influence. The town archives were housed in an ancient stone building which once served as a church or a monastery. All the hallways, offices, and especially the reading room, were very large and dark. I saw a few young people at the reading tables where they scanned huge tomes. They spoke in German. I was told that they were doing historical research. They looked cold, and probably were, because I was beginning to feel the chill and damp among those stone

138

walls which still retained their frigidity from the winter cold. In contrast, the well-bundled personnel who helped me to obtain documents about my family were warm toward Szmuel and me. They knew Szmuel very well. I surmised that Szmuel was a frequent visitor to the archives on behalf of other visitors to Lwów. I also surmised that Szmuel was a purveyor of documents and information. When I asked him about it, I got only one of his shattering laughs in return. Perhaps he was reminiscing about his former customers and about the money he got for his "poor Jews." By this time, I knew about his secretive nature and did not expect to be informed. Through Szmuel, I got a lot of information about my grandparents. In return, the archives obtained money to pay for utilities. I rewarded Szmuel monetarily, and he did not, in any way, have to justify the high cost of his service. In a sense, we were all winners. Szmuel may not love Stalin anymore, but he certainly is a well-trained product of Stalin's philosophy: screw them but make them feel that they like it. I liked the arrangement.

As I expected, the archives had nothing on Bogdan and Pani Natalia. Only real estate, financial transactions, and burial information were stored at the archives. However, Szmuel assured me that he and his contacts will try their utmost. Perhaps the Soviet files left from World War II days could be looked at, if…

Marek left this section incomplete; I do not know why. He and Karol finally saw the Soviet tanks roll down Lyczakowska Street and they were free.

Marek's mother miraculously survived as well. During the course of the war, she had had three different hiding places through three different benefactors. Since she was on the periphery of Marek's life at that time, he does not mention her ordeals in his written recollections. However, when we talked about those terrible times, Marek always referred to his mother as "the poor woman" or "that unfortunate, abused woman." There was affection in his words, to be sure, but I sensed pity more than anything else. Marek never elaborated and I did not pry.

The entire Mann family in Lwów was murdered, except for Marek and his parents. The Manns trailed behind the Soviet army as the war continued through today's Ukraine, Poland, and Czechoslovakia into the American occupational zone in Bavaria. On the way, Marek lost some of his fingers when a detonator from an armor-piercing projectile exploded. He contested that he was the only one to be blamed for it. The Mann family crossed the Atlantic Ocean in an American troopship during the bitter winter of 1946-47.

Chapter IX

———◆———

Oh Lwów, Lviv, Lemberg!

The bright sun blinded me as I stepped off the train in Lwów. Waves of people on the platform rocked as wildly as the train had done on its slow path from Poland. Everyone seemed to have an immediate destination except for me.

I stood by my bags, wishing I hadn't packed so many books and so much empty notepaper to try to fill during my four weeks in the city's archives. I turned my head from side to side—not too quickly, I hoped, trying to look composed. I was searching for a man, a relative of one of my professors, who was supposed to meet me and take me to an apartment. It wasn't long before I saw a gray-haired man dressed in denim. He eyed me cautiously as he leaned against the railing, smoking. He dropped his cigarette and approached me.

"Miss Martell?" he asked.

"Yes, yes," I said, and looked apologetically down at the bags. He laughed, picking them up against my protests and gestures to help.

"I am Sasha Korneichuk, Professor's Zbizienski's cousin. Welcome to Lwów, and to Ivan Franko University. You see, we are a Polish-Ukrainian mixture—we may even have few drops of Mongol blood. How do you say in America? Heinz 57 Variety, no?" Pan Sasha affably chattered in heavily accented but understandable English as he led the way out of the metal-glass shell of the station.

A tiny car carried us to the concrete apartment block. We walked up three circular flights of stairs, through a locked gate and a thick, triple-locked door into a small kitchen. A window framed a view across the electric streetcar lines and directly into another window on the other side of the street. Out of breath, the man showed me how to light the gas stove and furnaces, apologized for the dust in the bedroom, which was still being renovated, and then proudly opened the door to a newly refurbished bathroom.

"I know a little Ukrainian," I told Pan Sasha. "You may talk in Ukrainian. It will help me to learn the language."

"We have water," he said, "almost always. We just connected to pipes that the city doesn't shut down during the summer. Now and then, the neighbors might come with buckets."

I smiled. "Good, good," I said. The Ukrainian words sounded awkward to me as my mouth and voice shaped them, and I repeated them as if I were learning them for the first time.

"Unfortunately, you will have to evacuate the rooms in a month because the apartment was sold and the new owners will want to possess it," he informed me and looked at me apologetically.

"But I know a very *kulturalny* couple who need a little money and will be thankful to serve you food and give you a roof." Pan Sasha reassured me and added, "Vladya Novikov is a retired editor and he collects flowers. His wife bakes sweet desserts to sell for income."

The bed and breakfast arrangement will not be bad, I thought to myself, and besides, I will have local people around me which will help to immerse me into a native setting. For the moment, I feared being somewhat lonely.

"You remember, I am sure, tomorrow is a holiday and the archives will be shut." He added some dos and don'ts: "Walking alone, especially at night will be hazardous. Do not show that you have much money—only small grivne; never that you have dollars. We have a lot of bandits here. Make little conversation on the street, otherwise your accent will tell on you."

It was sunset when Pan Sasha left, and I walked downstairs after him so that I could buy a loaf of bread, a piece of cheese, and a bottle of water from a kiosk I had seen on the corner. Suddenly I felt exhausted. The week before I left Boston had been hectic. Not knowing what to expect in Lwów, I had packed and re-packed until I couldn't wait to get on the plane, just to be done with it. Now all I wanted to do was to put away my bags, climb into bed, and feel light.

The next morning I sat with my tea at the small kitchen table and looked across the narrow street. I saw a man, his shiny face and puffy eyes speaking of too much vodka the night before. His jaw was clenched and his lips were curled around a cigarette. As he leaned through the open window, his belly stretched through his sweaty, sleeveless undershirt and settled onto the sill. He quietly remained there for a half-hour. When a cigarette burned too close to his fingers, he would let it slip to the street below.

His wife appeared and stayed only for a moment. In her flower-print dress and stained apron pulled tight over her large bosom, she leaned heavily on the sill, watching the passersby through tiny eyes nearly hidden by the rough skin of her fleshy face. She smiled, or at least a fleeting moment of calm passed over her face, before she turned back to her chores.

An hour later, I still sat, distractedly leafing through archival guides. I looked periodically across the street, and was startled upon seeing a new face come to the window. She was a young woman, maybe twenty years old. A kitten was folded into each of her elbows, but one wriggled out to sit on the sill. The woman stroked the other one, not missing a beat as she stared absent-mindedly down onto the street, until that kitten, too, went to the sill. She cupped her chin in her hands, pouting, and then ran her fingers through her orange-red, permed hair. She glanced upward and across the street, and saw me. The young woman turned, leaned her whole body sideways against the window frame, and ignored me for a few long breaths. I, too, turned away, but not so far that I couldn't watch her out of the corner of my eye. The woman was wearing a smock over a small white T-shirt and navy nylon sweatpants. She and I stood frozen for those few seconds until the woman jerked the curtain shut. In the evening, I shut my own curtains for the first time.

The screech of the streetcar woke me up several times during the night. I felt tired and nervous as I left the apartment in the late morning. I had memorized the directions to the market on the central square. It was not far away, but I wanted to take a few detours off the main streets. I felt a rush of excitement as I walked down one alley after another. Finally, I thought to myself, I am walking these streets, getting to know the city that I have chosen to study.

An hour passed when my hunger reminded me that I wanted to go to the market, and I realized that I was lost. I stopped for a moment, leaned against the rough concrete wall of a small copy shop, and tried to orient myself using a torn-off section of my map. A café would be good, I thought. At least I could sit down and maybe eat something and pull out the rest of my map—maybe even write down some of my impressions thus far. I spotted a café sign just down the street.

I ordered tea and a roll at the counter and fumbled nervously with the coins when I paid. As I walked to a corner table, I thought I saw a familiar face off to the side. I became startled when I recognized the person as the young woman from across the street. She was deep in conversation with a solid, slightly graying man in a wrinkled, off-white linen suit. His brown leather briefcase stood on the floor between their feet. Its brass clasp caught the sunlight and flashed. The pointed toe of the woman's shoe knocked against it occasionally when she leaned forward. She clicked her painted fingernails nervously against her coffee cup as she spoke. Her lipstick was bright red and made her lips look wet. The man looked uncomfortable.

I slid into the chair at the corner table. My back faced the woman, who had not noticed me as I walked passed her. Another table was occupied by a young man who drank his coffee hurriedly. I pulled out a notepad and began to write: *Day 3. Out in the city for the first time. Must go to the archives day after tomorrow, but need to find the market, need to know where I am.*

I heard the voice of the woman above the scraping sound of chair legs on the floor: "This afternoon. Two o'clock at the women's clinic on Saint Yuri's Street." A few moments later, I suddenly got up to catch the woman's attention as she walked past me.

"Excuse me, please," I said, my voice shaking just a little. "Can you tell me where the main market square is?"

The woman stopped and turned. Her large hazel eyes were moist. She looked scared for a moment until she lowered her eyelids slightly and appeared seductive instead. The man at the table was watching her closely.

"You'll need to turn left outside the café and walk to the main boulevard," the woman said slowly. "Then turn left again and follow the boulevard to the second square. You'll see the market."

She eyed me a little longer and walked out. Her companion left within the minute and turned the opposite direction outside the door.

I shoved my notepad into my bag and swallowed the last drops of my tea. Walking ten minutes on the main boulevard took me to the market. Dark green canopies hung on thin poles and cast an uneven shadow over long rows of narrow metal tables. Farmers, mostly women from the outlying districts of the city, were selling their goods. Some stood next to high piles of apples or plums; others held out a single bunch of carrots or onions. A few men, traders from the south, sat on crates of bananas and watermelons, and smoked. Off to one side, women sold armfuls of roses and sunflowers, or stood by table displays of lace bras and used books. In back, behind the produce, flies buzzed around chicken legs and sausages.

I bought a sunflower and filled my bag with plums, a few bananas, a cucumber, some small carrots, and an onion. The sunflower vendor pointed me toward the street where I lived, and I walked home. My arms hurt by the time I recognized my apartment building, but I bought two more bottles of water, a bag of pasta, and a bottle of red wine at the corner kiosk before climbing the stairs.

The late afternoon light was filtering through the curtains of the kitchen window, and I opened them again. I put the sunflower in a glass on the kitchen table and leaned the stem against the wall to hold the weight of the flower's large black and yellow head. On my notepad, I wrote: *Bought a sunflower. Ready to work.*

A knock at the door stopped me. I turned the key in the wrong direction and was flustered by the time I opened the door. The visitor was already speaking, running her hands nervously up and down her apron as she talked. At her feet were two empty buckets.

"I live across the street. We need to use your water. My daughter is very sick. We know that you have water here. Please ...."

"Of course, of course," I said, gesturing the woman inside. As the woman filled the two buckets, I found two more in the kitchen and brought them into the bathroom. I filled them and started to follow the woman out of the apartment.

"No," the woman said as she shook her head emphatically. "It's not necessary. I will come back." She left quickly.

The daughter, the young woman of my acquaintance, returned to the window two weeks later. She seemed paler and thinner to me. One of the kittens, noticeably bigger now, jumped onto the sill and the woman scratched it behind its ear. The woman and I looked at each other, and neither of us looked away. I was intrigued by her, and I felt lonely. So the next day, I sat by the window and waited for her to leave the apartment, then I ran down the stairs. I slowed down just in time to appear nonchalant as I walked out of the building.

"Dobrii den," I said in my hesitant Ukrainian, greeting her with a polite "good day."

She answered with a smile, and in her melodious Ukrainian asked me where I was going. Having noticed her shopping bag, I told her I was headed to the market and asked if I could join her on her way downtown. She smiled again. She appeared tired but the anxiety of our previous meeting was replaced by warmth. Perhaps it was because the man was gone, or perhaps she was grateful for the water. Or perhaps, like me, she was intrigued.

146

We walked slowly and talked. Irka—as she introduced herself—spoke clearly, aware that her Slavic cadence was still a challenge for me. She gesticulated as she walked, and her expressive eyes and mouth helped me follow her meaning. Soon we had covered the basics: where I was from, and whether I was married. Most women that I had met here, and even some men, asked me this right away, and when I said "No, I am not married," they remarked on the difference between American and Ukrainian women: "You Americans wait so long! But don't wait too long to have a child!" Irka, however, did not add the comment about the child.

Often and indiscriminately she would break up her Ukrainian with "you know," her favorite English phrase. "*You know*, you must have a boyfriend, Maria." Or, "*You know*, tell me about where your parents live."

I knew that she already had an idea of what my family home would be like. It was a run-of-the-mill, middle-class, suburban tract house, but when such houses sprung up in Irka's Lwów, they usually belonged to the flamboyant new class of people with shadily earned money to blow. The gulf between these people and Irka was enormous. But I described our home to her, and told her about Jon. I noted that my voice carried little emotion when I spoke of him.

"But you know, when I was in high school, I met a man from Lwów," I suddenly said. I told her about meeting Marek in Washington on the Mall. As we approached the market she looked at me quizzically and said, "You like this Marek, don't you?" I smiled and nodded.

"Maria, we are real close to the *rynok*, the plaza that surrounds our *ratusz*, the city hall. *You know*, you must see the lions. The shopping can wait a few minutes."

There was no point in telling Irka that I already saw the *rynok*. With unsuspected exuberance she took me by the arm and we turned toward the looming tower of the city hall. We detoured a bit and found ourselves on the plaza in front of the two stone lions, symbols of Lwów, sitting on their haunches, guarding the portal to Lwów's municipal building.

"Touch them, Maria, for luck. Touch their paws. Come on, Maria. You will be lucky!"

"Hello, lions," I simply said. My innate timidity prevented me from doing what all the tourists are supposed to do. Perhaps, if I had touched the lions, my luck would have been different.

Irka became my friend during those first few months and I was so not lonely. She attached herself to me throughout my stay in Lwów, and I reciprocated to the extent that my time permitted. Even after I moved away and stayed with the *kulturalny* Novikovs, I still visited with Irka and tried to help her as much as I could by giving her small donations of money and occasional bits of advice.

∗   ∗   ∗

Days were long for me and consequently my nights were short. Like a child in a wonderful toy store, I read, abstracted, took notes, and listened, always wanting more—more documents, more written contemporary accounts, more interviews with those who lived in Lwów's twentieth century, and more visits to the historical sites.

On my first day in the archive I came across the 1894 yearbook of the Kaiserlich-Königlich Second High School, the first document from imperial Austrian times that I had ever touched. It was in remarkably good shape, a little yellowed and frayed at the edges, but perfectly legible. I smiled as I leafed through it. Everything was written in Polish, German, and Ukrainian, and I wondered how easily the students switched from one language to the next, or how easily students of different nationalities mixed in the school's hallways. Religious instruction did seem predominantly Roman Catholic. Was that evidence of the strength of Polish culture, as my history books had taught me?

Since my research focus was on World War II, I had to restrain myself from spending too much time on earlier documents, especially nineteenth century ones. Pan Sasha, the kindly professor who had met me at the train station, specialized in the interwar

148

period of the 1920s and 1930s, when Lwów belonged to Poland and relations between Poles, Jews, and Ukrainians set the stage for violence as well as humanitarianism under the Soviet and Nazi occupations. He came to the archive a few days after our first meeting and gave me a newspaper article that he thought would make a great anecdote in my dissertation. It was from the Jewish newspaper *Chwila*:

"At 10:30 p.m. on October 1, 1937, a man named Izrael Izak Reich was walking across Halicki Square with his wife Alicja and her friend. Two men suddenly closed in on either side of Reich. 'Heil Hitler!' one of the men called to Reich, hitting him in the back of the head. A sentry detained the assailant, who turned out to be a drunken Polish man. The man explained his action by saying, 'I met a man with the appearance of a Jew, walking in the company of two women. Because they did not want to get out of my way, I hit him.'"

I looked up at Pan Sasha and he told me the outcome of the incident.

"The Polish man had a choice of paying a fine or spending six days in jail. Not a huge punishment, eh?" He opened another file and pulled out a second article.

"So here's an article describing a bigger event: the funeral of two Jewish Polytechnic students who were murdered by Endeks, young, right-wing Polish students. Look at the picture. See the throngs of Jews at the funeral! Despite the turnout, it was a quiet, but powerful, protest."

Pan Sasha explained that there was indeed a large, vibrant, Jewish community which had prospered under Marshall Josef Pilsudski's regime, until his death in 1935. The Ukrainian population in the city had been growing and agitating for more rights under the increasingly nationalistic Polish government. Polish culture blossomed; *Lwówska Gazeta* overflowed with announcements for concerts, museums, and literature readings. Those who follow the European soccer scene today would be amazed at the intense rivalry that existed between the Polish (Czarni), Ukrainian (Ukraina), and Jewish (Hasmonea) sport clubs. They often brawled but they played nevertheless. I remember that Marek told me a long time ago on the Mall in Washington that on Sunday afternoons, his father Karol often took him to the soccer matches. There were tense moments, to be sure, but not the kind of violence currently witnessed, as when English clubs play in continental Europe.

So what happened? I don't expect through my meager research effort to provide the answers but perhaps to elucidate the demise of Lwów, Lviv, Lemberg as a town for diverse peoples. Were there any traits among the residents that facilitated the brutal destruction of both the Jewish and Polish communities, as well as the decimation of Armenians? Yes, of course, there were the Germans and their Nazi doctrine; there were the Soviets and their bestial Communistic imperialism. But to what extent did the local population contribute to this ethnic cleansing?

With a jolt, I realized that Pan Sasha was looking at me intently. "Maria, I'm having some friends from the university over for dinner tonight. Would you join us? Perhaps we can get to know each other better."

I felt flustered. I wanted to meet my Polish and Ukrainian colleagues, but I was uncomfortable with Pan Sasha's tone as he let the last phrase roll smoothly off his tongue. Even though Jon and I had agreed to see other people, an agreement made hastily during my frantic packing for Lwów, I felt cautious and self-protective. Besides, all I wanted was to work.

"Thank you, Pan Sasha, but I'm still getting used to the time change and I need to get to bed early tonight," I said. "Perhaps another night," I added weakly.

The next day at the archive I moved on to records of the German occupation. The most startling to me was the thick log kept by caretakers of the Jewish cemetery. Those poor wretches buried corpses, tried to identify them and occasionally jotted down the cause of death. They were hardly able to keep up with the flow. Many corpses turned up at the cemetery as a result of beatings. The log terminated abruptly, probably because the caretakers met the fate of many of the cadavers. But on the afternoon that I came to the log's end, I was ready to stop reading anyway. It had become too much to absorb, yet there were still so many more documents, there was still so much to learn. I looked forward to the coming weeks. But at that moment, I needed fresh air. Spring had turned to summer and I needed to remind myself that life around me continued to move forward.

I headed toward the Novikovs' home. On the way, I found myself thinking about Marek. Why? That was so long ago. It must be because of the Jewish cemetery documents, I told myself. But I could not deny that a warm feeling rose within me.

*　　*　　*

I had a sisterly affection for Irka, with me as the older, more experienced sibling. Yet in one way, Irka had far more experience. By the time she reached her eighteenth birthday, she had one abortion and several relationships behind her.

"You know, Maria, I didn't love those guys. You have to have a man so that the others will leave you alone, you hope. One guy scared me real bad. He threatened me with beatings—or worse—until I gave in."

Irka paused and looked down toward the decanter with cognac in her hand. I did not interrupt her thoughts but looked at her thin face surrounded by wisps of dyed-red hair. She had regular, classical features.

Sensing my gaze, she looked at me.

"Maria, you know, you are not listening and you are not drinking your tea. Are you thinking of your men? Are you happy, Maria? I am not."

"You know, Irka," I paused, realizing that I had fallen into her speech pattern. "You know, Irka, right now I am satisfied and, sitting here with you, I feel rather pleasant. But I am not fulfilled. I am still hoping...." But I changed the subject. "Do you fear even now? What do you fear? That man who was in the café?

"Oy, Maria. I am scared of him. He is very bad. He kills people. Oy, Maria! They are a gang and they are killing those who spied for the Soviets. They are big nationalists. They call themselves 'Bandera men' or 'Banderovtsy.' Sometimes 'Avengers.'" Irka filled her glass from the decanter and sipped thirstily.

"He tortures his victims before he kills them. He is a very violent man but now he has another woman and he doesn't come to me. At first I was attracted to him and his power, and of course, I was trapped. Now, yes, I still fear him. Oy..."

Irka was obviously distressed. She paused and looked into the nearly empty decanter. Then she lifted it up, tipping it toward her lips and letting the last few drops trickle onto her tongue.

"I feel bad, Maria. I am so sorry to spoil our party."

I took Irka's hand into mine and squeezed her small bony fingers. She trembled.

"Those Ukrainians who worked for NKVD during the insurrection after World War II, you know about them? The Avengers brutally murder them, even though the insurrection happened more than fifty years ago. Just two weeks ago, they found two mutilated corpses of old men. No one has been arrested. The police do not interfere; they look the other way."

"Maybe your man wasn't part of that," I interjected hopefully.

"He was, he was. He got drunk and stopped me on the street. He bragged that they have gotten most of the 'traitors' by now. He told me that there is still one, the worst, and that they will find him now that they can obtain NKVD files, documents from the Soviet times."

"Can I order another chut-chut, Maria? My man said that they know that the informer lived on Lyczakowska Street during the war. Now they will know more. The Avengers will find him and hang him by his *yayka*. Do you understand, Maria?"

Yes, I understood that *yayka* meant "balls." I understood much more: the brutality of the Nazi and Soviet eras has no end. It keeps marching on.

The African violets that abounded in the Novikovs' living room (It had been converted into my bedroom.) instilled in me a feeling of well-being when I awoke one bright morning. This feeling was reinforced by a vast breakfast that started with a plate of sardines, a fried egg, dark bread, and a piquant salad of chopped spinach, radishes, cucumbers, and onion. Just as I was finishing, Sara emerged from the kitchen with fried patties of farmer's cheese that she proudly served with her homemade sour cream and sour cherry compote. Five minutes later, she was back with a plate of last night's cake. I longed for coffee. The brew served by Sara was only coffee in color, so I learned to drink tea—very hot, green tea—in the morning, at cafés during my infrequent lunches, and again with the Novikovs after dinner. I even took a thermos of hot tea with me to the archives. The beginning of this day was not different from other days: I loaded up my backpack with my thermos, dictionaries, notes, and laptop. Vladya led me out and I was on my way.

Once I reached the street, that morning was not like the other mornings. For starters, I saw a partly deflated, worn ball in the gutter. In my exuberance, I took it out, laid it on the sidewalk, and kicked it. The ball swerved and took off from the ground, as did my imagination. I saw a well-formed sphere, decorated with many multi-colored, brilliant dots. The sphere grew larger and larger until it exceeded my field of vision and then it disappeared. Why did the memory of the Washington Mall return? Because of the ball I sent flying?

It was also an unusual day because it was to be my first visit to the city archives. My search thus far had focused on documents in state archives. It was recommended to me that I consult the city depository for more materials.

The morning was perfect. I felt excited about the prospect of finding something important. Indeed, I was not amiss in my intuition. After so many years, I found none other than Marek standing next to me in the reading room of the archives. Our paths had crossed again.

In the dark recesses of the expansive reading room, there were only a few people grouped together, probably foreign students. They bent their heads down over long, wooden tables as they read from bulky manuscripts. Silence. The only sounds were of occasional whispers when two heads turned to each other. Yes, they were foreign students. I easily discerned German words. The hall was very poorly lit and it was cold. The summer warmth did not penetrate the massive stone walls and little light penetrated the narrow windows. Centuries ago, this building was either a cloister or part of a church. In spite of the uncomfortable conditions, I was upbeat. In front of me were volumes of death registrations that dated from pre-World War II to the present. These tomes recorded the deaths of non-Jewish residents of Lwów. I knew by now that Uncle Willi had lived here. Could he have died here? Probably not. His name did not appear on the register.

Just then, a voice behind me said, "Excuse me. Your silhouette looks familiar. I thought that I recognized your hair. Are you—?"

I turned my head toward the speaker and, probably at the mention of my hair, I did as was my habit. With a jerk of my head, I flung my hair from my face.

"You are Maria."

"Yes," I responded, not recognizing the man immediately because of the darkness, but sensing something familiar in his bearing and in his face.

"I am Marek Mann, the artist. We met in Washington. What are doing here? You are Maria, right?" A second yes came out of me while memories flooded my mind.

"Quiet, be quiet, tiho, tiho," a functionary admonished us.

"Maria, I will be waiting, sitting in the café outside, to the right of the entrance. Finish what you are doing. It will be good to talk to you."

For the third time, all I could say was yes.

We sat across from each other, separated by a bright-red plastic table that advertised Chernihivske beer. With the noon sun slowly pushing away the shade, we began to talk.

"Why are you here?" I asked, suddenly feeling both awkward and excited. "Where are you staying?" I rushed to ask.

Marek brushed aside my questions. "I'm leaving tomorrow. Can you meet me tonight?"

"No, no, I have friends..." I started to say.

"Tomorrow? I'll stay. I can get a train the next day."

"Are you sure?"

"Yes."

"Okay," I found myself saying.

"At the Kupol, eight o'clock," Marek said. After a long, penetrating look, he got up.

The next day we met at the Kupol. The day after that, we took a tour of the town together, and had supper again at the Kupol. It was on that night that Marek gave me his chronicles and memoirs. Once I knew Marek's secret about his illegitimate, half-brother and learned of his father Karol's death, all barriers between us seemed to dissolve. In the mysteries of Bogdan and Willi, we each had a family story to complete. With each other, we began to feel whole.

Marek never did take the train out of Lwów.

*   *   *

Marek became my frequent companion, but I did visit the archives every day and my long hours of work paid off. Seemingly unpretentious bundles of one-sheet forms were handed to me one day by an archive functionary whom I befriended. He would feed me with documents that were stashed away in the basement and seldom brought out. He was a double amputee, a Red Army veteran who lost both hands during World War II. Thus, it would be more precise to say that he opened what remained of his arms and dropped a big, dusty bag on my desk.

Each of the several hundred forms was filled out by several persons and contained their signatures along with a brief statement by some ranking official. The handwritings were of different quality and some were illegible. The Russian and Ukrainian languages dominated, but Polish was also in evidence. I became engrossed in discerning the purpose and substance of the forms. Each group of signatories was organized to be an ad hoc committee, especially assembled to nationalize private houses in a specific region of town. Each committee was seemingly headed by a ranking commissar. All of the forms were dated in the fall of 1939, the exact period when the Soviets came to Lwów.

When I met Marek for our—by now, customary—supper, I gave him a kiss on the cheek and then showed him a sample of my acquisition.

"Do you know Vanya, the small pleasant attendant at the city archives who lost his arms?" I asked Marek.

"Yes, I can't bear to look at his naked stump when he wears a short-sleeved shirt. At least he wears a prosthesis on the other arm."

"I know exactly what you mean. My heart was breaking, Marek, when I saw how his stumps held onto the heavy bag by using sheer pressure against his chest."

"On my first visit to Lwów, I gave him a twenty-dollar bill, which was a lot a few years ago. Would you believe, Maria, he actually trudged a large box of copied court records for me all the way to the Grand Hotel where I was staying? All that paper! Those were records of my parents' problems. The documents concerned the house ownership and the fines that were imposed on my parents. My mother and father had financial problems. You know…."

Marek stopped and looked me in the eyes. I took his hand. He squeezed mine gently.

"Let me see this form, Maria," He reached across the table and took the form from me. He laid it next to him under the table lamp.

"Of course, you know that I love you, Maria." He whispered.

As we held our right hands tightly, we lifted our wines glasses with our left hands.

"To us." Another toast. "To us," we repeated together.

*   *   *

Together we deciphered the form. As I already knew, the half-page of cheap paper reported the nationalization of a privately-owned apartment house. The form stated the address and size of the apartment house: number of stories, number of total apartments, number of total rooms in each unit. The comment section was reserved for few words about the landlord. This particular form simply stated that the former owner was a capitalist, a proprietor of a grocery store.

"You don't know Maria, but when I was a nine-year-old boy, such a proletarian delegation barged into our apartment to dispossess us. I can still picture them. They were a pretty shabby crew, come to think of it."

"I can tell by the writing on this report that their education was not very high. Actually, I noticed on other forms that some people signed with a cross," I remarked, warming up to the subject.

"Seven or eight men. Two or three were in uniforms with rifles, obviously soldiers." Marek was excited by his memories and I leaned forward, interested to hear more. "I am sure that you saw pictures of Red Army soldiers wearing those conical caps. One of the jokes instigated by Poles was that the shape of the cap was designed so that lice could gather at the point of the cone for Communist Party meetings." Marek stopped, expecting a laugh but, frankly, I did not understand the Eastern European sense of humor at that time.

"I am sorry, my dear," I realized that I had used a term of endearment for the first time to address Marek. "I don't get the joke. But please, I am all ears. Go on."

"I remember best their leader, the commissar. He was clad in dark brown leather—leather jacket, leather cap like Lenin wore during the revolutionary era, leather riding boots, and leather britches. A leather belt girded his jacket. Some sort of map case hung from one side of it and a holstered sidearm on the other. A red star was pinned to his cap. Even civilians had a red star attached somewhere to their clothes."

Marek paused and refilled our glasses with the red ambrosia. We clinked our glasses but the romantic mood had dissipated. I assumed my usual demeanor of the scholarly historian bent on collecting information, while Marek crawled down into his memory cellar. Our hands loosen their hold. I began to fidget in my bag trying to locate a pencil and the small notebook I always carried. Marek held the form in front of him, but his eyes looked beyond me toward the window.

"The commissar read to Karol a formal statement thereby transferring our apartment house to the ownership of the People of the Socialistic Ukrainian Republic. Those 'People' of the proletariat in our apartment, in the meantime, took his words literally and began to rummage through every room. They took nothing that I could tell, but they behaved like the apartment was theirs: touching, opening and examining everything."

"Marek, wait. You said that most of them were civilians, right?"

"Yeah, they were local people."

"What do you mean, 'local'?"

"My father told us that he recognized two of the men. They were janitors from down the street. They were dressed in their Sunday best for this occasion but were not comfortable in their finery. They were not obnoxious; they just beamed with pride. They were imbued with the feeling of superiority over us, their former landlords. This was truly their day. The commissar barked orders. The committee hotly discussed something amongst themselves and then they signed just such a form." Marek shook the form in his hand for emphasis.

"There was more discussion followed by more directions from the commissar. The two soldiers got their orders, took red tape out their packets, and sealed off two of our rooms: Karol's study and my parents' bedroom. The commissar told Karol that these rooms and their contents now belonged to the People and that we were to respect the tapes—or else. We were not to enter those rooms without a properly authorized representative of the People."

The waiter entered our room.

"What then?" I tried to coax Marek.

The waiter began serving us *borszcz*, a soup that cannot be uniquely described. Every cook has his or her own recipe, but bone stock or bits of meat are common, plus any vegetables, which may, or may not, include beets.

"Enough about then. I want to talk about now."

And so we did. We held hands and we gently kissed on the lips.

*   *   *

The next day, Marek came early to the Novikovs' and we ate breakfast together. After a quick kiss on the cheek and a sumptuous meal in the kitchen, I was ready. With a pen and notebook in hand, I was poised to learn.

"That was pretty bad to have those rooms sealed. Were you able to retrieve any of your possessions?" I started the inquisition immediately.

"Maria, I don't know whether I love you more for your charm or for your lack of it when you are hot on a historical trail."

I got up and walked to his chair. I bent down and held his head in my palms. I wetted my lips with my tongue and then pressed them against his lips. Marek's lips were also moist. Today I would describe them as invitingly succulent. The Novikovs were unaccustomed to passionate displays of affection and they considered Americans to be quite sexually permissive. He and his wife allowed Marek and me a great deal of latitude in our behavior with one another during our stay in Lwów, considering their old-fashioned beliefs. Seeing us kiss, Vladya Novikov merely coughed, turned his head away, and we let go. Our minds back-tracked into the history channel.

"As far as I remember, we did not suffer badly. The two sealed rooms were assigned to Soviet military personnel who were pretty decent people. They let us remove some personal objects from the rooms. My grandparents and the Bielys were treated far worse. My grandparents were told by their dispossessors to take whatever they could carry on their backs and to leave everything else behind. That is how they were forced to live in the dank basement of their sheet metal shop. The Bielys fared even worse. They were kicked out, not only from their apartment, but they were denied residence in Lwów altogether. They had to live in a nearby village with relatives, like chattels."

"So these were the punishments meted to the bourgeois," I chimed in.

"Like hell 'bourgeois'! These were people who labored all their lives to save for their old age. Their only income was the rent. Sure, they were fairly well-off in comparison to ordinary laborers, but they had to work hard for what they had," Marek continued angrily.

"Why the different punishments?" I couldn't resist asking. "Do you know?"

"No. I would guess that it depended on the mood of each People's Committee and on the viciousness of their leader. Read the comments and dispositions on those forms. Those might shed some light on the subject."

I couldn't wait to get up from the table to tackle those forms. I dragged Marek out of the kitchen to the only table in the apartment not occupied by flowers.

"Vladya, could you help us? We need you to decipher some of the Cyrillic writings. Please, Vladya."

I cleared the table of disks, cassettes, and other electronic paraphernalia. Then we were able to spread out the forms. The three of us perused the forms sequentially. Whenever we came across one of the many Jewish names, we scrutinized it carefully. The shoddy quality of the forms—the poor paper, the smudged ink, the misspellings—also told us about the Soviet bureaucracy that imposed this nationalization regime.

Yet in the middle of the batch of forms, one writing distinguished itself by its neatness and legibility. The handwriting was almost calligraphy. The prominent signature was that of Wilhelm Menke, Captain, NKVD.

There were three other forms unmistakably signed by Uncle Willi. The fates imposed on the three dispossessed landlords were some of the harshest.

*   *   *

Now that I was certain of Uncle Willi's stay in Lwów from 1939 to 1941 when the Germans attacked the Soviet Union, my thoughts shifted toward the unfaithful wife, Halya Laski, Willi's paramour. I pulled out Tomek Laski's letter to Grandma Menke from my suitcase. Tomek specifically stated that Wilhelm Menke, an NKVD officer, had saved him from long years in Siberia, perhaps even from execution. Tomek gave no details but wrote that he himself resided in New York City, and god willing, he would like to meet my grandmother and tell her more. He alluded to a growing friendship with Willi and to an exchange of favors. Tomek did not say what those favors were. Did he turn a blind eye to the flirtation between Willi and Halya?

Tomek did describe his shock upon finding Halya's note on that "bloody memorable day" when the Red Army fled. Halya said that she was leaving Tomek to be with Willi. After all those years, he claimed not to hate Willi or Halya. Tomek wrote that he still loved his wife and would like to meet her and or help her if he knew where she was. Tomek was hopeful that, through Willi, he might learn of Halya's fate. "Mrs. Menke, could you please direct me to the whereabouts of Wilhelm Menke?"

Grandma Menke probably did not respond, but tucked the letter into the "Willi File."

Another day in the archives and another dinner with Marek. I was slowly falling for him. Our kisses became longer and more sensual.

"Marek, how can I learn about Halya? There must be traces of her in Lwów. Marek, give me the benefit of your thoughts." I noticed that I used Marek's name with increasing frequency.

"Have you met Szmuel Orloff? No, how could you. You are only a poor graduate student. Szmuel would take no note of you. But you must meet him. He is a magician and he will resurrect Halya for you. Tomorrow, I will make a date with Szmuel and introduce you. Hey, where is that waiter with the Georgian wine?"

We met with Szmuel the next day, and the day after that I held in my hands the location of Halya's grave at the Lyczakowski Cemetery on Ulica Piotra i Pawla, Section 4-C.

*　　*　　*

We walked to the cemetery although we could have easily taken the trolley all the way to the main gate. On this bright day, we were in a picnic-like mood as we started toward the cemetery. Andrey, Yulia, Irka, Marek and I joked and laughed all the way. After all, we didn't know Halya and she had died long ago. Our mood lost its joviality as we walked along the rust-colored walls that towered above us. The walls, decorated every few yards by foot-high triangular ornaments, occasionally gave way to grid-iron gates through which we glimpsed the cemetery. Its grandeur was overwhelming. I was awed by those hills, densely overgrown with grave monuments of varying sizes and shapes, in various stages of decay. The diversity and artistry of the gravestones was evident even from afar.

As we paused in contemplation across the street from the main gate, we were pestered by vendors. Some of these withered babushkas had small stands with flowers and a few small items; most of the women walked around selling bouquets. When they got the notion that we did not intend to buy from them, they began to hackle us loudly: "Polskie pany, Polskie pany." "Polish overlords," a vestige of Ukrainian resentment toward former Polish rule. Although we were neither Polish nor aristocrats, the chorus gave vent to their ire by expressing their contempt for us.

Andrey had had enough of their abuse or he simply thought that we should honor Halya. He turned around and bought a small bouquet of forget-me-nots which served to shut up one babushka. The rest continued to insult us as we crossed the street and entered the cemetery. Here we were immediately surrounded by a group of *stariks*. One of the withered, old men wanted money as an entry fee; others offered to guide us to the grave; some just simply begged. Andrey motioned to one *starik* and gave him the slip of paper indicating the location of Halya's grave. Seeing our flowers, the guide took a small, decrepit plastic bag out of his pocket and led us to a water fountain. He filled the bag and gave it to Andrey.

"For the flowers so that they will last at the grave," he told us.

Then we were off, leaving a trail of water behind us. I hoped that there would be some water left by the time we reached the grave.

"Andrey, watch it!" I yelled at him, as if he could stop the leak. "There will be nothing left for the flowers!"

"Okay, it's okay. The bag leaks mostly when full. Look."

There was, indeed, still some water on the bottom, and the water ceased to spout somewhat.

"Irka! Are you coming along? Are you well?" I turned around to see Irka way behind, sitting on a stone and holding her head in her palms. "Are you crying?"

"No. No, Maria. I am just a little sick again. I will be all right." Irka stood up. Appearing reinvigorated, she walked up the hill to rejoin us.

On a hill overlooking the military cemetery stood an unassuming cross among more ornate headstones. There was no stone whatsoever, only a mound of earth under the cross. The mound was overgrown with grass and ivy; a rusted can lay undisturbed under the branches and leaves. Halya's grave looked as though it had been neglected for several years. The tangled shoots of grass seemed to tell of her troubles. A single dandelion protruded through the grass.

We left the flowers in the can and knew that they would not survive long in the few drops of water that Andrey poured from the bag. We turned back toward the noisy entrance in silence, each of us deep in thought.

Andrey tossed the plastic bag onto one of the many heaps of trash that competed with the gravesites for space. Human remains and garbage. Trash, human remains and Halya. Not Halya! I couldn't think of Halya as trash. She was a woman who lived and loved. Jealous Hildegarde called her "Ukrainian trash." Not trash. Whatever Halya was, she was not trash.

Chapter X

Between Love and Death

Was I Maria or Jane? Was he Marek or Tarzan? Was this a large room filled with a vast collection of African violets, or was it an exotic jungle with thick succulent underbrush, vines of passion wrapping my body, and the intoxicating aroma of gorgeous flowers? Was it a merger of two spirits in need of companionship and mutual support, or a sexual release such as comes from shaming yourself by performing acts that seemed possible only in outrageous fantasies? It was all of the above, and more. It was love between a woman and a man as well as admiration for each other.

The second spring of my stay in Lwów was at its glory on that bright afternoon. My hosts, Vladya and Sara, had departed for their garden patch on the outskirts of town to plant tomato and onion seedlings, leaving me in charge of the apartment. The Novikovs were a very special, middle-aged couple. He was a very large Ukrainian man and she was a short, plump, Jewish woman. Vladimir and Sara Novikov had literary backgrounds. They were intellectuals with many diverse interests. Vladya collected African violets. Several hundred varieties of the species fully occupied their bedroom, my room, even the balcony—everywhere except for the kitchen. The kitchen was Sara's domain, the place where she created the most delicious *varenniki*, "stuffed dumplings." Just as Vladya prided himself on his phenomenal number of violets, Sara boasted of her many recipes for stewed *varenniki*. The Novikovs were good, warm-hearted people, but their hygienic facilities, ancient plumbing, and my rickety bed left a lot to be desired.

"Make sure that you bolt the door from inside," yelled Vladya from the antechamber as they were leaving. He was forever mindful of robbers. Normally, I would have walked out of my room after them and secured the door. But for some reason, I didn't.

A warm breeze swirled the unwashed, frazzled drapery back and forth through the open window. I sat on my trundle bed, at ease, feeling the warm air on my naked body. I began to apply thick lotion to my soft skin; I closed my eyes and inhaled the fresh air as it entered my room. I was in no hurry today. The combination of the cool moisturizer and warm, outside air was soothing and gave me a tingling, pleasant sensation. My mind wandered off to other pleasant scenarios: being undressed, being caressed, giddy with liquor, responding to passion. Rick, my first boyfriend, was persistent; he pleaded until I gave myself to him. Jonathan, my colleague at the Holocaust Museum was so serious in bed, as if performing a religious rite. There were other men who were not serious at all. We enjoyed each other's company and that was that. Another semester, another school, another job, another man, but never quite the fulfillment I hoped for.

I was applying a bit more lotion when a brisk knock on my door startled me. The door suddenly opened and Marek burst in. All I could think was that had I neglected to bolt the apartment door. Oh, my God, anybody could have entered!

Instinctively, my knees drew together and my hands cupped my breasts to conceal my nudity. As our eyes met, my heart raced. His gaze was so intense that I lowered my eyes. My nipples were hard and swollen. His presence began to arouse me. My hands dropped and I continued to gently rub the lotion around my legs and stomach. I lifted my hands to rub the cream onto my breasts, not feeling ashamed or embarrassed in any way. The sensation of being watched and allowing myself to explore my own body was sexually ecstatic—an experience so novel and so terribly thrilling.

166

Marek silently closed the door behind him and turned toward me. I looked up and our eyes locked. As he walked slowly across the room, watching my every move, I could feel my heartbeat quicken. I was moist with desire. Marek knelt before me and gently placed his hands on my thighs and squeezed them. He caressed me with his finger stubs; their tips felt soft against my skin and sent chills through my body. His gentle touch glided in between my legs and I lost myself.

The trundle bed creaked and rocked. The old mattress began to fold in half; the depression in the mattress became a chasm into which our bodies were thrown. It was not uncomfortable. I could have stayed like that forever with arms around each other and lips joined, but Marek fidgeted, disengaged, and then pushed and pulled the mattress to free me

When we picked ourselves up, I observed Marek's naked body and I liked it. It was thin, with graying hair, bony but sinewy, and his chest muscles were pronounced. I knew that I wanted to be his woman then, and for as long as we would last.

"Szmuel called me. He wants to see us right away. I tried to reach you by phone, Maria, but no one was answering. Your phone must be out of order. I came over to see. Szmuel sounded excited, but I detected worry in his voice. He says that he has something of great importance to show us. He can only do it in person."

Marek rambled as he dressed hurriedly. I slowly stood up and began to rummage between the flowers for clean underwear when Marek embraced me from behind and he briefly caressed me. I could tell that his mind was absorbed by thoughts of Szmuel's news. He let go and we finished dressing.

There was another kind of climax in store for us on that eventful day when we finally saw Szmuel. We climbed up Citadel Hill and then three flights of the stairs to Szmuel's apartment. The hill where the Austrian pre-World War I fortress is located is fairly high, and the stairs of Szmuel's old house rise high as well. We were out of breath by the time Szmuel unbolted the locks from inside and opened the door. He let us in without the customary niceties, merely saying, "What in Stalin's name delayed you?" Szmuel is the only person that I know who is so free with Old Joe's name. Perhaps it comes from the fact that his parents were unreformed Communists and that he himself was one. However, he claimed to be a Jewish Robin Hood: he took from the rich Western tourists and gave to the poor Jews of Lwów. This was, at least, what Marek and I wanted to believe.

"Your brother Bogdan was not killed by the Soviets in Rovno. He was captured and then became an NKVD informer. I will show you documents!" yelled out Szmuel. Then realizing that walls can have ears, he softened his voice.

"See? In 1944 he was interviewed by a commissar of the Konev's Ukrainian Front whose name I can not decipher. Later, that document became part of Bodgan's NKVD dossier. I have more to show you. First, let's have some good wine that I bought in the south."

Marek didn't say a word. I could tell that he was shocked by the news. I was also startled. Could it be? It would have been an incredible coincidence. My mind focused on the letter from Willi to Halya. Willi wrote that he had saved from certain death a Ukrainian SS soldier who claimed to be Jewish. Did it matter? No, but strange would be the ways of providence. Bogdan would know, but he would never admit to that sordid part of his past. I did not tell Marek about my surmise.

We both needed more than wine. Indeed, we finished off a half-pint of vodka *z pertsom*, "with pepper."

That was a day when, thanks to Bogdan, Szmuel, warm weather and a broken telephone, Marek and I became lovers.

*   *   *

Days passed pleasantly for us. Marek and I paused in our search and became tourists. We walked a lot and ate well. We visited Kupol Restaurant almost every evening. We had meals with friends who treated us to different varieties of Ukrainian *borszcz*. We sampled *piroszki*, known as *varenniki* in Russian. Whatever the language, they still were dough stuffed with a variety of delicious fillings that ranged from potatoes with cheese to meat. We had a selection of *golubci* (stuffed cabbage) and sweet *naleshniki* (crepe-suzettes). Having dollars and a favorable exchange rate, we imbibed excellent Moldavian, Bulgarian, Crimean and Georgian wines. We drank different vodkas and cognacs but Marek and I relished mostly the mutual love that grew with every day.

The preoccupation with Bogdan, Willi, and Halya gave way to a leisurely tourist life and all the pleasures of a handsome town with centuries of history. We lived and thrilled with learning about each other, the people around us, and eminent figures from the past. There was Adam Mickiewicz, the premiere Polish poet who lived in Lithuania but who inspired the Poles and was thoughtful of Jews. His statue still stands prominently in the main plaza of town. There was Bogdan Chmielnicki, the renowned Ukrainian leader whose fame is marred by pogroms against Jews. There was the Polish king, Jan Sobieski, who fought the Turks in the environs of Vienna and whose ancestral castle we visited.

Of course, there was Szmuel who made it a personal campaign to learn what happened to Bogdan. His intuition told him that Bogdan was alive and was doing well. After all, an unscrupulous, pliant former employee of a police state had a superb chance of being successful in the morass of the post-Soviet era. While Marek and I played, Szmuel and his retainers worked. We were told that Szmuel had to go to Moscow on a mission. Boris said that Szmuel was invited to participate in a symposium regarding the last decade of the Soviet regime. The conference was to be held in no less a place than the Kremlin.

Why Szmuel called the meeting the "Wannsee Conference" when, in reality, it was a lavish, festive dinner in Moscow, attended by former NKVD, KGB, SMERSH dignitaries, and others of similar ilk, was incomprehensible to us. The notorious Wannsee Conference, from which recorded proceedings survived, took place in Berlin in January 1942 in a palatial residence along Lake

Wannsee. The villa, the grounds, and the lake were normally used for recreation by the SS. The meeting took place at the height of Germany's power, under the direct patronage of Hitler. It was presided over by the powerful Nazi police chief, Heydrich, and was attended by high-ranking representatives of the German government. The objective of the conference was not to determine whether or not to murder all the Jews of Europe—mass executions were already taking place—but to determine who was a Jew. Would one or two Arian, non-Jewish grandparents define a grandchild as an Arian? Outside the formal agenda, the German officialdom was informed about actions already in progress against the Jews.

Why then the "Wannsee Conference" in the Russian capital in 2002? I guess Szmuel's perverted sense of humor again had its venue. He phoned us from Moscow, and when I asked him why he or they or whoever had chosen such an ignominious name, Szmuel only cackled roguishly and did not respond. Perhaps both occasions were attended by the most brutal functionaries. Yes, that must have been the connection, or so I thought.

"But I did locate Bogdan and that is all that counts," he smugly told us. He laughed uproariously and then abruptly hung up.

We had to wait for details until Szmuel returned from Moscow. The so called Wannsee Conference was not a symposium but a jolly meeting over appetizers, chut-chuts, and soldier's *kasha* (groats). (These served to remind participants of the food served in the trenches during the war.) Then more toasts, followed by sweets and still more toasts. The seventy-, eighty- and even ninety-year-old veterans of the secret Soviet apparatus, many wearing their medals and uniforms, had a day of remembrance. Somehow Szmuel was invited to participate. Was it his hunch that took him to Moscow? As Szmuel mingled with the crowd, he showed a photo of Bogdan as a young man and hoped that Bogdan would still be recognizable as a man nearing eighty. One inebriated colonel recognized him and unwittingly blurted out Bogdan's present name.

"Yes, Bogdan, as he was known then, was a good one to have working in our organization. That *sukyi syn*, son-of-a-bitch! He did well for himself, then as now. He will go to hell for sure. He is filthy rich, that corrupted oligarch. I dealt with him in Kiev but he cheated me. He is alive, still kicking, the bastard." Then, according to Szmuel, the richly medaled colonel murmured more juicy curses and staggered to the men's room.

Two days after relating to us his success in Moscow, Szmuel departed for Kiev to learn more about Bogdan with hopes of meeting him.

*   *   *

Three sharp raps on the door followed by a long, loud buzz jarred my placid train of thought. As usual, after a splendid breakfast with the Novikovs, we indulged in moments of private reflections. I, with a second cup of tea, was affectionately thinking of my sister Kathy, who was about to get married in Boston. Marek, who was living with me by then, was still munching on the *przylibka* of the crusty rye bread. To him, the end portion of a loaf of bread was a delicacy left to culminate a sumptuous meal so that the taste of the freshly baked bread would last through the morning. Sara was stroking Vladya's hand. This was the gentle way she nudged him to get up and clear the table. The raps and the buzz interrupted all of that.

"That must be Szmuel!" exclaimed Vladya, rising from the table. "Already back from Kiev! He must have important news to visit so early."

"Come in, come in, Szmuel Vissarionovich!" Vladya opened the door and sarcastically greeted Szmuel, slightly bowing in mock respect. Szmuel's father's name was David and so the proper Russian appellation, which incorporates paternity, would have been "Szmuel Davidovicz." Vladya couldn't help but to needle Szmuel by assigning him Stalin's father's name.

"Da, da. I found Bogdan. He is alive and he is rich," were Szmuel's first words. "Of course, he has changed his name. Igor, the man who runs Bogdan's not-so-legal empire, saw me immediately when I told him about Marek. We went out for a glass of cognac. Later in the evening, Igor entertained me regally."

"Did you see Bogdan?" Marek impatiently interjected.

"At our initial meeting, Igor told me that Bogdan was not in town but Igor said that he would notify Bogdan about you, Marek. He said that Bogdan would be pleased. Bogdan apparently knows about your relationship to him, Marek, but not that you are alive."

"How could he? Who told him? Natalia? Lesia? When can I talk to him?" Questions poured out of Marek.

"Not so fast, *pomalo*." Szmuel, the man for all seasons switched to Polish. "There may be a bit of a problem. I am sure that Bogdan will not be overjoyed by either Marek's or my knowledge of his new identity. I also suspect that Bogdan was in town and did not think it shrewd to show himself to me. They are cagey liars, those old *zuliks*. You must remember that Bogdan is a master of deceit, but so is the old, foxy Szmuel Davidovicz. I gave Igor a nice proposition for Bogdan. A few kopecks are nothing to such a rich man, but they will buy a mountain of potatoes for my Jews to eat in winter."

At this point, I expected to hear Szmuel's cascading laughter. Not this time. Instead, he repeated his name, clearly enunciating Da-vi-do-vicz, as if re-battling Vladya's slur upon his name. If there was anything sacred to Szmuel on this earth, it was his father, David, who was killed fighting Germany in World War II. After slowly repeating Da-vi-do-vicz, Szmuel fell uncharacteristically silent. He looked down upon the tip of his boots and brooded. I noticed that his hand was shaking and his face reddened.

All four of us fell silent also, even Marek who was merely fidgeting with the remainder of *przylibka* in his fingers. After a few moments, Vladya stood up and began to gather cups, utensils, and dishes into one big pile. The clanking roused us and we began to talk. Where? How? What? When? Szmuel remained silent, looking pensively at his boots.

"Come Szmuel, talk. Don't play games." Marek urged excitedly.

"What happened the next day? Did Bogdan send any messages via Igor? Did you see Igor? What did he tell you?" continued Marek.

"I tell you what," Szmuel came out of his stupor. "Bogdan wants to meet Marek but, before seeing him, I think he wants to test Marek's feelings. They may be brothers, but a lot of things have happened. Remember the meeting between Isaac and Esau, Marek? Do you remember how distrustful those two brothers were of one another?"

Wow, Szmuel's reference to the Bible was unexpected.

"He is sending Igor to Lwów to sound off Marek and then to report back. We are invited to meet Igor on Saturday at Galicia's Ozero Euphoria, about thirty kilometers west of Lwów. It is a new, very exotic complex with a restaurant and a hotel. It goes without saying that the place is well-guarded and is extremely expensive. I hear that this is where all the voracious *zuliks* meet to carve out their fiefdoms and divide the spoils." At last Szmuel was becoming himself and he began to laugh.

"I will tell you more; really not much more, at least not now. I must see Marek alone." Szmuel rose from the table and then, as if talking softly to himself, he added, "Yes, it should be fun." But there was no joviality in his voice.

*   *   *

At first, I was excited by an invitation to the Ozero Resort. Marek insisted that he be represented as a successful, well-connected American. Szmuel agreed. Marek would play the role of a Westerner, traveling in my company. I was to portray myself as an up-and-coming academician at a respected university. In the presence of others, Marek was to address me formally as "Pani Profesorka Martell." I had to suppress my smile every time I heard him refer to me or introduce me as "Mrs. Professor Martell."

To match the honorific title that I had not yet fully earned, Market said that he would be honored if I would agree to dress in a manner befitting my status, and to follow the sophisticated European model of female elegance rather than my casual, frumpy, American style. I was taken with the way the privileged class dressed in Ukraine. In fact, I was perplexed by the number of Ukrainian women who dressed in the latest Italian fashions, fashions which were the cutting edge in Europe and had not yet reached the upscale clientele in the USA. I learned how this was possible when Marek arranged for Olga to take me shopping.

Pani Olga, now a successful entrepreneurial dentist, was beautiful to the point of looking like an Olympian. Pani Olga was so stunning that people would literally stop to watch her when she passed them on the street. Other women wore impossibly high stiletto heels with discomfort, but Olga floated on them and they never caught in the deep crevices between the uneven cobblestones of the ancient streets built in the days of the Austro-Hungarian empire. She could wear a see-through blouse and custom-made lingerie, give you a second to gasp, then begin to talk and force you to meet her gaze as she controlled the conversation. According to Marek, once upon a time she was a struggling single mother, barely surviving on a dentist's salary. He confided to me that after his first visit to Lwów years ago, upon seeing the destitute way she lived, he wired her one thousand dollars, which was a fortune at that time. He was adamant in claiming that he received no favors in return.

I asked him how he met her, and why he did it. He explained that at the time of his first visit, she was living with her child and her grandparents in the very same apartment where he had lived with his parents prior to being forced into the Ghetto. Nothing in the building had been repaired or replaced since. Water leaked from the faucet of an enamel cast-iron sink that was chipped and stained and falling away from the wall. Marek had been touched by the utter innocence of Olga's little boy. Marek had been the boy's age, with a few months of innocent childhood left, when he lived in those very rooms and played in the yard below. Marek never asked how Olga's grandparents obtained the apartment.

One of Marek's remarkable qualities was that he held no grudges. If he had a grievance, it was specific. He did not blame all Germans and all Ukrainians for the horrific events of the Holocaust.

I could see how Marek could meet Olga and respond to her plight. Life under Communist rule was harsh. Marek corresponded with Olga and decided to help her because he could. The cash he sent gave her enough of an advantage to catapult herself out of poverty. Using her knowledge of the system, her skills as a dentist, her charm, and a second marriage to a clever dental technician, she had become a successful businesswoman, the head of a private practice with business connections in Canada.

Olga loved to shop. She now had plenty of money and time. When I turned to Olga for assistance, she volunteered without hesitation to help me prepare for the upcoming trip to the Ozero Resort. Did I know it was on the water? Of course, I thought, Ozero meant "lake," so it would be near water. Olga spoke ungrammatical but acceptable English, which was great. It meant that if we spoke English, no one around us would understand what we were saying. Most of the time, we spoke Russian. Russian was a useful language, the one I had studied in the United States. Russian is very close to Ukrainian, so I could understand basic Ukrainian. Under the Soviet regime, Ukrainians who were Olga's age had been in schools run by the Soviet system, and were all fluent in Russian. I had more trouble with Polish, but I got bits and pieces. It was certainly easier to read Polish, which used the Latin alphabet, than Ukrainian, which used the Russian Cyrillic alphabet. Olga started off by asking me to show her my wardrobe so that we could supplement what I already had. She stared in frank disbelief at my clothing, which I had packed compactly in my lightweight rolling suitcase: two pairs of jeans, a few sweats and T-shirts, three decent-looking mix-and-match blouses, one navy skirt, two presentable slacks, and one wrinkle-resistant black dress. Olga asked me why I didn't have anything nice. I was, after all, a rich American.

"You are Pani Profesorka. That is a big deal. Don't you care how you appear? Don't you care about looking good for Pan Marek?"

Men, she explained, liked to show off their women. Women were proud to appear to their greatest advantage. Olga said that even when she wore her white lab coat for patient procedures, it was pressed and starched, and beneath it was classy clothing that she could wear without hesitation to the fanciest restaurant. It was a point of pride to be presentable at all times. I asked her the question on my mind: How could so many Ukrainian women wear the latest European fashions? How could they afford it? Olga laughed. Pirated and inexpensive copies of the most up-to-date fashion magazines were sold discretely to the well-informed. Lots of women knew how to sew or had competent tailors. Many young professionals she knew had only one or two outfits, but they were top quality, and the women took meticulous care of them. Appearances were high priority. If you had to choose between buying one stylish suit or being able to eat out for the next three months, most women would choose to invest in the suit. Less money in the budget for enticing restaurant food was good for the figure, anyway. What was this she heard about all Westerners being overweight and on diets? Had I seen any over-weight people in Lwów?

"No, actually, I haven't."

Olga nodded and continued, "Only if you had lots of money would you buy something of quality off the rack."

"That's exactly what we must do because time is of the essence."

I needed to look my best for Marek, and he wanted to show me off at the exclusive Galicia's Ozero Euphoria Restaurant. Did I realize that we were supposed to impress his brother's representa-tive and maybe Bogdan himself? If Bogdan will not come, what did I want this representative to report back about Marek and his woman? Olga said that I should look alluring and elegant. She gave a deep, throaty chuckle. Olga suggested knowingly that the way to cater to a man's fantasy was to dress well. As soon as Olga said this, I knew she was right. I did love him, didn't I? I decided to be Marek's vision of a sexy woman.

My mission with Olga turned out to be fun. We flitted from one expensive store to another on Ulica Svobody, Lwów's Fifth Avenue, and then to a few side streets where dollars could buy you a lot. First, we bought a pair of high heels. I wanted something lower in order not to tower over Marek, but Olga assured me that Italian pumps were the best for my appearance. Well-dressed and acting imperiously, Olga was obviously a member of the hoy-poloy. The portals of the stores were opened immediately for her. The standard security precaution of "only four customers can enter at time" was waived for us. We did not stand in line on the street in front of the store; the beefy security guards erased their customary suspicious looks. I have to admit that Olga also had an excellent eye. After visiting a number of stores, she selected an exquisite long dress made from Italian silk and tailored in a classic sheath style with a collar. It was black, with silver and gold threads that formed subtle patterns. It hugged my hips and accentuated my feminine curves. It looked stunning with my new pumps. Minor alterations were needed to adjust the bust and the length.

"Will you have it ready by Friday?" Olga asked the sales woman in Ukrainian.

"Yes, madam, but it doesn't give us much time. Our tailor is very busy. I cannot make any promises on such short notice," replied the woman.

"I understand," responded Olga, who then turned to me, asking in English, "Do you have three single dollars on you? That will assure that your dress will be ready to wear by Thursday."

I slipped the three singles into the salesperson's hand, bowed my head, and said "Diakuiu, thank you." The dress cost my whole month's university honorarium paid to me by my research grant. Relatively little in American dollars, but more than most had to live on here.

The shopping spree with Olga had turned into a most positive experience. Packages in hand, we walked to Pani Stefa, a classy ethnic eatery, and were presented with a plate of beautifully arranged *kanapki*, elegant cousins of the canapés served at Western cocktail parties, along with strong hot tea in clear glasses to tide us as we waited for the main course. I contemplated the experience as we sipped our tea in satisfied silence. I had learned a lot about style and what worked for me, and also had gained an insider's view into the business world of Lwów. It was good to connect with another woman, especially one who, on the surface, was so different. It occurred to me that this meeting with Bogdan's representative had many layers, and that I was in unfamiliar territory. So, feeling certain that Marek would not mind, I plunged ahead.

With no preliminaries, I asked Olga, "Will you and Vasily join us at Galicia's Ozero Euphoria on Saturday?" Quickly, I explained, "Remember, we told you about Bogdan, Marek's half-brother in Kiev? He invited us there, and said he would meet us there if nothing pressing comes up in his business. If he can't meet us, he said he'll send his top assistant. I know that Bogdan is very important in whatever he does, and I hear he is very rich and influential. Nevertheless, I think it is odd that he is setting up a meeting in this way. I mean, Bogdan and Marek have not seen each other since the middle of the war. Why would he send a representative? Does he want someone to look us over before deciding to invite us to Kiev? I think I'd feel better if we had some Ukrainian friends with us."

Olga's expressive eyes gleamed, and it didn't take her long to reply: "Yes Maria, I have always wanted to see that place. You know, you need very high connections to get in there. Vasily and I would be honored to be with you on that occasion. You and I will astound those *zuliks* from Kiev. They will drool, watching our bodies. I should have said our figures. I will also wear something tight-fitting. How much skin should I show, do you think? You know the word *zulik*, don't you?"

"Aren't they criminals, sort of chiselers who became rich on illegal deals?"

Olga nodded: "Yes. Some are bigger than others. What should I wear, Maria?"

"Olla, last time you invited us over to your villa, you were stunning in your simple miniskirt. Miniskirts suit you very well. But how did you manage to walk on those stilettos?" Uninvited, I had called Olga by the diminutive, Olla. Olla no longer seemed unapproachable, she had become a friend.

When we finished our tea and *kanapki*, the costumed waitresses at Pani Stefa presented us with sumptuous luncheon delicacies. At first, Olla had appeared to be aloof: living on a high scale, wearing very high heels, and possessing a supermodel's willowy build. But she was not the forbidding goddess I had taken her to be; she was down-to-earth and was quite humorous, especially when deprecating herself. Now it was shear camaraderie between us. Over *naleshniki* (crepes), we broached many topics.

"My husband Vasily is smart. He has a stream of orders for false teeth from big dentists in Canada. They pay him much less than they would have to in America, but he is still doing well. Vasily has ten workers grinding out teeth." She laughed. "It is funny. Those patients across the ocean have no idea that their teeth once were enveloped by the garlicky breaths of Vasily's workers. It comes from the tasty sausage, *kielbasa*, that our people eat."

After our meal, we shared the customary drinks which are habitual, even amongst women. We took turns toasting: "Chut-chut, one more sip!" Olla and I burst out laughing. She often laughed spontaneously. She enjoyed life.

"We will show those Cossacks from the Dnieper what we *Lwówianki*, women from Lwów, look like."

"But Olla, I am not...."

"But, yes Maria, you are now one of us. I saw your nipples when you tried that dress on. So let's give those old, filthy men a thrill. Just a taste will suffice. By the way, Vasily and I will drive by ourselves in our Mercedes, and will meet you there at seven o'clock. I know you and Marek will arrive with Szmuel. He'll bring his guards, his goons, in his minivan. I don't want to drive with them. Anyway, there won't be room for all of us in it. By the way, will you be staying there overnight? The hotel is supposed to be very luxurious."

"I don't know. I thought we were going there just for the dinner. Marek and Szmuel have been rather secretive about this meeting. They don't tell me much, but it doesn't matter. It's about Marek and his brother, and I know he'll work it out in the best way."

Olga did not respond to my concerns about the nature of the meeting or of the relationship between the brothers. She was still thinking about the advantages of the resort as she continued, "I was told that they have excellent Western showers and lots of hot water in each suite. Think of that, Maria. If I were you, I'd pack an overnight bag. We will, too. Do pobaczenia, until next time."

Then, Olga hesitated before entering her automobile, and she added, "I hope you realize, Maria, that these big shots from Kiev cannot be trusted. They can also be dangerous. Vasily had some unpleasant dealings with one of them. Tell Marek to keep his eyes and ears open. Marek is a good, trusting man, and I hope his brother will not disappoint him. Well, Do pobaczenia again."

The normally humorous Olga was stonily serious when she warned me. Her parting remarks worried me. The picture was blurry and it was not getting any clearer. There was Szmuel and his entourage. Goons, Olla had said. There were Bogdan's goons, with or without Bogdan. What were we getting into? What was *I* getting into? Did Marek have any idea? The pleasure of the day faded as the sun set, and the dull, yellow lights from windows barely illuminated the dark streets of Lwów, which seemed more foreign and unfathomable than ever.

It was raining and unseasonably cold on that Saturday in June. Six passengers crammed tightly inside the smelly minivan, considering that two spare wheels, two large jerry cans of gasoline, and other equipment bundled in canvas occupied the back, where presumably the third seat once was attached. Boris was our chauffeur. Szmuel and his tiny wife sat next to him. I squeezed between Marek and Moris in the remaining passenger seat and tried to ignore the uncomfortable ride. What a chariot for a woman in her finery en route to a gala dinner! With or without

Bogdan, surely with good company and the promised luxuries of the Ozero Resort, we were guaranteed a memorable experience. A limitless supply of hot water at the end of a fine evening of dining and dancing seemed like icing on the cake, especially on this dismal night. I looked forward to the company of Olla and Vasily. I hoped for excellent live music in the restaurant and for a chance to dance. Marek bragged about being a good dancer. Well, now he would have a chance to prove it, I thought. He had been proving a lot to me. The day before, he had bought me a necklace of pinkish amber. It was imported from Poland and it must have cost Marek a pretty penny, or plenty of zlotys or grivne. It was made of irregularly-shaped amber beads tastefully arranged by size. It looked stunning against my black silk gown, which was ready on time, as promised.

As the minivan rattled on the cobblestones on the way out of town, Marek sneaked frequent admiring glances at me, while I snuggled closely against his shoulder. I could tell he loved the contact and that he took this closeness as my expression of affection for him. It was, but I was also cold and I savored his warmth. It was very chilly. The van had no heater, and my gown was thin. I saw that Szmuel also had his arm around his wife. Was this a typical sign of affection between them, or were they also cold? I sensed in myself a changing attitude toward people. It felt good.

Three days earlier, on our shopping trip, I had bonded with Olga and was pleased to now have her as a woman-friend. In that short time, we began speaking daily on the phone, and had even begun to confide in each other on personal issues. "Girl-talk," we would say back home. It was good for me to have a professional, sophisticated, bright Ukrainian woman of my age, who spoke English, as a counselor and confident. As I observed that bear of a man, Szmuel, with his arm wrapped protectively around his wife, I detected some kindness in me welling up toward him. He lived in a world that I could not really understand. I spoke the language and was an expert in some specialized topics, yet on a personal level, I had not penetrated the cultural barrier of that world.

That night, I even felt a scintilla of admiration for the ever-somber, obedient, and uncomplaining Moris and Boris. They were like faithful henchmen. What were their lives like? Did they really want to be out on an evening like this, observing the ultra-rich playing power games? Didn't they have families or lovers with whom to spend this gloomy evening? Were they really faithful protectors of Szmuel and his designates? Amidst all these musings, I wondered if I was really in love with Marek. Had our relationship also passed from lover to beloved? Was it true that love begot love? What about Bogdan, and to a lesser extent, the wheeler-dealer Igor? Would I always mistrust and fear them? Had I been fabricating their dark nature because I was in a foreign culture? I wondered what Marek truly thought of Bogdan.

I paused in my musings to notice again the miserable weather. It was foggy. The Siberian rain pounded on the windows, making it difficult to see the road or anything else. I could tell from the increasingly rough roads that we are almost out of the city. We had long passed the apartment houses from the fashionable central districts of the town. The real center of Lwów remained from medieval times. Around the center were beautifully constructed apartments and building where the upper class lived in Austro-Hungarian times when the city was called Lemberg. Those districts were still fashionable and convenient parts of town, but they were in varying states of decay, as minimal maintenance was done in Soviet times. Beyond them, built to accommodate a huge population influx from the Soviet Union, were miles and miles of seemingly endless apartment complexes built of rough, unadorned concrete. They were barely visible through the fog, and looked like slumbering, shadowy, prehistoric beasts.

The van swerved around the ever-present pot holes of the poorly paved streets on the perimeter of the city. The bouncing increased as, further outside the city, the road transitioned to into a wide, unpaved path. Shabby country cottages appeared less frequently as we drove further away from the town. At one point, we actually had to stop for a flock of sheep and some cows to complete their passage across the road, herded by a hunching, water logged peasant. Here and there, a few new houses appeared. We passed through villages with churches, easily spotted because of their onion-shaped domes, characteristic of Eastern Orthodox churches.

Suddenly, a bright, red brick wall became visible. In contrast to the dark and foggy night, the wall was illuminated by spotlights from watch towers that looked eerily like the walls and towers of the death camps that dotted Eastern Europe in the not-so-distant past. I didn't want to think of that. I knew that we had arrived at Ozero, the walled compound of the very rich.

*　　*　　*

As we drove closer to the wall, we could see glass shards imbedded on its top to prevent undesirables from climbing over. We were stopped at the entrance, where a formidable guardhouse stood filled with guards and snarling German shepherds. Across the road was an electric fence, the first that I had seen in this country.

"We are expected by Pan Igor from Kiev. Is he here already?" asked Szmuel as an armed guard approached us.

"Please, do come out of the car. Are you Szmuel Davidovicz and Mister Marek Mann? May I see your passports? You are welcomed here but we must make certain." Pleasantly but firmly, the young guard made his request.

"No, no. Not you Szmuel Davidovicz. Not Mister Mann. You don't have to get out. Just hand me your passports, please. Certainly, neither the ladies need to step out on this night," said a senior guard who glided to the window and displaced the younger guard.

"We just would like the driver and the other man to step out of the van and identify themselves. The rain has eased," added the senior guard, oozing with hospitality.

"Please come out and follow me to the guardhouse." The younger guard stepped up to Boris and Moris and began talking to them through the open window.

"Is that necessary?" asked Szmuel, as he stepped out of the van and interposed himself between the vehicle and the senior guard. "These men work for me and I vouch for them."

"We know that," soothed the senior guard, "but Pan Igor insisted that that we check them out. Everything here must be peaceful, proper and enjoyable. Pan Igor did not arrive as yet, but we expect him any minute now. Please…"

Boris and Moris walked to the guardhouse where they were frisked for weapons. None were found. Another guard, acting as a valet, parked the minivan in a fenced enclosure abutting the guardhouse. Walls within walls. One could not leave without permission any more than one could enter. Thus, Boris and Moris, our two protectors, were separated from us. They were driven in an Ozero vehicle to the main restaurant, where we were assured that they would be treated well.

The four of us were taken in another Ozero vehicle in the direction of the lake where several wooden pavilions were erected for the dining pleasure and privacy of the guests. They were really just garishly decorated cabins imitating the very old dwellings of the Hutzuls, the Carpathian mountain people who lived within the borders of Ukraine. Inside our cabin was a massive, oblong wooden table surrounded by eight throne-like chairs. How else can I describe those heavy, tall, ornately-carved wooden seats with side arms? Despite being furnished with velvet cushions, they were uncomfortable; their backs were straight and their scale was massive. It was difficult to relax in this restricted environment. We were seated, leaving the head and foot seats empty, presumably for Bogdan and Igor, and two vacant seats across from me for Olga and Vasily.

To pass the time, I conjured up an image of myths from the distant past. We were seated at King Arthur's table, in his medieval dining hall, as he presided at the head of the table directly opposite Sir Lancelot. I shifted my imagination to the near future, just a few hours ahead, and visualized Szmuel and Marek defending us from snarling German shepherds as we tried to sneak away from the compound, gain access to our van, and barrel our way out of this strange complex. That scene was too threatening, so I returned to medieval times. I imagined the dogs wagging their tails and rubbing themselves against the king's legs. They licked Arthur's fingers in expectation of a handout. Was Bogdan going to resemble King Arthur and throw bones to the dogs? Were we the dogs? Where were Bogdan and Pan Igor?

As I continued my fantasy, Marek and Szmuel spoke quietly, while Szmuel's wife looked out of the window toward the lake.

"Isn't it beautiful here?" She broke the silence, talking to no one in particular. Our male escorts were too engrossed in their conversation to answer.

I responded in Ukrainian in agreement, "Yes, the grounds are landscaped very attractively. Too bad that rain is obscuring the lake. I can barely see the boats tied at the dock. The rain has certainly picked up again. Don't you think it is cold in here?" I chatted.

"Yes, I am cold also. Szmuel Davidovicz! Is there anything you can do? These walls are so very flimsy. The rain is actually leaking through there in the corner. Pani Maria and I are very cold." Pani Szmuel turned to her husband who looked around as if he had just stepped into the pavilion and was only now noticing the puddles and the leaking walls.

"Yes, it is very brisk," acknowledged Szmuel.

My thoughts shifted to poor Irka. What would she think of the opulence around us at Ozero? That unfortunate girl probably wouldn't care by now. At eighteen, she was diagnosed as HIV-positive. Being unable to afford expensive treatment, she will probably die, I thought sadly.

The atmosphere lightened when we were joined by Olla and Vasily, a truly regal-looking couple fit for any royal table. The ambiance warmed considerably after we all had two rounds of libations. Waiters brought in hors d'oeuvres from the central restaurant located somewhere out there in the chilly rain, in another building. Two more toasts and we could have almost forgotten the cold, but not the purpose of our trip.

"Pan Igor called and asked us to tell you that neither he nor Pan Bogdan will be able to join you here tonight, but please do not have any concerns," announced a man in flawless Ukrainian. "Tonight, Pan Igor will call you and will explain. Your stay here is paid for. You are his guests. You will be staying here overnight, yes?" He wore a tuxedo and had just entered the pavilion with another man.

"Are you the manager?" responded Szmuel in Russian.

"No. My name is Leon Illich," the man replied in Ukrainian. "Pan Igor sent me here to make sure that they treat you well. Allow me to introduce my comrade. This is Pan Danko. He will attend to you at all times to make sure that Pan Mann and his guests have all their needs met."

It was clear that Danko was a strong-arm man. Did we need protection? Leon Illich proceeded to provide some justification by telling us how crime was rampant in Ukraine.

"Not so much around Lwów. Mostly east—in Kiev—but unfortunately, here, too. Ukrainian patriots, the old Bandera supporters, are avenging themselves on those who were working with the Soviets, spying for the NKVD. Other scores are being settled as well. We have protective associations which are like your Mafia, Mister Mann. You Americans call them syndicates. Am I right, Mister Mann? Did you hear—"

"No, no, nie nuzhno. Please Panie Leonie, we came here to enjoy ourselves, especially hoping that my brother would join us. We don't want to hear about your crime and murders," Marek interrupted him in studious Russian.

I could tell that Szmuel was listening intently and was doing some rapid calculations. So was I. Was this a scare tactic? Could Igor's absence be an intentional insult or, perhaps, a warning signal? Why, I wondered. Szmuel was deciding how to respond and what to do. Marek looked concerned, and it was he who chose the direct approach.

"I came here all the way from America to see my brother, and Pan Igor, who works for my brother, was supposed to be here in order to arrange a meeting between us. I insist to know why neither Pan Igor nor my brother have come. I am angered and feel imposed upon," Marek exploded in rapid English.

"I no speak English good. I not know who is your brother. I know nothing of what you say but what I understand I tell to Pan Igor. He talk at you tomorrow, so please, to enjoy yourselves here. We serve to you good dinner. Because it cold here, you, dear guests, want come to big restaurant? Warm and nice. Yes?" Leon Illich answered unperturbed, smilingly. Warmth, at least, would be good, and Marek readily agreed.

We were driven to the main building. There at the bar, Moris and Boris were happily situated with several young people. Two musicians and a male singer did their best to reproduce the worst of American culture. "Iaika, Iaika, Iaika," screamed the singer into the microphone, over and over again, bending, twisting, and shaking his torso as he touched his crotch with each "Iaika." Then, to connect with us, the coveted Western guests, he repeated his performance, screaming "balls, balls, balls" into the microphone, barring the opportunity for any conversation. Hearing and seeing this spectacle, I knew that there would be no dancing for us this evening.

We were practically the only guests. Only two other tables were occupied by groups of well-dressed men. The staff had seated us at another regal table with eight thrones, a place for the six of us, and who else? Regardless of what Pan Leon Illich had said, perhaps Pan Igor or Bogdan would still show up. Appetizers came, followed by a decent dinner of tender baked duckling with plums. There were more tumblers of vodka for all and attempts to be convivial, but the mood was apprehensive. Why this dinner, with its elaborate setting? Another man in a tuxedo with an Ozero badge on his pocket slid his way over to us and introduced himself as a public relations representative. He would be pleased if he could take some pictures of us, their distinguished guests.

"Please, please, you lovely ladies. Sit close to the lovely gentlemen. These shots will be wonderful publicity for us."

Marek and Szmuel wore very serious faces, obviously worried about the turn of events, while the well-dressed men at the other tables gawked at Olla and myself.

"Please, gentlemen, Pan Orloff and Mister Mann, please smile." But no smiles from those two. So the photographer addressed himself to Olla and me.

"Please, pretty please, lovely *Lwówianki*, please stand here so that your lovely, exquisite dresses will show. You both look absolutely gorgeous. Yes, it is lovely. The pictures will be super lovely. They will be hanging right at the bar so all can see what lovely women come to Ozero. Please, Pani Maria, rest your hand on Mister Mann's shoulder. Yes it will be lovely."

The obsequious, "lovely" man began clicking away with his camera. He bowed, and again said "please this, please that" and finally departed. But how did he know my first name? Did any one else in our party notice? I couldn't ask, for fear of being overheard if I raised my voice above the blaring music.

Boris staggered to our table, apparently soused. Szmuel looked at him severely and began to reprimand him, but Boris winked and continued his act. Before he staggered back to the bar, he gave Szmuel a note that Szmuel, in turn, surreptitiously showed us: *Don't like what is going on. We must leave as soon as possible. Will explain later. Don't talk seriously. They are listening.*

We suffered through our dessert and cognac. Olga, who turned out to be a wonderfully consummate actress, went to the bathroom several times, making a slight detour in order to be seen and admired by the well-dressed men at the other two tables. Each time, the men interrupted their confabulation to stare at her longingly. She looked terrifically attractive in her miniskirt, nylons, and heels. At our table, she again attracted attention by loudly complaining of the sudden onset of a terrible migraine and faking other pains as well. I did my best to contribute. I gagged, as if about to vomit. It was not entirely an act, because I truly was beginning to feel unwell.

When the staff was unable to cajole us to stay overnight in the hotel, we were finally led to our automobiles. Leon Illich extended the deepest regrets of the staff in his most flowery Ukrainian, and again assured us that Pan Igor would certainly contact us as soon as his business would permit. He did not apologize for Pan Igor or Bogdan. He was very formal. He acted as if he were following orders. The three dogs barked furiously when our van was brought back to us at the gate. The guards, who had obviously been prepped, said nothing and waved us through. Outside of the gate, we bid goodnight to Olga and Vasily, promising to meet them soon.

"Please follow us. It will be a comfort to have your Mercedes behind us on the way to town. I will try to explain the situation to you as soon as I figure it out myself. Olla, you are quite an actress. Diakuiu, I really mean it, thank you," were Marek's parting words to Olga and her husband before they drove off.

On the way back Boris told us what he had learned from Danko when the two sat together at the bar. Apparently, upon instruction from higher up, Pan Igor was supposed to show Szmuel Davidovicz and Mister Mann how powerful his organization was and how much clout Bogdan had. We were to be photographed and our conversation was to be bugged. Something was supposed to happen later that evening. Danko did not say what. Danko's revelation was most likely part of an elaborate scare tactic. To scare whom? Marek? Szmuel? Both?

Moris, in the back seat, turned around to examine one of the canvas bundles in the far back of the van.

"Those bastards opened up the van and searched it! I had my Weston 38 there and now it is gone. Those mother—! Sons of bitches!" he cursed.

One look at Szmuel was enough to make me realize that this boisterously confident man was plenty worried. He said nothing, and Marek did not pry.

"I will talk to you tomorrow," he said to Marek when he dropped us off at the Novikovs' apartment.

Too bad that we weren't able to enjoy the pleasures of a Western-style hotel with a giant-sized bed fit for King Arthur and plenty of blessedly hot water running directly from the tap. We did enjoy the intimacy provided by the creaky trundle bed at the Novikovs', though. My silk dress with the slit on the side certainly satisfied Marek's fantasies. He undressed himself and then felt my body through the tight-fitting black silk. He placed his hand under the silk and caressed my thighs. He slowly took my dress off, then my nylons, and finally my panties. Who needed the Ozero?

*   *   *

The unexpectedly bitter Siberian weather front is finally moving away. The rain ceased. It is not so gray but it is still chilly and damp. Maria is out, researching at the archives for her seminar at Ivan Franco University. We are supposed to meet later before going together to Szmuel's apartment. So I have the whole afternoon to myself. I need to be alone for a while.

First, I have to brush out those thoughts and feelings from the main compartments of my life. To be sure, the love that Maria and I have for each other floods my heart. In the core of my being, I am happy. On the periphery, I am uptight. A not-so-subtle premonition envelops my brain. It has been two days since our debacle at Ozero and Szmuel wants to see me again this evening at his house. I just talked to him yesterday! My gut senses that something even more worrisome must have happened. Will that cunning man tell me the truth—the whole truth?

*   *   *

I sit from atop the remains of an old defensive wall, just above Szmuel's apartment house. I am on a once heavily fortified hill, Citadella. The bastion consists of a series of mutually supporting forts, dating back to Austrian times. The location is fabulous. Situated practically in the center of Lwów, there is a fine overview of Old Town and the surrounding hills in the distance. I am sure that some day it will be studded with very expensive apartment houses. Today, except for a few attempts to convert some of its massive buildings into office spaces, Citadella is a gigantic heap of trash where

190

garbage and dog droppings abound. It seems that every dog owner in Lwów walks his pet here.

From my vantage point, I can see the windows of Szmuel's spacious third-floor apartment. He has a fine view of the city. To have obtained such a desirable apartment during the Soviet times must have been extremely difficult. What did Szmuel do to become its owner? Whom did he dispossess? Were the previous owners exiled to Siberia, and did Szmuel have anything to do with it? More likely, he paid a lot for it in bribes. From whom did he leech that money?

Szmuel is a puzzle, wrapped in enigma. Above me hover memories of stout Polish resistance to Bolsheviks and Ukrainians after World War I. More pervading are ugly remembrances of recent German atrocities. Here, very near where I sit, hundreds or maybe thousands of Italian, Soviet, and, I think, Polish officers, were all brutally massacred, their bodies buried in the moats which once protected the forts. There are plenty of ghosts around here. The most recent ghost is that of a high-ranking Ukrainian official, a minister of railroads. He was an extremely rich oligarch whose massive, newly-built red-brick home surrounded by walls I can see next to Szmuel's apartment house. The minister was found dead with two bullet holes in his cranium but his death was declared to be a suicide. Such is the power of Mafiosi and zuliks and such are the risks of being one. Leon Illich did not minimize the extent of crime in Ukraine.

Bogdan, my half-brother, is of the oligarch-Mafia category. So said Szmuel after his return from Kiev a few days ago. Yesterday, Szmuel saw me privately and we had a talk right here on this very hill. Szmuel confided in me that Igor had called to warn him not to press Bogdan about anything, especially donations. Apparently, the events at Ozero were to be a preview of the power that Bogdan, the dark eminence, wields through his front man, Igor. It was a threat. No wonder that Szmuel appeared to be scared.

"Szmuel Davidovicz," I told him yesterday, "you are not so clever! Why in the name of Stalin did you have to mention your poor Jews to Igor? Couldn't you have resisted the temptation of soliciting Bogdan for money? No wonder you are worried. Should I also worry, especially after the sinister signs yesterday at Ozero?"

Szmuel told me that he would make amends. He would telephone Igor immediately and apologize for his brashness. I hope that it does not have a bearing on my reunion with Bogdan. Perhaps tonight, after contacting Kiev, Szmuel will tell me when, if ever, I will see Bogdan. I wish I didn't have to go through Szmuel. After tonight, I will take the matters into my own hand.

It is hard for me to flush out and sort out my feelings about Bogdan. I started my quest fired up by curiosity, to be sure, but also with an inherited sense of loyalty toward my tribe, toward my relative. During my initial visit to Lwów, when I didn't know that Bogdan was my brother, in my eyes his sins were those of abandoning me as a friend and then enlisting in the viciously brutal SS division. I could have lived with those two blotches on Bogdan's character, and I could have attributed his SS enlistment to youthful foolishness. But now, I have learned that my brother's transgressions were far more grievous. Simply put, he is a very bad man. Reason dictates that I should drop my attempt to see him. And yet… He must have family, children and grandchildren. There is a temptation in me to be called "uncle." I am nobody's uncle and never have been. Am I so tempted to have more of a family?

My children and grandchildren live far away from me, according to the American model prescribed for well-to-do professionals. We spend little time together and our infrequent visits lack purpose. We all are perpetually busy. My wife lives separately from me and is pretty much involved in her own life. The American Dream has resulted in loneliness and unfulfilled aspirations. Life is harsher and starker in Ukraine, yet more intimate and cultural; perhaps here, on the periphery of Bogdan's family I could somehow enter my last stage of life.

Maria, my wonderful Maria. I sense you in the innermost crevices of my being. You are my heart of hearts, as Uncle Willi would say. When you snuggled against me in the minivan and put your head on my shoulder, I was ecstatic. I knew that you loved me. Yes, Maria you looked enchanting in your silky dress with a slit. Yes, Maria, you are a gorgeous woman, like a rose in full bloom. You are desired by all, but accessible only to me. That night after Ozero, I did not desire your body, but your affection, my heart of hearts. I know that we must eventually part. My constellation Virgo will beckon me to the galactic vastness and I will have to obey. Professional opportunities, many future years of life and study, will beckon you, Maria, and you will obey. I came here to this beautiful town to uncover Bogdan's history and I did; but finding you, Maria, is the zenith of my life. My brain tells me that my expectations to reconcile with Bogdan are not so very good. Yet, let tomorrow come, for as long as I am with you Maria, I will live happy and die happy.

"On the day, rainy and gloomy; from Citadella, children of Lwów are descending from the hill. In rows upon rows, they march to scatter around the world."

This is the refrain of a popular pre-World War II Polish song. Its melody and patriotic words haunt me today. More than half a century ago, my parents and I left Lwów, vowing never to return to this scene of so much pain. Yet I, a crumbled cookie of fourteen, who was scattered and blown westward by the Siberian wind, am back here, loving and being loved by a woman whose two German uncles died so that Nazis could smash my family and my people.

Let tomorrow come. Perhaps Bogdan, too, feels loyalty toward members of his tribe, toward his half-brother. Maybe we could be reunited. But, it is a long chance. The clouds are receding as the evening approaches. Their orange lining becomes more vivid as the sun sets behind them. My spirits brighten and as they do, the Citadella ghosts disperse.

I walk past a trampled but unpolluted patch of grass, rare for Citadella. I think of the Mall in Washington and the life that I left behind me. I visualize myself kneeling right here on this hill, Citadella, with a brush in my hand. I imagine scooping viscous cadmium orange with it, and then twisting and twirling the brush in ever-increasing circles as I apply the pigment. Oily globules of orange merely dribble onto the canvas, hardly as neatly textured spirals. How sloppy my work, especially compared to my "Summer Barn" of long ago, with its exquisitely brushed, straight lines. I shudder at my imagined clumsiness and walk away to meet Maria.

Summer Barn

                              *   *   *

"The day after tomorrow I have an appointment with Bogdan in Kiev. By Stalin's mustache, he is now anxious to see us." Szmuel jubilantly greeted us as we shook hands. We took off our shoes, as custom dictated, and situated ourselves on the sofa. "I just received another call from Igor. I sweetened him up. In turn, he assured me that everything will be all right and that our little business is on the right track. Igor expressed regrets for not being with us at Ozero. He also apologized for the ransacking of our van that evening. He will make sure that the revolver is returned to us."

Szmuel was not the intimidated, scared Szmuel of yesterday that Marek described to me prior to our coming here.

Szmuel walked out to the kitchen. Marek turned to me and, with his lips mussing my ear, whispered in English, "Can't believe that this is the same Szmuel. I know that he is mercurial but what do you make of this apparent niceness on the part of Bogdan and Igor? What brought this about? Yesterday, Szmuel was worried sick." And then, loud enough so that Szmuel could hear him in the kitchen, Marek asked, "What did Igor say about Bogdan and me? If you and Igor cannot arrange a meeting between us, I will contact Igor or, even better, Bogdan directly."

Excited, Marek now yelled out as he switched from Russian to English which came easier to him when upset. "Come on Szmuel, I reimbursed you for finding Bogdan. I demand first consideration. Your additional dealings with Igor and Bogdan trouble me."

"Relax, Marek. You will meet your brother. Here, first we will toast." Szmuel came back from the kitchen and handed us shots of cognac. He continued, not looking at us. His eyes focused on the diminutive Mrs. Szmuel who unobtrusively came in and sat by us on the sofa.

"Bogdan *does* want to see you, Marek, but Igor was quite adamant that I should not bring you with me tomorrow. Igor told me that Bogdan wants to welcome his brother properly and does not want our little business session to interfere with a family reunion. Igor also cautioned me not to reveal Bogdan's identity at this time, even to you, Marek."

Szmuel shifted his head toward us but looked down, not meeting our eyes.

"These rich *zuliks* can be very persuasive and assertive. Bogdan is business, all business. Even the contribution that he promised to make to the poor Jews—he considers it 'business.' Ha, ha, ha. I am the only one who knows who he really is. I must remember not to address him as Bogdan. He sure was startled and furious when I first called him and intimated that he was Bogdan."

Szmuel laughed as only he could do, with his stomach shaking and his palms rubbing each other. It was a hearty laugh, as if he envisioned thousands of grivne passing through his hands. However, I didn't think that Bogdan's philanthropic contribution was a cause for frivolity. Something had occurred since our debacle at Ozero to so alter Szmuel's mood.

Marek thought that Bogdan was attempting to befriend Szmuel in order to gain his good will as well as the incriminating NKVD documents. Szmuel told us that Bogdan had simply volunteered to give money to the poor Jews of Lwów because he wanted to impress his half- brother by appearing charitable. As I learned later, alas too late, it was a sordid scheme by Szmuel to extort a fortune from Bogdan. It was a crude black mail: Bogdan promised to pay a lot of money for the incriminating NKVD dossier and for Szmuel's silence. At that time, neither Marek nor I knew that a carefully negotiated deal between Szmuel and Bogdan had already been agreed upon and that it was to be consummated in Kiev. For now, it was Szmuel's show, and he relished it. As the saying goes: Gods make their victim mad before killing him.

"Ha, ha, ha. If Batko Stalin was alive, he would certainly commend me for my cleverness. I have Bogdan by the balls," Szmuel laughed even longer and louder with his mouth opened wide.

I have seen older people with golden teeth in Ukraine but Szmuel had a wealth of them. I was never fond of Szmuel and considered his mannerisms to be quaint at best, but at that point, his overbearing joviality became abhorrent to me. I had an uneasy feeling in my gut. The room itself was enough to make me feel that way: The bust of an unsmiling Lenin stared at us from atop Szmuel's desk. A tattered red banner with a brownish yellow hammer and sickle emblem draped over an ornate standing coat rack. Faded, three-inch, yellow triangles made of cloth were framed under glass and now hung on the wall behind Lenin. At one time, they were worn by an Obóz Janowski inmate, just like the one that Karol wore sewn to his camp uniform. All these were grim symbols of man's inhumanity toward men. But Szmuel continued his outpouring of levity and self-congratulation.

"Can't wait to see my poor Jews eating caviar for breakfast and stewed duck for dinner. Even tender young *kurki*. Get it, Maria? Little chickens. I think in America they call them 'pee-wees.' Those poor old Jews have no teeth and will enjoy the soft meat."

Perhaps the image of the toothless old wretches brought Szmuel back to reality because he became serious. Turning to Marek, he said, "Bogdan doesn't want you to come with me, but it is better that you do come, Marek. You must come. Absolutely."

Marek, who was sitting on the couch next to me, was deep in his thoughts, as if in a world of long ago. After all, he came back to Lwów to learn about Natalia. He was hoping that Lesia was alive and could be located. And then, most importantly, there was the shred of possibility of meeting his half-brother. He must have been recalling the tales that Karol told him about Hryniu and his childhood memories of Bogdan; once a neighborhood friend, now his brother. I was sure that Marek was thinking back to the days when Bogdan was his friend, when they fashioned tiny boats and played with lead soldiers together. It would be so characteristic of my beloved Marek to give Bogdan the benefit of the doubt, especially considering the overpowering events that might have influenced Bogdan in his deplorable past. At that time, we did not know the worst about Bogdan. Had Marek known what I later learned, this tableau in Szmuel's dreary room would not have taken place.

"It will be good to have Marek with me in Kiev. Bogdan will face his Jewish ancestry. He will be more accommodating."

"But, Szmuel, I don't understand. What do you mean 'accommodating'? Didn't Bogdan say—," I started to express my fears about this enterprise. I did not trust Szmuel's motives nor did I believe his words.

"No. No, *Kureczka*. You and Marek need to relax."

Szmuel gave me that pet name the first time we met at the archives. At first I found this nickname demeaning but after he explained with a charming smile that I am as delicious as a young chicken, the local food delicacy, I did not protest.

" No, *Kureczka*. We will have our two *ganiffs* with us for protection." He meant our two bodyguards.

"But you, *Kureczka*, cannot come with us. Bogdan must believe that only Marek and I know about his past. That ugly past is surely pinching him, like Stalin's corset. Of course, you must know that later in life old Joe wore a corset to look fitting in his marshal's outfit."

At the constant mention of the dictator's name, whatever remained of Stalin must have been churning in its grave. I mused about the murderer Stalin for a moment and equally sinister thoughts invaded my brain. Szmuel the Mercenary and Bogdan the Brutal could make an explosive concoction: a Molotov cocktail. Damn it. Foreign minister Molotov was one of Stalin's most subservient flunkies. Why did Stalin have to pop up again? This time it was me, not Szmuel, who thought of the brutal dictator. My history-trained subconsciousness recalled the famous weapon of World War II: a bottle of gasoline, well-shaken into emulsion, with air and a rag for a fuse. Light the fuse and throw. A powerful ball of fire enveloped many a German vehicle that way.

Szmuel suddenly turned serious, "Bogdan must dispose of his NKVD dossier if he is to save his life. The descendants of Misko and of others whom he betrayed to Soviet authorities would kill him. Remember those mutilated corpses they have been finding in Lwów's Kaiserwald for the past two or three years? They found another one recently. People speculated that it was revenge against those who were working for the Soviets during the Ukrainian insurrection. You and I know what they would do to him, Marek, especially if they learn that he is a Jew. All of his money would not help him. Most likely he would be killed by his own crowd."

Szmuel was now addressing himself directly to Marek, who finally stirred, put his arm around me, and brought me closer to him. While we pressed against each other reassuringly, Szmuel paced rapidly about the room with his head pointed in our direction, waving his hands in agitation. He sensed that I would not let Marek go without me.

"Marek, you must tell *Kureczka* that she will be in danger. Bogdan must not learn that another person knows about his ugly past. You are his brother. Likely, he will learn to trust you. The day after tomorrow you will know about Natalia and maybe, if Bogdan genuinely regrets his misdeeds, you will gain a brother. Me, he will not trust, but he knows by now that I am a reasonable businessman." He stressed "businessman" by giving it a good American pronunciation.

As if on cue, Boris, the senior *ganiff*, walked in and took Szmuel to the side. He whispered something in rapid Russian. All I gathered from it was "minivan" and "have to repair." Without the minivan they will not be able to drive to Kiev tomorrow, I thought. There was something ominous about that trip and I hoped for postponement. Perhaps another day or two and Marek would be able to talk to Bogdan on the phone and find out if really Bogdan desired to meet him.

The whispers became a rapid, loud discussion concerning a malfunctioning carburetor and possible causes for its sudden break down. Who could repair it overnight? It appeared that their trusted repairman was away in Brody for his sister's wedding. They would have to resort to another mechanic.

"Check with the new garage opposite where you live, Boris. It will be convenient for us. We could pick it up easily when they fix it, and then we will be on our way," concluded Szmuel.

While they were still arguing about the merits of the new garage, I pulled Marek from the sofa and pushed him toward the door. I had had enough of Szmuel, of Bogdan, and of the stern Lenin looking down upon us. All I wanted was to be out of these cheerless surroundings and back in amongst violets and *varenniki* at the Novikovs' apartment.

"Marek, you must be ready tomorrow at six in the morning. Boris will pick you up. And Moris will take you home now to the Novikovs," were Szmuel's final instructions.

We did not wait for Moris to escort us, but opened Szmuel's door into the pitch-black staircase and slammed it behind. Then, step by step, holding onto the banister, we carefully descended three flights into the street.

Without saying a word, we walked down the dimly lit streets hand in hand, my fingers interwoven with the stumps of Marek's fingers. We climbed three flights of another very dark stairwell to the Novikovs' door. Vladya identified us by peeking through the slit. He opened one lock with a key and slid off a thick bolt. He opened another lock and the door was finally ajar, although still secured by a heavy chain. Vladya peeked at us again. When absolutely satisfied, he unhooked the chain. We were inside our haven. While Vladya busied himself in securing the door again, we took off our shoes for the last time that day.

*　　*　　*

In our violet-filled room, sitting on our rickety bed, Marek prolonged his silence. That night, he was not Tarzan and I was not Jane. He was in serious contemplation of coming events. I was silent and worried, but the whiff of odor that came from under my arm made me think of a bath.

"I need a bath," I told Marek, "You know you will have to help me."

The mention of a bath jarred Marek from his trance, and a feeble smile appeared on his face.

I am sure that all lovers throughout the world have fond memories of bathing together, sensual recollections of their naked bodies, partly submerged in warm water, pressing against each other in varying positions—sitting, laying, standing—as they scrubbed each other's backs and soaped each other's bodies.

As I write these words, I cannot help but to think of Professor McKenzie's inspired lectures on Roman history. He would pace the floor in front of us students as he described the decadence, treachery, brutality and, yes, luxury in the lives of the Roman upper classes during Emperor Caracalla's era. His favorite dissertation centered around the symbol of those "good" times: the Baths of Caracalla. As a tourist, I visited the ruins of this imposing edifice, and forever after, I aspired to luxuriate in a small, ornate, marble pool that could be filled with lots of water of just the right temperature. I was greedy in my fantasy because I also visualized a personal slave who would soap, scrub, rinse, and towel me.

Most certainly, the bath at the Novikovs' has nothing in common with the baths of Caracalla. The Novikovs' bath cannot even claim kinship with most Western European baths and I doubt whether something like it exists today in the United Sates. Yes, a bath at the Novikovs' was an experience without an equal, especially with Marek as my slave.

I had to admit to myself that I was no longer the shy "goodie-two-shoes" from a decade ago. I had changed dramatically, especially in Lwów. I had become much more worldly and outgoing. Intimacy with Marek added conflicting traits to my personality: I became serious and utterly realistic, but also childishly joyful and much more receptive to life's pleasures. The transformation was startling to me. I even used words that would have made me blush a short while earlier.

My vulgarity was particularly evident in the Novikovs' bath. I even exceeded Marek in pungently expressing my sexual desire as I undressed myself. The rags, socks, and underwear that were forever drying on crisscrossed wires suspended from the ceiling, the dangling rubber tubes, and the uninterrupted dripping water all lent themselves to my off-color comments.

The Novikovs' bathroom was five-by-four feet at most. Its four-foot-long tub was situated at the narrow end of the roomette, right under a very large window that looked out to the balcony spanning the back of the apartment house. The glass window would intimidate anyone who tried to fit into the tub; Fortunately, the clear panes had accumulated enough spider webs, cracks, and dirt so that they acted as a screen to shield the bather from the snooping eyes of neighbors who shared the balcony. Even so, I felt like I was being observed whenever a human silhouette appeared beyond the window. At least at night I couldn't tell whether anyone was peeking. Marek wasn't concerned at all. His response was typical, "Let's give them a good show, Maria. Let's make it worth their while." I'm sure we did.

Between the window and the door was a small basin that was once used for washing hands, brushing teeth and the like. The sink faucet began to leak decades ago and was never fixed. The Novikovs had permanently attached the faucet to a black rubber tube that ended inside a bucket placed on the floor. The collected water served to flush the toilet during low water-pressure periods which happened every day with regularity. Each one of us took the bucket from the bathroom to the adjacent toilet room. There we poured the accumulated water on the excrement, hoping it would flush down.

The object that really dominated the bather was a gas heater that hung right over the tub. The flaming gas enveloped a metal coil through which cold water passed, thus making the bath possible. The heater had to be ignited ahead of time, and then the resulting hot water had to be collected in the tub prior to situating oneself in the tub. The unevenly heated water dripped slowly into the tub through a long, red rubber tube. Once the water reached the outflow level, barely covering the thighs of medium-sized person, it was wise to turn off the gas in order not to be scalded by an occasional burst of steam. From then on, one had to be satisfied with slowly cooling water in the tub.

Marek, however, would relight the heater while I was still soaking. He would add hot water and, using the red rubber hose at the end, he would rinse me off. The hose would gurgle, ejaculating its alternately hot and cold contents. Here, Marek the artist showed his ingenuity. He would sense the extremes of temperature while holding the hose and would divert the water away from me. He was good at distributing the pleasantly warm water over the various parts of my body.

I am sure that it was the thought of the rinsing-off process that caused Marek to finally act his normal self, to stand over me as I squeezed, partly submerged, into a fetal position. He caressed me with the dripping end of the hose. The warm spurting water felt good from my neck to my buttocks, from my breasts to my thighs. Being Marek, he gave named the red hose *huy*, Polish for "penis," because it reminded him of the Angus bull's partially inflated member.

That night, I convinced Marek to purify himself, too. This meant that in order to save gas and water, he had to use my tub water and simply add more hot water to it. Then came my turn to rinse him with the "*huy*." In spite of my concerns for the next day, I was as playful with him as he was with me. I became aroused but couldn't budge Marek. He seemed to be back in his blue funk. We went to bed and held each other tightly.

After some minutes, I slid upward in Marek's arms, my breasts at the level of Marek's face. I expected his tongue to fondle my nipples and, as times before, I expected his large, moist lips to engulf my breasts and suck on them. The expectation was elating and for the second time that evening, I felt a surge of wetness between my legs. I also felt the wetness of Marek's tears on my breasts.

"Marek, are you crying? What is wrong? I love you. Marek, I want you."

Marek remained silent and softly sobbed. Why this emotional collapse? Perhaps he thought of us parting at the end of our quest—he returning to America after his trip to Kiev, and I flying back separately months later. Maybe the difference in our ages hit him and suddenly he realized how fragile our future would be. I tried to comfort and reassure him.

"Marek, I love you. I know that I am truly in love. I am happy with you here and now. Marek, I am your woman. Marek, love me. Marek, come to me."

As I was saying these words, I realized that we had no contraception. Strangely, it did not matter that I was not protected. I wanted Marek. I wanted that unique man. Somehow, subconsciously, I was thrilled by the thought of being a mother. After so many years of unfulfilling relationships, I yearned to create something special with the man that I loved so much. I pulled Marek closer to me.

"I love you. You are my man. Be my man. Satisfy us as you did before. I will be forever yours."

With my arms, I pressed him even closer to my breasts. I kissed his head and twined my legs around his hips.

Marek lifted his body, rising ever so slowly. He entered me, and in a slow rhythm, he rubbed my inside, making it even more pleasurable. I felt a profound intimacy: sensual joy, combined with my yearning to have a child with this man. Marek and I began to throb. After all those years, I had finally experienced the sacred ritual of procreation. To make love and to love with tenderness has no equal. Afterwards, we kissed, hugged, clung to each other, and finally fell asleep.

Surrounded by the early morning light and the friendly faces of Vladya and Sara, life looked good to us. It made sense that our quest should finally end, but we made promises to meet in the United States. At the same time, it made sense to me that Marek should not go to Kiev that morning. But the minivan was repaired on time, and Marek did go in spite of my pleas. I was persuaded by everyone to stay behind.

Irka came later that morning to tell me about the tragedy. I prayed that it was not true.

Official news about a vehicle accident near Rovno with four fatalities appeared the next morning. No one survived the accident; fire consumed all. The report speculated that a jerry can full of gasoline somehow caught on fire. I rang the American Embassy in Kiev. Eventually, the local police admitted that a more powerful blast than one possibly caused by a container of gasoline, blew the minivan to smithereens. I went to the morgue and identified Marek's mutilated corpse. I did not need to look at his face. The stumps of fingers on his bloodied left hand were the last thing I saw. My knees buckled under me and I fainted into the outstretched arms of Vasily and Olga.

Marek ended his journey through the galaxies of human beings. Now he navigates in the firmament of suns and planets, not among the multitudes of people. Another cookie crumbled.

That Bogdan engineered the murder of Szmuel and Szmuel's bodyguards was obvious to the few of us privy to Bogdan's background. I wanted to believe that Marek died in the explosion incidentally. Marek died not knowing the critical role that Natalia played in saving his and Karol's lives. Thankfully, neither did he know what a beastly part Bogdan played in robbing and murdering the Jews in Lwów even before joining the SS Galicia.

The investigation of the killings and the shipment of Marek's remains to the USA required all the emotional energy that I had, but, in a way, all that activity numbed my ache. My friendship with Olla was forged; during those terrible days she helped me and she soothed me.

The name of a possibly implicated "important Ukrainian industrialist" was not mentioned officially or in the local press. When the trauma and pain abated somewhat, I took it upon myself to complete Marek's mission.

I wanted to find out about Natalia's fate, during and after the occupation. The historian in me also wanted to reconstruct the events which led Bogdan to join the SS Galicia Division which, in the end, could have brought him face to face with Willi. Before departing from Lwów, I had one final mission here: I wanted to pay respects to the memories of the Bielys and Halya. I was drawn to the quiet surroundings of Lyczakowski Cemetery.

Chapter XI

Willi and Halya

I sat down on a flat, rather unimposing, heavily eroded grave-stone next to a tiny parcel of weedy dirt, enclosed by a low ornamental wrought iron fence with a small gate. Inside the enclosure was the mound of earth covering the remains of Franciszka and Piotr Biely. An amateurishly wrought metal stat-ue of a very bony Jesus Christ on the cross faced the mound. Jesus' head, with a large crown of thorns, hung low, looking down at the mound. Nothing more stood out at the gravesite, except a bouquet of mixed flowers in a blue glass jar weighted with two field stones. Pan Oksan must have visited the grave because the flowers were merely wilted. The site was shaded, letting little sunlight through. It was dark here, cool and quiet, far away from the noisy main entrance. I sat for a long time with my somber thoughts, crying. It seemed that I was totally alone in this vast cemetery with only my memories. Time elapsed, maybe an hour or two, as I sat on the stone. The emotional turmoil inside of me gave way to a dull ache. I halved the bunch of flowers I brought and threw them on the mound. Where was Halya's grave?

Up and down I went, along the twisting paths, among spectac-ular old graven sculptures and large tombs, and came back to the newer section of the cemetery. Here there were no crosses and no religious figures; only emblazoned likenesses or encased photo-graphs of people in their prime were on many of the vertical gravestones. The inscriptions often boasted of the deceased's prominence. This was a burial ground from the Soviet era. Down toward the Polish and Ukrainian military cemeteries was Halya's grave. Not much had changed at her gravesite since our first visit. The rusty can, now overturned, still lay at the bottom of the mound. The forget-me-nots died, and with them the lonely dandelion flower. We were a joyful fivesome when we visited the grave last time. Now I was standing here alone and Marek was gone forever. A tide of sorrow engulfed me again. I scattered on top of the mound the rest of the flowers that I had brought. I had no water for them. I stared at the grave for a few moments without sitting down. Then I turned around to walk away.

Yet, I couldn't leave. It was as if Halya's life story was forcing itself upon me, binding me to her grave with the threads of yesteryears. Halya's past penetrated the austerity and gloom of her grave to reveal to me a young, beautiful woman, who was deeply in love with a vile, but basically compassionate, man. He was a man who suffered, and a man who learned how to hate and how to avenge for the wrongs done unto him. He was a man who probably loved her passionately; a charming, handsome, complex man; a man worthy of an attractive, intelligent, and caring woman such as Halya probably was. Is that what you were trying to tell me Halya, from beyond your grave?

I tried to imagine those traumatic events in June 1941, as if you were standing next to me, Halya, relating them to me. The day before, the Soviet borders were overrun by powerful German motorized columns that caught the Soviet border units in a total surprise and destroyed them. Lwów, reeling under bombardment of the Luftwaffe, was in close proximity of exploding artillery shells. The Soviet army was in retreat, clogging the main thoroughfares leading eastward. These two days and nights you were in the basement of your apartment house, in a bomb shelter. Weren't you, Halya? Your husband Tomek wasn't with you. Why? You heard the clanking of tanks on Lyczakowska Street. You heard the rumble of straining motors of cars and trucks. Then you heard the staccato of machine guns and the bursts of exploding grenades. These were the NKVD internal security troops trying to escape but they were ambushed by Ukrainian paramilitaries. The troops suffered casualties and retreated, not eastward, but back to the center of town. With bitter anger, the NKVD contingents entered the jails that were still in Soviet hands, and slaughtered all the inmates. You didn't know about those atrocities yet. Your thoughts were with two men: Tomek, your decent but dull husband, and Willi, your passionate lover. A door to the shelter opened and in burst a tall Soviet officer, alert with a pistol in his hand. Yes, I know that you recognized him immediately. He saw you and took you by the hand.

"Come, Halya, not a moment to lose. I have a truck with comrades waiting on the street. Come with me. You are the only woman I want, the only one I ever loved. You will be good for me. You can make me into a good man. I beg you, come."

Willi embraced you in his arms and tried to kiss you, right?

"Hear those machine guns burping? These are your people, not Germans. I must flee or they will butcher me. I just committed some unspeakable deeds. I had to take revenge on the Bandera beasts."

Willi sat down and placed the pistol behind his belt. And then looking upward to your face, he begged you. Am I right?

"Come, Halya. You will not regret it. I beseech you Halya. You can restore me to sanity."

That is what he must have said, and you went with him. You had just a few moments to scribble a note to your husband. I like to think that you, Halya, were a truthful person and that you wrote Tomek honestly about your decision. You knew that Tomek loved you, but…

As I recreated in my mind Halya's dramatic escape with Willi, a summer storm came fast upon the cemetery. Lightning flashed against the blue sky and illuminated the neighboring graves. And there it was: a simple rectangular stone that, years ago, had been tilted from its original vertical position by the elements of nature. That tall stone, fashioned of black granite, leaned in my direction. The eerie light created by the storm produced an unusual shadow affect, and outlined the eroded inscription: 31 VI 1911 – 14 XII 1987. The birth date was that of my granduncle, Wilhelm Menke, but the name on the stone was not. The coincidence was overwhelming. So Willi and Halya were in death separated by a mere few yards; lovers even at the end.

*   *   *

What drove Uncle Willi? In his youth, he believed in ideals: a fair deal for the working class, absence of hatred among the people of the world, acceptance of people as individuals based on their own merits. Justice and freedom? Perhaps. I never will know. Those graveyard sculptures—stones and crosses—guard the secrets well. I want to believe that Wilhelm Menke was a fine individual who, however, was imbued with hatred against those guilty of tormenting him. He served that one master who abetted vengeance and brutality in return for utter obedience: Stalin. How dare my family remember fondly Uncle Gerhard who also served a brutal master! Hitler, too, demanded unquestionable service, which Gerhard gave him. Is it because Gerhard died and Willi lived? Are we so angelic as to condemn Willi for his role on behalf of the Communist Party, to sentence him to oblivion, to destroy his memory, while speaking fondly of Gerhard?

In this eerie light of the summer storm, the thousands of grave markers were indeed sentinels guarding the secrets buried with their dead charges. Way, way above them, swirling in the galactic torrents lie the souls whom Uncle Willi either helped on this earth or sent to hell. Let the heavenly balance weigh the good against the evil that Willi accomplished. All I know is that he loved and was loved by a worthy woman. That says a lot for him.

It began raining severely, and I was soaked and dripping. The raindrops and my tears mixed on my cheeks and tasted salty.

The emotional impact of Marek's death and of subsequent events is still so severe that, even now, I cannot describe it. My curiosity persisted, however. While I was still in Lwów, I determined to learn something about Sergei Velikyi, alias Wilhelm Menke.

After I unearthed the name that Willi used during his last sojourn in Lwów, I hoped to learn more about him and Halya. My time in Lwów was running short and so was my emotional stamina.

I did learn, and I am glad. Halya indeed escaped with Willi into the recesses of the Soviet Union. But, sometime in 1943, in the middle of the mighty struggle against Germany, Halya was arrested somewhere in Asia. It was impossible to learn why. Reasons for arrests were easily fabricated in those times. Perhaps it was because she was a Ukrainian from Lwów or because she simply didn't want to accommodate a local Lothario. She disappeared into the gigantic punitive system of gulags and jails, without ability to communicate with anyone. Willi erroneously assumed that, in the turmoil that was war, Halya had discarded him for another man. Twenty-three years later, when the Soviet Union began to crumble, Halya was released and returned to Lwów. Tomek was gone, and the few relatives she once had had disappeared. She began a life of economic and emotional struggle alone, as a ghost from the past. Fortunately, she maintained her married name. Thus, when Willi was cashiered from the GDR and pensioned off as a former NKVD officer, he looked for her and found her in Lwów. For nearly two decades they lived inconspicuously, avoiding any political or community involvements. One of the very few neighbors still living who remembered them told me that they must have been deeply in love.

"He was tall and very dignified. She was nice and trim. She dressed simply but with flair." The neighbor woman told me with detectable envy. I did not wonder, seeing the shabbily dressed, corpulent babushka in front of me.

"They were in love and they kept to themselves. They were happy together. They went to markets together, they stood in queues together. They took walks together." The babushka stopped and sighed.

"I wish that they were friendlier to me. You know, I wish they talked more to me. When she died, he became totally withdrawn, a hermit. He was a German, you know. His Ukrainian and Russian were good, but everybody could tell that he was a foreigner. Of course, he might have been a Jew. No, if he were a Jew he would have had money. But he lived from his pension, like the rest of us."

"How did he die?" I interposed.

"Quickly, and without a fuss, shortly after she did." Here babushka became pensive. I let her think.

"You know, he did have special connections. Two foreign men, I guess German, came and arranged the funeral and must have paid for the stone. None of us in this house could have afforded such a luxury. Yes, now I remember. As sick as he was in his last few days, he took a taxi to the post office, probably to phone someone. Do you think he called a relative abroad or a former comrade?"

As his life was ebbing away, did he really attempt to reach Grandma Menke, who had already immigrated to America? Grandma never mentioned whether or not Willi called. Her silence would not be surprising because for a long time she did suppress the "Willi File."

Chapter XII

Bogdan, the Flawed Son

When Marek was alive, he especially wanted to know Natalia's fate. Marek always felt affection for Natalia because of her civility toward him when he visited Bogdan in the Kapista's apartment, but more so because she helped him and Karol during the hiding. The story of how affectionately Natalia ministered to Karol during his siege with typhoid fever has affected me profoundly. This story defined for me the essence of devotion and love by a woman for a man, no matter how dire the circumstances. After years of trying with many men, I finally experienced with Marek the selfless dedication and the enhanced thrill of love. When we were still together, we took for granted that Natalia was dead. We hoped that the last years of gentle Natalia's life were not unpleasant and that her death was easy. My premonition at that time, and perhaps that of Marek, indicated otherwise. About Bogdan, I knew already a lot of bad things, but not everything. My intuition that Bogdan was a biblical Cain gave me no respite. I had to know. Perhaps I could shed more light on Bodgan's vicious and immortal personality. Perhaps, I could even learn something positive about Bogdan. But, how? Natalia's daughter, Lesia, might have some answers. If only she could tell her story. I vowed to find Lesia, if she was alive.

Certainly, Bogdan should have known the fates of Natalia, Lesia, and Pan Kapista, but would he tell anyone anything about his past? Of course not. I would not have had the stomach to approach him even if I knew the name he used. Without

Szmuel, Boris, or Moris, I could not know Bogdan's true identity. There were too many oligarchs and criminal syndicates in Ukraine. Probing into Bogdan's past could have been fatal for me in Ukraine. I surmised that if Lesia Kapista was alive, she could be induced to talk. It was reasonable to think that Lesia knew who Bodgan was and where he lived. I could not tell what I would do with that information, but in my gut, I wanted to know.

Lesia was the only possible witness to those events of the last winter of the German occupation of Lwów, the tragic winter of 1943-44. Lesia Kapista, Bogdan's half-sister and Natalia's legitimate daughter, surely had witnessed a great deal. At least she could tell me what induced Bogdan to join the SS Galicia.

I had already learned that the Kapista family, with the exception of Bogdan, had run away before the Red Army troops arrived in July of 1944. It was logical to assume that if Lesia was still alive, she would be in Austria.

The escape from Lwów must have been a jarring experience for the Kapistas. My uncle Gerhard, a member of the Waffen SS who was near Lwów that summer, wrote an introspective letter home which focuses on the flight of families such as the Kapistas. It is fanciful of me to imagine that the girl Gerhard befriended at that time was Lesia, but no, that would have been impossible. Lesia Kapista was twelve years old then. Gerhard describes an older Ukrainian girl, albeit in a similar circumstance.

Uncle Gerhard's letter reveals the paradox and the pathos of those days: the foolish optimism of many of the Germans and the avalanche of terror that was engulfing those who collaborated with them.

> *...Everyday we realize more strongly that the war must end quickly. We must employ radical measures before it is too late. In the future, history will admire the nation that survives in this immense struggle. History will absolve us of some of the necessary actions. Our enemies would do*

the same if they ever broke through to our homeland. I think that you do understand me.

We Germans cannot make a choice similar to that of the Italians. As for us here at the front, we intend to muster for every situation, no matter what the demands may be; yes, muster the strength and optimism that have always characterized the German soldier.

It is heartening for us to know that the local Ukrainian people look upon us as saviors from the Judeo-Bolshevik threat. Their men now fight the Soviets side by side with us under the same SS standard. Unfortunately, the families of our Ukrainian comrades and many other Ukrainians are suffering now. They are fleeing in fear of the Bolsheviks. Many lorries and even horse-drawn carts filled with scanty possessions drive westward on the roads. I do what I can to help and to inspire them with hope. Surely, within a few weeks we will strike mightily and will regain our positions around "L" and with new weapons manufactured by the homeland, we will win the war.

You will remember from my last letter the Ukrainian family I was friendly with in "L." Well, they have already left for Vienna. They hope to wait out the war there and then to return to "L." I gave them the address of our relatives in Vienna in case they need some assistance. You are probably wondering why I am concerned with that one family. Well, as you might guess, it is a woman, a girl, actually. With death constantly around the corner, I finally gave in to temptation and I am not sorry for it.

A few weeks ago, you should have received two packages from me: one with a can of meat and a can of butter, the other just with butter. I don't know when I will be able to send you anything again. But now, I must give this letter to a comrade who was lightly wounded and now goes on

*leave. He will mail it to you in Germany. Don't worry
about me, but do write to me. Your letters are important
to my well-being. You can be sure that I will do my duty.*

Your loving son, Gerhard

Uncle Gerhard indeed did his duty. This was one of his last
letters to the family. He was killed in action a few weeks after he
wrote it. I also did my duty. I contributed to the knowledge of this
fine but tragic town: Lwów, Lviv, Lemberg. It was time for me to
leave. I stashed Gerhard's letter together with Marek's memoirs
and chronicles and other important documents to take along
with me. I boxed up the rest of the papers dealing with my
research and left them with the Ivan Franco University to be
shipped later. I was going home, but on the way I had to try to
find Lesia. Austria seemed like the best bet.

*   *   *

I took an overnight train from Lwów to Budapest in
Hungary, and then a bus to Vienna. By now, the trains and
public facilities of Eastern Europe no longer shocked me. Not
all were terribly bad, but you could not count on a clean restroom. I brought my own toilet paper and hand cleanser for this
trip, and I did not look at the filth. I felt lucky to find a seat
attached to the stool in the W.C. of my sleeping car. The train
rocked. I had to roll up the legs of my pants before I squatted
so that the hems would not dangle in the stinking, sloshing liq-
uid that pooled on the floor. At least on the train there were
no ever-present attendants to demand coins for the use of the
restroom and to charge me for paper by the piece. The cleanli-
ness of my Pullman compartment was trivial in comparison to
some concrete joys in passing from East to West. I was served
hot, boiling tea in glasses fitted into ornate metal holders, and
I slept on laundered bed sheets; they were starched and pressed
to perfection.

The passport checks on Eastern trains and border crossings reminded me of travel in the war years, and I hadn't even been there. I hadn't even been born. But, all my reading and research sparked my imagination when I crossed from Ukraine to Poland. It was the middle of the night, pitch-black, and the train had stopped. Marching sounds came from the corridor outside my sleeping compartment. There were barking voices and someone wailed in agony. Shouts. The sound of a door opening and slamming. More marching. Then loud knocking on my compartment door. Someone demanded in Polish for my passport. The border guard examined it, page by page, under a glaring light torch. He ran the magnetic strip of my American passport through a contraption on his belt and asked in broken English about my reason for traveling to Poland. I was so intimidated that if I had been involved in anything illegal, my face would have given me away. I wondered what had happened to the unfortunate person whose cry I had heard minutes earlier. Had some illegal stow-away been caught and ousted from the train? I thought back to a time some fifty years ago when many persons almost made it to the "free" border before being detected. Those unfortunates were turned back to German-occupied territory, thus sealing their terrible fate as tragic victims of Hitler's Final Solution.

My train journey from Ukraine to Hungary was by far less traumatic. In Budapest, I transferred to a bus bound for Vienna. After umpteen hours of travel and one last border and passport check in Austria, the bus arrived at the central station in Vienna. I felt so exhausted and crusty from the long hours of tense travel that I did not know how I would be able to muster up the energy I would need for the coming quest. From my window seat, I could see the signs on family businesses, evidence of centuries during which Vienna received immigrants from the east and south: Slama Gallery, Kerekes Electrics, Zaleski Books, Dolenko Meats. Although I can read the Cyrillic alphabet used to write in Russian and Ukrainian, my eyes were always happy to return to the familiar Latin alphabet used in English, Polish, German, and the Romance languages. It was so easy to scan shop signs and street signs and advertisements. My tired brain found it easy to process the information. I kept looking for "Kapista," as if by some miracle it would be easy to find Lesia.

The bus station did not reflect the cosmopolitan population of Vienna. The station was filled with gypsies. Mothers carried babies in slings while girls and boys ran among the passengers, hands outstretched, tugging at sleeves and handbags. I brushed past all of them, ignoring their pleas, and went immediately to the telephones and opened a directory.

What tremendous luck! I found Lesia's uncommon Slavic name was under the Ks in the telephone directory. How lucky for me that she never married, or that for some reason she had retained her family name. There was only one "Kapista" listed, and there was an "L" as the first initial. It had to be Lesia.

I figured out how to use the phone. Every country had its own system to master, be it special coins or cards. I was glad to be in the bus station, which had all the necessary components to make a call. I remembered being in Poland, being told to get a special card at a post office, finding the post office, waiting in line, being told to go to another line for a phone card, and finally obtaining the card only to have to walk back blocks to the public phone, which did not work. I dialed the number for "L Kapista" and then again, and again and again. There was no answer. Even the gypsy children gave up pestering me once they realized I was not an easy target and would not give them my change. I ran out of coins and walked into Nordsee, a seafood chain restaurant.

After ordering a 'Tee mit Rum', I sat down near an elderly cou-ple who looked rather out of place among the Formica tables and bright lights. They wore traditional Austrian dress, perhaps they were on their way to a celebration. The woman wore a dirndl; the man wore a wool vest and a feathered hat hung from a hook in the corner. I shook my head and wondered once again if I was in a time warp. I added more sugar than usual to my tea with rum, and felt the concoction warm my weary body.

Half an hour later, I tried Lesia again. Ten tries and another hour later, Lesia answered. I told her that I was an American historian writing about Lwów. I didn't give her my reasons for the call. I told her that I learned about her family and about the heroism of Bogdan through a chance acquaintance living on their old street, Lyczakowska. I had to prevaricate because I feared that the atrocious treachery of Bogdan as an NKVD informer would be so painful to Lesia that she would clam up. My rehearsed introduction had no effect. She adamantly told me that she did not want to see me. She was unmoved by my story and was not interested in talking about Lemberg. "Nein, nein, nein." No, and that's final.

I played my trump card. "Marek sent me," I stated gravely. Lesia gasped. She was speechless for several long moments, and then burst out with a staccato of questions about Marek and his father. She wanted to know everything that I knew. I satisfied her immediate curiosity with half-truths, saying nothing about Marek's death. I asked her about Natalia. She sighed.

"My mother is dead, of course. But why don't you come over tomorrow."

We agreed on the time, and I anxiously waited for the next day to arrive. A taxi took me to a small hotel where I had stayed once before, during my days as a graduate student. Then, I took a long walk to clear my head and to help pass the hours. I lingered near some sausage stands where old men gathered to swap stories and drink beer. I felt Marek at my side, and knew he would not have been able to resist stopping and purchasing one or two Hungarian Debreziner sausages filled with horseradish. He would have been as hungry for European street culture, for company of the local people and for conversation, as he was for the spicy European meat and good bread. I was tempted by the aroma, but the tourist in me wanted a *Wienerschnitzel*. Around the next corner, I chanced upon the Stephansplatz, looked up, and saw the brightly tiled roof of the monumental St. Stephen's Cathedral against the gray, cloudy sky. I walked in.

I am not a regular churchgoer, but the cathedral's grandeur affected me profoundly. I sat down and looked upward at the great Gothic arches. The weight of the events of the past few weeks bore down on me, and a searing sadness swept through me. Seeing light through the highest windows, I wondered when I would feel relief. My only consolation was that Marek died so suddenly that he should have felt no pain or suffering. I prayed that he had died a happy man. The words escaped unintentionally from my lips: "God grant him peace and please make me strong."

That evening, I had my *Wienerschnitzel* in a colorful ethnic restaurant and drank a stein of local beer, while a costumed accordionist played folk songs. After a fitful sleep, I met Lesia in the morning. She lived on the other side of the Danube, away from the city center, in one of the city's newer suburban districts. It seemed sterile and lacked the charm of the older neighborhoods. The taxi driver, realizing that I was a tourist, took me past the giant ferris wheel at the Prater before driving to Lesia's apartment house.

Lesia was a small, trim woman with a badly wrinkled face. Although she looked to be in her seventies, her voice was clear and strong, her movements were resolute, and her handshake was firm. She looked me in the eyes a long time before we sat down at the kitchenette table in complete silence. Her eyes were intelligent and searching, though sad. She closed her eyes, composing herself for a while and then, out of the blue, softly said, "I wonder what you would call my relationship to Marek. I am not Marek's sister, am I?"

Prior to meeting her, I imagined that Lesia had some inkling about Karol and Natalia, although I did not know how much she knew. Still, her direct, unembellished question startled me. I did not have a ready answer. I started to mumble something about Marek and Bogdan being childhood friends. I wondered how to indicate that her "brother" was really a half-brother both to her and to Marek, but Lesia did not wait to be answered. Hers was a rhetorical question. She knew about Karol and Natalia. She plunged into her memories.

"War was a tragic experience for us all," she began. "You may not know that I am named after our heroine, Lesia Ukrainka, the late nineteenth-century writer who did a great deal to promote the Ukrainian language. My father was an ardent Ukrainian nationalist but not my mother. My father was absolutely elated when Germans occupied Lviv."

Lesia pronounced "Lviv" softly, as if she were speaking Ukrainian to me. Actually, she spoke in High German. She must have been well educated in Austria and felt comfortable speaking German.

"My father's joy affected all of us. We were sure that Ukraine would become an independent state under German protection, and that cities like Lviv, where Polish culture once dominated, would be rightfully recovered by Ukrainian nationalists. We hoped for an independent Ukraine. However, Bogdan was much more influenced by my father than were my mother and I. At home, my father used to grumble about how Jews—like our Jewish landlords, the Manns—were buying up all the property and were running the city and squeezing out Ukrainians. But he was politic enough to be polite in public until the Germans came. On the whole, he was not very talkative anyway. I remember when Marek came in pre-German days to play with Bogdan. My father avoided Marek as if he were diseased, and always left the room. Not my mother. My mother was always kind to Marek, especially whenever my father was not present. Marek even came to us during the first few weeks of the German occupation, but then my father yelled at my mother and threatened to call the Ukrainian militia to take care of "that dirty little Jew." The next time Marek wanted to enter our apartment, mother obediently shut the door in his face. Bogdan watched but did not intervene. I'm sorry to say that I just watched and accepted it, too. I was merely a child, but I can't forget that I didn't do anything to help. I felt sorry for Marek."

Lesia paused and looked down at the floor.

"What was the occupation like for you?" I wanted her to relax a little and thought that it might help to move the topic briefly away from Marek. I wanted to know about Natalia and Bogdan. As if reading my thoughts, Lesia plunged ahead into her family's tragedy. Clearly, this was a topic she had been dwelling on repeatedly over the years, decades after the war had ended.

"Of course, on that horrible day in December 1943, I learned the reason for my mother's niceness to Marek. I am convinced that my father did not know about her relationship with Karol before the occupation. Perhaps even later, when we moved to Austria, he never learned about Mama's love for Karol. Certainly, my father had no inkling that Bogdan was not his son. I kept the secret knowing that my father would kill Mama if he knew. In Vienna, my father became so embittered by the German defeat and by our refugee status that hatred and frustration seethed inside him. Like always, he said very little, but once in a great while his hot venom would erupt. In those moments, he was capable of the worst violence. His only consolation in the remaining years of his life was his belief that Bogdan died killing the hated Soviets. Bogdan became my father's idol. Tell me what you have heard of Bogdan's death. What are the people in Lviv saying? Did he really die a hero? I heard something to the contrary from one of the emigrants who came to Austria after the War. I do not know what to believe. What have you learned?"

I hesitated, not knowing what to say. Fortunately, Lesia was too absorbed in telling her story to wait for an answer. It was like she had silently rehearsed her painful story to herself so many times that she was relieved to finally say it out loud to another human being.

"Actually, I liked Marek. I was a brash little girl of seven or eight, while Marek was a shy little boy of about ten. Marek took some liberties with me but did not go too far. On the other hand, Kazik, the other little boy in our apartment house, was more persistent and ventured farther. So it was. Those weren't bad days in Poland or even under Soviets."

Lesia raised her hands to her head and massaged her temples with her fingers. Then, she placed her hands back on the table and looked at me as if seeing me for the first time.

"You want to know about Bogdan? Is he important to your history?"

Once more, without waiting for an answer she began.

"Bogdan liked Marek, at least he did in the beginning. When my father forbade Marek to come up to us, Bogdan went down to the Mann's apartment to play with Marek but that did not last long either. Because of my father's views and the German propaganda, Bogdan began to dislike Jews. He saw how Jews were being beaten and robbed without resisting. He lost respect for the Jews and began to take advantage of the Manns and other Jews in our area. For example, since Jews would not often go out of their apartments into the street, Bogdan would run errands for them and charge large amounts of money for his services. He associated more frequently with Misko and some older Ukrainian boys in the neighborhood. These boys roamed in town together and became inseparable. To Mama's despair, Bogdan spent less and less time at home. When he did come home, his breath smelled of alcohol and his behavior was insolent. Because of the special love she had for Bogdan and perhaps because of the guilt she carried, Mama did not complain to father about Bogdan's misbehavior.

"In any case, my father was frequently absent from home; he traveled on behalf of some German agency. What work he did was unclear to me. All I knew was that his job was important and that it helped the German war effort. Bogdan always had cash. He showed me a camera once, another time a gold watch and a pearl ring. He said he got them from Jews. How he obtained these and other precious articles he did not say. Mama was in agony suspecting that he and the other boys were stalking Jews and robbing them, perhaps beating them and even killing them. She had no power over Bogdan. He sensed it and became more arrogant. Bogdan was always a good big brother to me and I respected and loved him. But by the time that he was seventeen, his insolence and drunkenness grated on me, and my affection and esteem for him lessened."

Lesia continued recounting what she observed early during the German occupation of Lviv.

"In the summer of 1943, Ukrainian militiamen led by a plain-clothed German policeman entered Pani Yanka's apartment.

Pani Yanka was our neighbor on the first floor. Shrieks and a woman's cries were heard throughout the house. Mama, Bogdan, and I came out to the balcony just in time to see Pani Yanka and Pan Szapiro, her Jewish lover, being prodded with rifles, through the courtyard to the street. Mother and I were dumbfounded to see Tusiek. That is what Pani Yanka called Pan Szapiro. Anyway, Pani Yanka had evidently been hiding her lover-coworker in her apartment all these months. They lived in such close proximity to us, and yet neither my mother nor I suspected she had been hiding anyone. They stood in the yard, holding hands. Both of them wore their white dental coats, but the coats were reddened with blood. The militiamen had beaten them without mercy. Pan Szapiro's head was bleeding profusely. Pani Yanka dragged her bum leg; she was barely able to walk. Mama couldn't stand the sight and went inside to our kitchen. She sat down on a stool and covered her face with her hands. But Bogdan watched intently, his eyes gleamed strangely, as if he savored the tragedy. I looked at him and could not believe that this was Bogdan, my brother. Somebody must have informed on Pani Yanka, but who? Could it have been Bogdan or Misko? My mother cried. Hers were not soft, gentle tears. They were tears of anguish as her body convulsed with grief and disbelief. I tried to console her but all to naught. Her pain came from the depth of her being. I am sure she was thinking of the terrible danger that Karol was in, and of the flawed son they had begot."

"Are you comfortable? " Lesia asked me. I nodded and she continued.

"This was the time that I began to dislike Bogdan. My hatred for him began later when he came home tipsy in the winter of 1943-44, saying that he had confirmed that Jew Mann and Jew Marek were hidden at Franciszka's, a few blocks away from us. Upon hearing that, my mother trembled, lost her balance, stumbled, and collapsed onto the sofa. Bogdan, sensing his emotional supremacy over Mama, proudly went on to tell us that he had suspected something odd at Pani Franciszka's for some time. Bogdan had been playing soccer on the lot abutting Franciszka's house when he saw a person standing next to the window in a room that was not supposed to be occupied. That happened once again, which made him very suspicious. So, he audaciously barged into Franciszka's apartment and confronted no less a person than their former landlord: Karol Mann. He came home and yelled to us, 'I found Jew Mann there with stinking Marek skulking behind. That Jew even wanted to touch me with his filthy hand. Phew. It's disgusting!' Bogdan wouldn't stop. 'He is there and we will get rid of him. Screw Jews! Kill those rich sons-of-bitches. They and the damned Poles bled us Ukrainians for centuries, and now we'll finally get rid of these vermin once and for all!' he screamed. Oh, I remember Bogdan's angry outpourings very well. They stuck in my memory and haunt me even today."

Lesia took a deep breath.

"What happened?" I asked, hearing my own voice quiver.

"At Bogdan's vicious words, my mother completely broke down, prostrating herself on the sofa. She sobbed, uttering, 'Bogdan, Bogdan, Bogdan,' over and over again. But Bogdan rattled on, spewing hatred. He bragged that it was he and Misko who had informed on Pani Yanka and the Jew Szapiro. 'Tomorrow we will go to the militia,' he boasted, 'and they will apprehend Mann and those pathetic old Poles, the Bielys. We'll be rid of them, and be rewarded for it, too. Don't you dare interfere!' Bogdan advanced toward my mother. Now standing above her, he threateningly waved a finger at her."

Lesia's eyes became moist and her voice altered as she imitated her mother. "Bogdan, Bogdan, Bogdan. Don't do it! Don't do it! Have mercy. Remember Marek. Marek is hidden there also. You liked Marek. He was your friend. You played together here, and at his house, too. They will take him with his father and will shoot him."

Lesia lowered her voice; it became harsh while she looked stonily at the floor.

"Bogdan was somewhat taken aback, but then he yelled even more threatening words. 'Jews, we must kill them, that vermin. I don't care what you say! They are Jews and they must not live in the same world with us Ukrainians.' Even today I can see the superior smirk on his face when he said, 'If Papa were here, Papa would be proud of me. He would approve.'"

The soft, pleading voice returned, and Lesia sat up straight on the chair, as her mother must have done on the couch.

"'Bogdan, you don't know,' my mother said. 'If you denounce Karol Mann, you will be murdering your real father.' Bogdan backed away from Mama as if he received a stunning blow on the head. Her words visibly shattered him. The smirk disappeared from his face. At first he swayed under the impact, but then he stood silently erect, apparently digesting the meaning of Mama's words. After some seconds he fell into a chair and a shrill, unintelligible scream came out of him."

Lesia dramatically lowered her voice. To hear her, I pushed my chair closer to hers.

"Bogdan seemed to have wilted, but with a gust of energy, he yelled out again, even louder. Brutal words came out of him. 'Jews, we must bury them in the ground, filthy vermin. I don't care what you say and who they are. To me, they are Jews, and they must not live in the same world with us Christians!' He seemed to have regained his self-assurance. Even today, I can picture the smirk that reappeared on his face when he repeated that if Papa were there, he would be proud of Bogdan and would approve. However, at the mention of Papa, like a lightning bolt, realization struck Bogdan that Papa was not his father. His reaction was a burst of invectives directed toward Mama."

Our shoulders were touching and Lesia's body surged with emotion. She trembled and so did I. Lesia took a deep breath and pain filled her throat.

"'You bitch, you false, whoring bitch! You deserve to die with that Jew! I will kill you both! You fuckin' bitch! I always sensed that you were soft on Jews. I will tell them about you and they will take you too, you shit-smeared cattle!'" Lesia ended in Ukrainian, imitating Bogdan's curses. Then she switched back to German.

"Mama strained to pull herself from the sofa. Her knees were visibly shaking but she got to her feet nevertheless. She stepped forward toward Bogdan, who was sitting, and with all of her strength she smashed his jaw with her fist and then punched him again and again. Bogdan stood up, stunned. Mama had never hit him before. Not pausing, she grabbed him by the hair and brought his face close to hers. Softly, regaining her composure, she whispered, 'Bogdan, you are a Jew. The Germans will kill you, too. Karol would never tell on you even were they to torture him, because he loves you. But if they take them all, Pan Biely is likely to incriminate you in order to save his own life. Both he and Franciszka know about me and Karol. Can't you see? You rat on them and you, too, will die. You are a Jew, Bogdan. To Nazi eyes you are a Jew!' Then my mother let Bogdan's hair go. Bogdan was devastated. He was of medium height but his emotional and physical collapse made him appear to be shorter than me. He fell to his knees and clutched the sofa with his hands. He was a very clever boy and he must have recognized the truth in my mother's words. She sat down on the sofa and caressed his hand with hers. Bogdan abruptly withdrew his hand and quickly stood up. With curses and threats to us, to the Manns, to Jews, to Poles and Soviets, and surprisingly to Germans also, he ran out of the apartment. The next morning, we learned that he had enlisted in the SS Galicia Division. Mama and I never saw him again, but my father did visit him, perhaps twice, telling us about Bogdan's exploits on behalf of Ukraine.

"We understood that he was killed with many other SS men in Rovno. It is a tragedy because Bogdan was a smart and creative boy, perhaps he could have been an artist if the German occupation and our father had not warped his mind. He definitely did have at least part of a Jewish head on his shoulders. Yes, half a Jewish head.

"If only Karol would have contacted Mama after the war. I am being foolish; it was impossible, I know, but—. Did he try to find her? Do you know? Mama died an unhappy woman, may she rest in peace."

Lesia stopped and looked at me quizzically as I abruptly moved my chair away from hers.

"Now have you heard enough about my family?" she asked. She looked concerned and asked, "Are you ill?"

I was sick in my heart and my stomach. It had finally all come out. Bogdan was the incarnation of evil. Bogdan was the avid imitator of Nazi hatred and brutality. Bogdan was a traitor to those whom he thought to be of his blood and a tormentor to those who actually were of his blood. I could not relate all of this to Lesia, nor could I tell her that Bogdan was alive—prosperous, and dangerous. I left Lesia abruptly, thanking her and wishing her well, excusing myself on account of the sudden nausea that had overcome me.

That night, I lay sleepless in the dark and agonized over my new knowledge. So, Bogdan was not what Marek had hoped him to be. Marek gave his brother a huge benefit of doubt. Marek tried not to see Bogdan's ugly, anti-Semitic warts. Marek persisted in remembering that although Bogdan knew where he and Karol were hiding, Bogdan had not reported them to the police. In Marek's mind, that one memory outweighed all the terrible flaws of Bogdan's character. How deluded Marek was!

I became physically sick. My head hurt and I vomited. I could feel sweat seeping through my blouse. I regurgitated Lesia's story and spewed out into my cranium the monstrous thought that had been lingering in my subconscious ever since Marek's death. Marek was not killed by accident. Bogdan knowingly had Marek murdered. That thought splattered all over my feverish brain and gained on credibility. Of course, it made sense. At first, Bogdan despised Marek and Karol simply as landlord Jews. Then, he wanted to eradicate his Jewish connection by denouncing his hidden father and Marek to Ukrainian Militia. Well, he had finally severed that link. Marek was dead, but I knew Bogdan for what he was: Cain.

What was Bogdan's actual name and where did he live? Obviously Lesia didn't know, and neither did I. Those that knew—Szmuel and his men—had been disposed. Igor, yes Igor!

Bogdan's lieutenant knew. Igor was being investigated for the four deaths but with Bogdan's power behind him, I was sure that the authorities would prove nothing and that it would be one more unrecorded assassination. They would be sure to maintain that an accidental explosion of a jerry can with gasoline was responsible for those deaths. They could fabricate anything. Like that case of a minister of transportation who was found with two bullets lodged in his head, and whose death was pronounced a suicide!

Morning finally came and I knew that Bogdan had won. Only Lesia and I knew of his Jewish blood. Only I knew of his hideous past as an NKVD informer. But did he really win? If so, what did he win? Perhaps he secured for himself luxurious prosperity for his last days. He was a cookie made of faulty dough that was cut out by a perverted cookie-maker. The cookie rots; it will not crumble. Oh God! If I could someday crush Bogdan!

With an aching head and feeling utterly miserable and traumatized, I boarded a plane for the USA. The thought of the work ahead kept me going. I had enough historical material to publish at least three good articles on the interaction of Lwów's residents during World War II. Of course, I had more, much more. I had my memories and Marek's writings. Yes, I agreed to myself, I would write a book, a book about us, and about Marek and his paintings. Maybe then, I thought, I would be able to turn Marek's ambitious dream of becoming a famous artist into reality.

Chapter XIII

Cookies for Good Luck

July, 2005. The pre-opening reception was tonight. The evening was muggy after this hot and humid D.C. day. Tomorrow, a temporary exhibit of Marek's paintings will open to the public in the West Building of the National Gallery of Art. The crowd of well-wishing guests thinned out. It was nearly closing time as I stood on the corner of Madison Drive and Fourth Street, near the main entrance to the West Building, watching people emerge from the gallery, animatedly talking to each other. A number of visitors waved their hands or nodded at me in recognition. Some approached me to say a few complimentary words.

A group of adults with teenagers stood apart talking amongst themselves, but periodically they snuck surreptitious glances at me. Those must have been Marek's children and grandchildren, and perhaps his wife if she is alive. Marek seldom talked about his immediate family with me. Then, again, we had so little time together. I am glad they came. Perhaps someday we will get to know each other, although that might be a bit too optimistic.

Olga and Vasily stopped by me very briefly. "We will see you later. Okay, Maria? We will celebrate. Okay? Don't be sad. And don't forget: come tomorrow to our hotel."

Vasily chimed in seriously. "I really like Marek's work. Will we be able to buy? Well, we talk tomorrow. Yes?"

The cheerful Olla and the attentive Vasily have been of great help during the last few days in Washington. I enjoyed the pleasant moments we had together in Lwów. Here in D.C., as in

Lwów, we also shared somber thoughts. Olla bore tragic news: Irka had at last succumbed to AIDS and died. Olla has become a true friend to me. We vowed to meet again, next time in Lwów.

Next, a plump woman of medium height with a mop of silvery red hair and dressed in a business suit approached me and squeezed my arm. She said nothing, but I could see her face twitching with emotion as she looked into my eyes. Her eyes glistened and tears appeared. The Lady Orange, I thought. "Are you Anna?" I asked. She did not respond by gesture or words but I sensed that it was Anna, shamefully remembered by Marek. I wondered what she recollected of Marek and of her homeless days ambling up and down the Mall, raving and cursing. Had she forgiven Marek his apparent insensitivity to her longing? Her grip on my arm slackened and she walked away. After taking a few steps, she turned around. She said something but I could not hear. She pointed to the West Building with her right hand, and with her left hand she touched her lips and sent a kiss in the direction of Marek's encampment on the Mall. Then I knew her for Lady Orange and I knew what she felt.

Phil came to me. I knew it was Phil. I met him one day after I returned from Lwów when we both happened to be wandering aimlessly on the Mall. Without looking at me, Phil took off his ski cap and bowed. He held a bunch of blackberry branches; some were still flowering, but most bore small, green berries. Their stems were wrapped in translucent plastic and taped together with several Band-Aids. He extended the "bouquet" to me by its stems so that I would not be scratched by the thorns. It was a precious gift that left me speechless and crying. Indeed, Marek must have meant something to those people. Phil abruptly turned away, and with giant steps he walked toward the West Building, faster and faster until he broke into a run. He turned right into the gallery stairway, and then leapt over several steps at a time until he reached the portals. Down and up and down again. He must be nearing fifty now but the energy and the "devil" still reside in him. Finally, having exhausted his strength or anger or both, he walked slowly away toward the sun as it set behind the National Monument.

I noticed Violet, the Korean cripple, slowly making her way toward me. She was with an elderly Oriental man who carried her crutch and gripped her arm in support. I walked toward them and tried to compose a few appropriate words of thanks. But her round black eyes stabbed me and I said nothing. I was only capable of bending down and giving her an affectionate kiss on the head. This lovely child responded, "Thank you, much thank you." They, too, walked away, and for awhile, I was alone.

Next came a dark-skinned, lanky man wearing a wrinkled brown suit. He reached into his pocket and pulled out a small, crumpled print with an image of Marek's "The Messiah."

"I am the Messiah," he told me. He pointed to Marek's signature on the card.

"Marek knew that I am the Messiah. That's why he painted me. See, my head is on the Bible. But it wasn't me who knocked that trash can down. The cookies I gave Marek came from heaven, maybe from the galaxies—not from the trash can."

He stashed away the print in his suit and looked toward the sky.

"It is going to rain but I don't hear Figarroo singing. He must be dead. I don't hear Marek calling Figarroo anymore either. I heard Marek's voice from above many times, but in the last year it has been blocked off, probably by Park Police. Is Marek also dead? Who is going to paint me now?" Muttering to himself, he shuffled away.

The last person to approach me was a tall, elegantly dressed black woman with the finely chiseled features of an Ethiopian. Her gait was slow and stately, like that of a princess. Behind her was an elderly white male with gray hair that fell to his shoulders. He was shorter and less imposing than the "princess." From Marek's chronicle, I surmised that she was Yvonne, the stewardess. She looked me up and down and flashed a warm, embracing smile.

"Yes, Marek did well. Very well. You were his woman, right?" she said and handed me an elegantly packaged box.

"These are cookies for good luck. I baked them myself. They may have crumbled, but I hope you enjoy them all the same." She left without waiting for me to respond.

I was and I wasn't Marek's woman. In some ways, I disappointed and hurt him, but I also loved him dearly at the end of his life. I fulfilled my vow to Marek and I fulfilled one to myself: Great-uncle Willi is "out of the closet." What he was, he was. At least, my parents and I can talk openly about him and about the brutal forces that spawned him, nourished him, and then discarded him.

Should I also walk into the setting sun? I have accomplished a lot and I have learned a lot about many people. Willi attained a peaceful end with his cherished Halya. I am glad and now I may close forever the "Willi File." Willi should not embarrass my family anymore. What was it that Marek wrote in his memoir? "We are all different, obviously not shaped by the same cookie cutter."

I deserve a comfortable niche in the history department of some university. However, in my heart there is hate and pain. I must seek revenge. No matter how mighty Bogdan is, I must bring him low. This treacherous scum, this ugly murderer needs to be punished. I have to find convincing evidence. This killer of Pani Yanka, and her lover Tusiek, of Misko, of Szmuel and his bodyguards, of Marek, and assuredly of others must suffer. Should death take him away before justice prevails, I hope that hell swallows him and torments him forever. I do not fear for myself anymore, as I did that day in Lwów when I let Marek go to his death. I must go now. I have work to do. But right now, I have to pick up my son—Marek's son, our two-year-old Billy—from the babysitter.

Historical Background

This story originates in the 1930s with the rise of the National Socialist (Nazi) Party in Germany. The narrative develops during World War II in the 1940s, and culminates in the late twentieth and early twenty-first centuries.

After World War II, the map of central Europe changed greatly. A comparison between a 1930s map and one of present-day Europe (see pages x and xi) illustrates these border transformations. World War II and its aftermath caused massive, often tragic upheaval to countless inhabitants of central Europe, including to the residents of the city called Lwów in Polish, or Lviv in Ukrainian.

In the 1930s map, Lwów is situated well within the territory of Poland, while by 2000 it is an integral part of Ukraine. The population change in Lwów has been just as dramatic as the political dynamic. Except for a handful of survivors, the Jewish community was murdered. The majority of Polish people were evicted or also murdered. The historically important Armenian presence has also diminished, while gypsies have altogether disappeared from the streets. The majority of present-day Lviv residents are descendants of those who resided in Ukraine prior to World War II, and Ukrainians who came from the countryside or from eastern Ukraine during World War II.

The upheaval in Lwów, and for that matter in all of Eastern Europe, began in September 1939 when Germany attacked Poland, thereby initiating World War II. Within three weeks, the German army had overcome Polish defenses and its motorized formations battled their way into the suburbs of Lwów. As the fleeing Polish soldiers tried to escape the German onslaught, the Soviet Union entered Poland from the east and occupied Lwów. The German-Soviet secret agreement, known as the Ribbentrop-Molotov Pact, was being carried out. The pact engendered a short-lived alliance between the two dictatorships. Stalin believed that cooperation with Germany would end on his terms and according to his timetable. Hitler also needed time to finish his destruction of France. Hitler struck first.

In June 1941, powerful German armies broke through Soviet border defenses and plunged into the Soviet Union. Two days later, German units entered Lwów. Brutalities abounded. The departing NKVD, the massive Soviet secret and uniformed police, murdered many prisoners. Local residents and some German soldiers blamed the Jews for collaborating with the Soviets, and retaliated by torturing and slaying numerous Jews. This was the beginning of the Holocaust experience in Lwów.

From June 1941 until late July 1944, when Lwów was reoccupied by the Soviet Red Army, about ninety-nine percent of Lwów's well over 100,000 Jews were murdered in the town or shipped to extermination camps. The Jews were collected periodically in hunts which were called "actions." There were a number of German police organizations that participated in the extermination of the Jews. Most prominent were the SS (Schutzstaffel), Schupos (Schutzpolizei) and Gestapo (Geheime Staatspolizei). Ukrainian militia also cooperated with the Nazi design to exterminate the Jews.

The Jews of Lwów were quickly reduced in number. During 1942, the remaining Jews were forced to the Ghetto where disease, hunger, and continuous deportations gradually took their toll. The brutal Janowska concentration camp was established where Jews worked in inhuman circumstances. Many were tortured and executed. In June 1943, the Ghetto was burned; the remaining inhabitants were murdered or assigned to Janowska. The Jews in Janowska did not survive much longer; in November 1943, the camp was liquidated.

While Jews and many others in Lwów and in a multitude of other occupied locations were being annihilated, a global war was raging. On the Eastern front, the Red Army was at first defending itself and then began its attack. Stalin resorted to barbaric measures against would-be deserters and against those who were real and potential Nazi collaborators. A special organization, SMERSH, which stood for "Death to the Spies," was formed behind the front. The function of SMERSH was to execute captured spies or assign them to penal battalions. The single bloodiest act perpetrated by SMERSH (or its predecessor) was the massacre of nearly 10,000 Polish prisoner of war officers.

Hitler depended on tough Waffen SS Divisions to strengthen his forces. These SS men were imbued with Nazi doctrine and fought fanatically. The Ukrainians from Lwów and the surrounding area, Galicia, organized a Waffen SS Division called the Galicia Division. Under German tutelage, the Galicia Division fought Soviets near Lwów but was thoroughly defeated and lost most of its soldiers. Some of the weapons, however, were saved by the Ukrainian Underground Army for its future struggle against the Soviet regime. Indeed, as the Soviets retook Lwów from the German Army in July 1944, they almost immediately faced insurrection by Ukrainian nationalists, known as "Banderovsty." The insurrectionists took their name from a Ukrainian nationalist hero, Stepan Bandera.

While the Banderovsty were spilling their own and Soviet blood, the Soviets established a Communist regime in their occupation zone in Germany. The Deutsche Demokratische Republik (DDR) became an obedient satellite of the Soviet Union. The German Communist Party, the ruling Socialist Unity Party, was already organized during the war in the Soviet Union by German Communists who had escaped Hitler. Now, with the assistance of a vast police apparatus, STASI, they became the governing body of the DDR. They lasted in power until the Berlin Wall was dismantled in November 1989. Prior to that time, the DDR was a major player in a military pact forged with the Soviet Union, the Warsaw Pact.

The Ukrainian insurrection lasted surprisingly long, but was finally crushed by 1950. Insurrectionists, as well as their families, were sent to Siberia. The Soviet Union as such lasted until 1991, when Ukraine, along with other formerly Soviet republics, became an independent state. Lviv is now a Ukrainian town with a unique flavor because, at one time, it was truly multiethnic.

About the Authors

Marek Mann lives on through this book and his paintings. Maria moves forward in her teaching career. To learn more about her Holocaust research and to view Marek's artwork, please visit www.marekandmaria.com. *Crumbs* is their first novel.